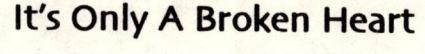

It's Only A Broken Heart

It's Only A Broken Heart

Paul Vasey

Black Moss Press
2000

Published by Black Moss Press, 2450 Byng Road, Windsor, Ontario N8W 3E8, Canada. Black Moss books are distributed by Firefly Books in Canada and the U.S.

Black Moss would like to acknowledge the generous support of the Canada Council for the Arts for its publishing program this year, as ell as the financial help from the Ontario Arts Council.

This book was edited for the press by John B. Lee.

Cover design by John Doherty.

Canadian Cataloguing In Publication Data

Vasey, Paul
    It's only a broken heart

ISBN 0-88753-343-4

    1. Title.

PS8593.A.78188 2000   C813'.54   C00-900567-6
PR9199.3.V387188 2000

FOR ADAM, KIRSTEN AND MARILYN

-ONE-

A middle-of-the-night dog-walker had found a body beside an abandoned car in a river-facing field down in Balmy Beach. The dog walker had wakened a neighbour. The neighbour had called 911. The dispatcher was dispatching the Ident unit and half a dozen cruisers to the west end. Which got Garth and me on our feet in a hurry. On our feet and headed for the newsroom door.

The clock rubbed its eyes: ten to two.

Eleven minutes later we were rooster-tailing past Bronson's Tavern on the sorry side of town, gravel chattering in the wheel wells. Garth managed a nice four-wheel slide around the corner onto Chappus, heading for the river and the car-dumping, body-dumping river-facing field.

When the call came in, it must've cleared out half the donut shops in town. By the time Garth and I arrived, there were six cruisers and three unmarked cars parked at odd angles, doors open, lights flashing, on Water Street, a dirt road that borders the field which extends to the riverbank. Beyond the cars the cops were setting up the Mobile Command Unit.

Some constables were looping yellow tape from tree to tree so Alan Sears and his partner Dennis Brown from the ID crew could do what they had to do before someone messed up the scene with footprints or tire tracks.

Alan Sears, when he's working a crime scene, is a madman for detail. Like all those who love their work, Alan Sears loves talking about his. He can talk crime scenes for hours. And I mean hours. ' I read a story about Ted Williams one time. He was talking about batting. He said when he was really in the groove and that ball was coming toward him, it was like a beach ball. He said he could actually count the stitches. That's how focused he was. That's what I get like, when I get to the scene. It's like I have a different way of seeing things.'

There isn't much that escapes the attention of Al Sears. And he doesn't care how long it takes to get the job done.

This doesn't always endear him to the boys on the death squad. They always want to get in, get the prints, bag the body and start banging on doors.

As far as Al Sears is concerned, the door-banging can wait. Doesn't make much sense to corner the bad guy if you don't have the evidence to tie him to the scene.

Which is why, among other things, Alan Sears spoons a bit of soil into a baggie and why he also bags samples of the grasses and plants from the crime scene. When the dicks collar the bad guy, Alan grabs the shoes, socks and trousers, puts them under the microscope. If he's lucky and not too much time has passed and the bad guy hasn't visited a laundromat, Alan might find tiny traces of soil or grasses or plants that would match as perfectly as two bits of a pane of glass that's been broken. When Al and his partners go into a crime scene, they go in almost catlike, careful to observe everything at their feet on the way in. One of the things they look for is the impressions of shoes in the grass. Al can tell by the way the grass is bent which way the guy was walking - toward the crime scene or away from it. He can tell by comparing the depth of foot impressions whether someone was carrying something toward the scene, but not away from it. A body, for instance. Same with tire tracks. Al can make a cast of tire tracks going to a scene. Then, once he's done, they can run the car over the same dirt and he can take another cast and he can tell by the difference in the depth of the casts whether there was something heavy in the trunk on the way in that wasn't there on the way out. Like a murder victim.

I could listen to Alan Sears for hours.

But the one thing that impressed me, apart from all those details, was something he said the first time I interviewed him: 'When I'm at the scene, I'm not working for the police. I'm working for the victim.'

8

Well, Alan Sears had himself another client. And there was no way anyone was going to get anywhere near the scene - contaminate the scene, as Al likes to say - until he and his crew had finished what they started.

Which was going to take a while.

Which seemed to suit the crowd just fine. It looked like pretty well every man woman and child still living in Balmy Beach was on the far side of the road on the far side of the yellow plastic tape, gawking and jostling, joking and smoking.

Balmy Beach is a forlorn outback of shanties and shacks. It's so far down in the west end it's almost out of town. It's so far down on the economic scale it doesn't register.

Once upon a time, Balmy Beach was a summer place. Then it fell on hard times. Not what you'd call a precipitous fall. Back in the 20s and 30s there were fourteen one-bedroom clapboard cottages on the riverbank. At the south end of the row of cottages there was a snack stand and a livery where a man would rent you a metal rowboat, twenty-five cents an hour, buck for the day. A couple of years ago, I interviewed that man. His name is Abel Kane. 'Say this for my old man. He had a sense of humour. My mother, conversely, called me Albert, though Albert ain't one of the names she gave me.' Abel Kane still lives in the neighbourhood, a little ways back from the river. He's on his last legs now and those legs don't take him down by the water much anymore. No fish to be had these days anyway. None you'd want to eat. Not like those earlier times. During our interview, Abel loved to talk about those earlier times. A little rummaging in closets and drawers and he'd come up with some snapshots of strings of fish to prove his point: 'If you couldn't catch a fish, you could always catch a breeze.' The rent on those cottages was reasonable and The Beach was within easy reach of Detroit, where most of the vacationers came from.

All in all, Balmy Beach had been a little corner of heaven, if you couldn't afford a real summer place and you didn't mind the scenery and the smell. Stretch out on a chair in front of one of those long-ago cottages and what you'd be looking at and smelling was Zug Island, directly across the river, less than a mile away.

Zug Island is a nightmare of steel mills and foundries. Every so

9

often, you'll hear a siren wail and then the stacks begin to spew plumes: purplish, some of them, yellowish, black and white. What billows up out of those stacks and then drifts downwind is anyone's guess. But put it this way; you wouldn't want to lick your finger after dragging it across the hood of your car.

Behind Zug Island there's a forest of refineries and gas fields and mills and incinerators and who knows what else. A lot of lethal-looking plumes, for sure. The channel that cuts around behind Zug Island caught fire one time. Abel Kane remembers watching the fire boats foam it down.

By the late fifties, pollution had taken care of the fish and time had transformed the cottages into shacks - dog-eared shingles, blistered paint, plastic-covered windows - occupied by people who'd been shoved or had fallen from the next rung up. Balmy Beach is pretty well it in terms of rungs. One more tumble, you'd be sleeping in an abandoned factory or the back seat of an unlocked car and lining up with all the other saggy asses for lukewarm meals dished out by all the middle-aged church-attender volunteers down at The Mission. By the sixties, a few dozen tiny houses had sprouted up between the river and Front Road, a mile or so inland, and Balmy Beach had become a kind of tatty gravel-roads lost-souls neighbourhood.

The old cottages are long gone - most of them razed, a couple of them dragged out on skids by people who turned them into backyard sheds - and only twenty-seven houses still stand in the rest of the neighbourhood. The area has been designated an industrial park - your oxymoron of the week - and the city is buying out the last of the homeowners one or two at a time whenever it can find the money or whenever a particular homeowner starts bitching too loudly, calling The Spectator about the lousy living conditions. Whenever the city buys a house, the works crews come with their bulldozers and back-hoes and dump trucks and knock it down and truck the remains away to the dump.

So Balmy Beach now consists of a mothballed coal-fired power plant and a brand-new state-of-the-art gas-fired power plant across the road from it, a Ford engine plant, a steel fabrication mill, a scrap yard, a salt mine and that won't be the end of it.

The whole area has a weird countryish feel about it - birds and bugs and distant barking dogs - and an unobstructed view of Zug Island across the river.

10

You've got to admit that at half past two on a star-scattered morning in May, Zug Island is beautiful in a depraved sort of way: all billowy plumes and winking lights and wailing sirens and vague gruntings and huffings and steaming slagheaps. It's like something Dante might have imagined and Blake might have sketched. Stand on the riverbank, stare at that tangle of mills and foundries, and their reflection on the river, and you get the sense you're standing at the last edge of the world, waiting for The Boatman to come and row you across.

Turn your back to the island and you're looking at a moonlit minefield of old tires and roofing shingles, engine blocks and busted toilets, aluminium siding and rusted-out mufflers, washers, dryers, freezers, sofas, three-legged tables, two-legged chairs and anything else it would cost you ten bucks to truck to the dump.

The garbage, and the occasional body in a ditch, is what the last of the homeowners bitch about when they turn up at City Council asking that their house be next on the buy-out list. Who could blame them?

Counting this latest one, it's three bodies so far this year. And it's only May.

The latest one was under a yellow plastic sheet beside a late-model Mustang ragtop whose arse-end was just visible above the edge of the riverbank on the far side of the field facing Water Street.

An inspector named Tubby Taylor - 'if you're going to quote me, call me Theodore' - was in charge of things out on the road.

He'd asked Dispatch to run the plate through the computer and see what came out.

He told three cops to start scouring the fields on either side of the taped-off area, take a walk down the beach, check under bushes, check the ditches, the usual. Make themselves useful.

He told the rest of the boys to fan out and question the curious, find out if anyone saw the Mustang go down the lane toward the river, or if anyone saw a person or persons walking back through the field toward Water Street, or if anyone saw a vehicle leaving the area. Anything unusual. Anything at all.

Then Tubby wedged himself behind the wheel of his cruiser, with

11

the driver's door still open, pulled a pack of Players Lights from his pocket and lit one up. He sat there for a couple of moments, smoking and surveying the scene.

I sidled over, leaned against the front fender, fired up a smoke myself. "Looking for a killer, Inspector?"

"No," he said. He gave me one of those looks cops reserve for reporters. "We're looking for the Easter Bunny."

"Nothing personal. I get paid to ask."

"Yes you do. And I get paid to put up with assholes. Nothing personal, of course."

Of course.

It was starting to smell like a story to me. Which I mentioned to Garth, as he was motioning for the dog-walker to move a little closer to the rear end of one of the open-door cruisers, and to stop smiling for a moment.

"A story? No shit? Honest to God, Hemingway, you're as quick as a hare. I can't imagine what you'd be like if you had an entire brain."

The dog walker was a 50-ish guy named Walter Harris. Lots of gut, not much hair. "You can call me Wally." Wally and his German Shepherds Pooch and Rover - who could make this up? - had come down from the Old Town, which is a bit of a hike, maybe three miles. "I cut in behind Bronson's and take that lane to the river and then walk along the river right down to Morton Terminal and then we take a break. I have a smoke and they have a dog biscuit. Then we head back home."

Wally Harris is on permanent four to midnight at a stamping plant. Finger factories, they call them. No joke. By way of proof, Wally had a stump where his left pinkie should have been. Every night after he got home from work, Wally would have a TV dinner - chicken last night, though he really prefers the beef but he'd had the beef four nights running and enough was enough, eh? - and he'd have a couple of beers, one with his supper and one right after, and then he and the dogs would head out for their middle-of-the-night ramble: rain or snow, heat or cold. "The only thing we don't walk in is freezing rain. Ice is hell on their foot pads."

Tonight, they'd followed their usual route and it was just after they'd reached the riverbank behind Bronson's that Wally thought he

12

saw something a little unusual up ahead: a Mustang peering into the river. "I thought, holy smokes, someone's had a bit too much to drink. I figured for sure I was going to find a body in it or something. Like in the movies, eh?"

Well, not quite like the movies. But it was a body, and it was quite dead. As soon as they'd caught a whiff of it, the dogs practically dragged him around to the far side of the car. It was all he could do to drag them back from the body.

The body was naked from the waist down. She'd been beaten, and then some. It was enough to make you sick, which Wally had been. Then he'd run across the field to the first house he could find and told the woman who answered the door to call the cops.

The home owner's name was Leslie Ambrose. Tough little item, five three or five four, maybe a hundred pounds. Her home is right across the road from the river-facing field, not two hundred feet from the body. It was her house we were standing in front of, Garth and Wally and his dogs and I. Her dogs, a couple of mixed breeds from the looks of it, were inside the screened-in porch, barking their arses off.

Leslie Ambrose was looking in the direction of the Mustang and the body. "It's too close to home," she said. "People will be scared to go out the door now."

And then she said: "I don't agree with the life they live, but they don't need to be killed. She might have been a hooker, but she didn't deserve this."

I wrote it down, word for word, then looked up at her. I asked her why she thought the dead woman was a hooker.

"The cops told me."

I asked if they said how they knew that.

"They found her purse. Beside her body. Wallet, I.D., the works."

Whatever the motive, it wasn't robbery. "They said there's seven hundred and some odd dollars in the purse."

I asked Leslie if the cops had mentioned a name.

She shook her head. "They said she hadn't been positively identified. But they did say the ownership to the Mustang was in the purse beside the body. They said the owner of the car was 'known to the department'."

Then Leslie said again how the victim might have been a hooker, but it was no reason for someone to murder her. And then she said again how she'd be thinking twice about wandering around the neighbourhood after dark.

Wally had a leash in either hand. His dogs were getting antsy, so he'd better be getting them home.

I thanked him for his help.

"Is my picture going to be in the paper?"

Leslie Ambrose gave him a look. "A woman's lyin' there dead under a sheet and you're wonderin' if your fat face is gonna be in the paper. Ain't you a fuckin' prize." She turned and headed back to her house.

Wally recoiled, like he'd been slapped, turned his palms up and shrugged. "I was only wonderin'." I told Wally he'd have to keep on wondering until the early edition hit the street.

Garth had his camera bag up on the trunk of one of the cruisers. He was changing rolls. He'd fired off one within five minutes of parking the car up on Water Street - some nice grainy long-lens shots of the Ident guys down by the Mustang and the body - and then he'd taken another of Wally and the dogs, and then Wally and Leslie. From the looks of things, we'd have the top of the front page to ourselves and he wanted to make sure there was no shortage of shots to choose from.

Nothing makes us happier than seeing our pictures and stories above the fold on Page One. We are quite frequently happy. They don't call us Prima and Donna for nothing.

Garth shouldered his camera bag and headed down Water Street to shoot the crowd.

Behind the yellow tape, it was party time. The folks were capering and gossiping and conjecturing and craning their necks for a better look at the car and the body. Even old Abel Kane had hobbled down, cane in one hand, cigar between the fingers of the other. Almost imperceptibly, the crowd shuffled forward until they were right up by the yellow tape. Then one of the cops barked them back but pretty well as soon as the cop turned away they started edging closer again. It was sort of like a little game. Then the cops gave up and ignored the crowd and so the folks just huddled there smoking and talking and laughing and whispering and waiting to see what happened next.

What happened next was, Deke Dupuis jounced his tip-bed tow truck around the corner and down Water Street and pulled to a stop behind the clutch of cruisers. He ignited the rack of rooflights and lit the scene up like a Hollywood set. He left the engine idling, stepped down from the cab, took a look at the crowd, hooked a finger in a belt loop on either side and hiked his blue jeans up just under his gut. He hawked a good one into the dust, wiped his lips on his shirt sleeve. They don't call him Deke the Geek for nothing. He strutted over to see what Inspector Taylor was up to. Taylor told him to cool his heels until Ident was done, then they'd tell him what they wanted done with the car.

Next thing you know, Freddie Miller was pulling up in his black Chrysler mini-van. Freddie runs the City County Removal Service. His licence plates read BDY WGN. His business cards feature his name, the name of his company, his phone and fax numbers and this reminder: When You're Dead, Call Fred. A little bent, admittedly. But it never hurts to have a sense of humour when you're in the death business. And Freddie can afford to joke and screw around: he has a corner on the market. There aren't all that many people willing to go out all hours of the day and night, seven days a week, twelve months a year to haul bodies out of car wrecks and ditches and burned-out houses and lakes and rivers and hospitals and bedrooms and basements and cart them to the morgue or the funeral home. Bodies didn't bother Freddie. 'Me'n the dead get along just fine.'

They should. Freddie grew up in a small-town funeral home. His old man had always hoped Freddie's brother would take over the business and always feared he'd wind up having to turn it over to Freddie. The brother had taken off, long years since, and it looked as though Freddie had lucked in. But then the old man sold the place to a funeral-home chain, took his winnings and retired in Arizona. Freddie had lasted about a month under the new funeral-home manager. He'd bid the fellow a two-word farewell then went out and bought a van and went into business for himself.

He parked the body wagon then ambled over to see what was what.

Tubby told Fred the same thing he'd just told Deke. "Cool your heels. It'll be a while."

"I got all the time in the world," said Fred. "And the body ain't goin' nowhere without me." He lit a cigarette and leaned up against the fender of Tubby's cruiser.

Garth took a shot of the three of them: Deke and Fred and Tub.

"You get me a copy of that, Garth?"

"Sure, Fred."

"And can you take one when we lift the body."

"No problem."

Freddie loves to have his picture in the paper. Garth is more than happy to oblige.

Half the tips we get about dead bodies we get from Freddie.

An hour or so later, the ID boys were all wrapped up. Tubby told Fred to go get the body. Freddie didn't need to be told twice. And he didn't waste any time. Eighteen minutes after he backed his van across the field, he was driving back toward us, the body in a bag on the gurney in the back.

We waved as he went by.

Then Tubby told us we could go down and get a couple of shots of the car. "But make it quick. We wanna get this thing hauled out of here."

The Mustang was a year or two old, a rag top, candy-apple red, white leather interior, mag wheels, 5.0 litre, dual chrome-tipped exhaust, the works. Someone loved that car, for sure: wash, wax and buff. It was gleaming under all the spotlights and headlights. Didn't seem to be a scratch on it. So, kind of funny to find it where Wally had found it early this Tuesday morning, tag end of May - its rear end on the riverbank, nose in the gravel at the water's edge, grille filled with weeds, headlights shining into the minnowed water.

The top was down and the driver's door was open. A single key was in the ignition and the ignition was in the on position but the engine wasn't running.

When Al and Dennis arrived, the hood was cool to the touch, so the engine hadn't been running for a while. The gas gauge was three-quarters full, so the engine had probably stalled out when the car hit the beach. The radio was still on. It was tuned to FM 89.9. Public radio. A gravelly voice - Muddy Waters? - was singing something faintly bluesy. Five would get you ten, the car hadn't been stolen. At least not by kids. Any self-respecting car-stealing kid would have tuned in to one of those head-banger stations. Alan Sears would lay you odds the driver was middle to upper income, fairly well educated, 30 or older and, given the position of the driver's seat, under five eight in height. He would also put a buck on the fact the driver hadn't been wearing a seatbelt, had banged his or her head against the steering wheel and was sporting a noticeable cut between the bridge of the nose and the hairline. Thus the drops of blood on the front edge of the driver's white-leather bucket seat. The driver was probably left handed - he or she had touched the cut, then opened the door. There was a smear of blood on the door handle. Given a hair they'd found, and the height of the driver, Al surmised it was a woman. But maybe not. Maybe some shortshit of a guy.

The body had been face up on the riverbank, about twenty feet behind the car. Like Wally had said, there hadn't been much left of her face. Someone had pounded it in with a rock.

Talk about your coincidences.

Three weeks earlier, in a ditch about two hundred yards away, Al and Dennis had been taking photographs of a partially-clad badly-beaten female body.

That victim was early thirties, a single mom who'd been supplementing her welfare cheques by turning tricks on Wendell Street, clear across town. She apparently hadn't had the smarts to smell a psycho when she opened the car door and climbed in. Her name was Melissa McBride. Wasn't much left of her face when they found her, either.

The guy had pounded her with a rock the size of a bowling ball.

The rock was embedded in her skull, where her face had been.

I covered the story. It was front-page for three days. I interviewed Melissa's sister. 'Poverty shouldn't be a death sentence,' she'd told me. No, it shouldn't. However, there's a pretty wide gulf between what should be and what is. We're a long way east of Eden. Especially these days.

Melissa's body had been found in the ditch that runs alongside Water Street. The body was about fifty yards from the head of the laneway which leads to the riverbank, the lane once used by the cottagers who came to Balmy Beach to get away from it all. The lane's pretty well weeded over now and it's one pothole after another and if you're not careful it'll rip off your oil pan, or your muffler, or both. The only people who use the lane these nights are lovers with a case of the hots or kids with a case of beer.

And the driver of the Mustang.

Late-night lovers and underage beer drinkers you can understand.

But you have to wonder who in their right mind would take a good-looking Mustang like that down a lane like this and then drive it over the riverbank.

You'd have to conclude it wasn't the person who spent a lot of recent hours wiping dust off the paint job and vacuuming dirt from the floor mats. At least not voluntarily. Or not without good reason. A very good reason. Seems Alan Sears and the rest of the cops were of the same frame of mind.

So Alan Sears and Dennis Brown had spent the last couple of hours taking still photos and videos of the car and the area around it; dusting for prints, making casts of footprints and tire tracks; taking soil samples and picking plant and grass specimens, checking for blood elsewhere in the car, bagging cigarette butts from the Mustang's ashtray and a book of matches found under one of the seats and some strands of hair on the driver's side floor mat and anything else that might come in handy in court some day.

Now Garth was prowling the same territory.

Alan Sears was watching, with professional interest, while smoking a cigarette he'd bummed from me.

I asked him if the cops were thinking serial killer.

"Could be," he said.

I asked him if he happened to remember the name on the Mustang ownership.

He said he thought it was something like Cindy Lou Gilmore. "One L in Gilmore."

I asked if he happened to recall an address.

He mentioned a street name, and number. It was an up-tempo part of town - Southland Gardens - doctors, lawyers and used-car dealers.

18

I asked if it was safe to assume that the body Freddie was carting downtown belonged to Miss Gilmore.

"You're old enough," said Alan Sears, stepping on my cigarette, then grinding it into the dirt, "and you should be smart enough to know that you never assume shit."

As a matter of fact, however, the Inspector had dispatched a unit to Miss Gilmore's residence. The unit had radioed in that the place was in darkness, nobody home. The Inspector had told them to wait right there until someone showed up. Someone had shown up, about ten minutes ago. The boyfriend, apparently. A certain Wayne Vincent. He wondered what the hell the cops were doing staking out his house. The cops had told him. They asked him if he knew where Cindy Lou might be. She might be in bed asleep, he said. They asked him to check her bed. Her bed was empty. The cops wondered if Mister Vincent might know where Cindy had gone. He said he didn't know. Alan watched me writing all this down. He waited until I stopped. "He appeared to be very agitated by the news that his girl-friend's car and purse had been found beside a body on the river-bank. He's apparently on his way down here."

"Oh," I said. "Any idea who Mister Vincent might be?"

"Let's put it this way. He's not her parish priest."

"Oh," I said.

"Oh, indeed," said Alan. "And now, I've got to get back to work."

Garth got a couple of frames of Alan Sears and Dennis Brown wrapping the Mustang in clear plastic and another couple of frames of Deke winching the car up onto the flatbed. He promised Deke a print if the picture turned out okay. Then we headed back across the field toward the staff car.

A few minutes later Garth nudged me on the shoulder. "Have a gander."

A Jaguar purred around the corner, the driver doing his best to avoid the potholes on Water Street. He pulled to a stop just behind the Inspector's car.

Fine-looking late-model Jag: XJS, V12, wire-wheels, British racing green with a beige convertible top. The driver got out without turning off the engine. Couldn't help but notice the licence plate: I SELL. He was apparently successful at flogging whatever it was he flogged:

gleaming loafers, knife-edge trousers and a leather bomber jacket that was probably worth more than everything I had on my back. The shiner on his pinkie was definitely worth more than my car.

He walked up to the first cop he saw and announced himself. He nodded in the direction of the Mustang, shrouded in plastic on the flatbed of Deke's truck. "That's my girlfriend's car." Before the cop could say anything, Vincent wanted to know "what's going on here? Who's in charge?" The cop told him to go see the Inspector, and pointed him out. The Inspector looped his smoke into the field and told Vincent to get in the passenger side and shut the door behind himself. Then the Inspector got in and shut his door.

They spent the next ten minutes or so in what seemed to be a pretty animated conversation. At one point Vincent was pointing his finger at Tubby and making little poking motions, as though to punctuate a point. And then Tubby made a few poking motions, too, but his finger was poking Vincent on the shoulder. Things got spirited. You could hear their voices rising. Seemed Vincent didn't much like the tone or direction of the interview. When he got out of Tubby's cruiser he gave the passenger door a smart slam. He started to walk toward the lane that led into the field but before he got there, Taylor was out of his cruiser: "You can't go down there."

"My girlfriend's car is. . ."

"You can't go down there."

"I can go where I want. My girlfriend's ..."

"That field is a secured area. You take another step in that direction, and you'll be under arrest."

Vincent looked at the car and then he turned and looked at Inspector Taylor and then at the crowd which was looking at him and then he took what was left of his pride back to his Jag.

Didn't slam his own door.

"Whaddya think?" Garth was busy reloading, having shot a roll of Vincent and Tubby Taylor.

I was thinking several things, actually. I was thinking Wayne Vincent, whoever he was, was a weasley looking little shit. Also a very nervy little shit. I was wondering why he was so anxious to get to the scene, and have a look at the Mustang on Deke's flatbed. And

I wondered why he didn't ask what had happened to his girlfriend, or demand to see her body, or even ask where it was.

I was also thinking what a condescending prick Tubby Taylor could be, without even trying.

I was also thinking that Wally Harris could do with a brain transplant.

And I was also wondering what would emerge if I sat down and had a few cigarettes and a few beers with Leslie Ambrose.

But mostly what I was thinking was, I wanted them to get a positive ID on the body which was on its way to the morgue; and then I wanted to start typing.

"What I'm thinking is, I think we might have something that will fill up a corner of Page One."

"God, Huntzie, you are such a genius. Were you born this smart, or did your mother supplement your diet?"

Garth was doing the driving. Quick trip back to the office.

It was almost dawn by the time I finished my story.

I called the cop shop one last time.

Still no positive I.D.

I asked the dick on the desk when they might have one.

"Your guess is as good as mine."

I thanked him and hung up.

I handed in my story then went back to the darkroom to see how Garth was coming along with the pictures. He was coming along just fine - printing the last of the shots. When he was done, we brought them out and spread them around on the editing desk.

"I got a hole at the back of D Section." This was one of the early-morning rim rats. "It's a toss-up between a ribbon cutting and this shit. Pick up the early edition and see who won."

He was laughing as we left. It's what happens, you spend twenty years editing stories. Your brain gets a little twizzled.

Garth and I were just about out the newsroom door when the jokester called my name.

21

"Some lady called."

I asked him if there was a message.

"She said to tell you you were in deep shit."

I asked him if was my girlfriend, or my wife.

"If you have to ask, you're in deeper shit than you think."

-Two-

"What do you think happened to her?"

Betsy was curled up at one end of the couch, wrapped in a blanket. I was sitting at the other end. My toes were working their way under the blanket. Betsy was squirming. But she wasn't complaining. "Huntzie!"

So, I wasn't in deep shit after all. I could have been, but as soon as I walked in the door, Betsy came up to me, all sleepy-eyed and slinky in her see-through nightie and gave me a big kiss and one thing led to another, which was not exactly what she'd had in mind. What she had in mind was, she wanted to check my breath, see if Garth and I had stopped off at MaryMary's for a little of Hiram Walker's finest and a couple of hands of poker.

MaryMary runs an after-hours place on Ouellette Avenue, right across from Hotel Dieu Hospital.

The Sisters of Mercy, we call it.

Once upon a time the place had been the home of one of the town's upstanding citizens, a doctor I think, or a judge. One of those country-club types.

Word around town was that MaryMary was this guy's illegitimate daughter, which is how she'd come to inherit the place. A house is one thing. Taxes and the cost of living are another. Poverty is the mother of invention. It's also the mother of blind pigs and whorehouses.

MaryMary had installed a bar and some fridges in the basement and hired some girls to make use of all those upstairs bedrooms. It's

a classy joint. But what else would it be? Even at seventy-something, MaryMary is a classy broad: high heels, satin gowns, pearl necklaces, Bette Davis cigarette holder.

MaryMary's been in the entertainment business all her life. For a while, after the Second World War, she worked at The Rendezvous Roadhouse as a kind of lady of the house. She was boss of the kitchen and the wait staff and the bar staff. She greeted you at the door and said good night when you left. Slip her twenty, you got a table by the windows with a view of the lake. Get in her bad books, you'd get a table at the back with a view of the kitchen's swinging doors. Cause a hassle, she'd have your ass fired out into the parking lot.

MaryMary knew everyone who was worth knowing and many who weren't. She knew some of them well and others very well indeed. She does not deny being caught in the sack - this was back in the 50s - with His Worship The Mayor when Mrs. Worship The Mayor returned unexpectedly one Saturday morning from what was to have been a weekend trip to Chicago. It is said, and MaryMary won't deny it, that she pranced across the bedroom in the altogether and lounged in the tub for an hour before dressing and leaving.

Mary could have put on airs. But that's not her style. Despite the pearls and finery, she's a pretty down-to-earth old broad. She has a knack for making you feel right at home when you walk into her place, so long as you don't start cheating at cards or getting ugly with the girls. Cause any trouble, and you'll find out in the blink of an eye that MaryMary can be just as contrary as her namesake. You'll also discover how quickly One-Eyed Louie can take care of business.

One-Eyed Louie resides in a maroon-leather lounge chair just inside the front door. When you walk in, Louie gives you the eye: shutting his good one, which is blue, and staring at you with the glass one which is green and at least two sizes too large for its socket. It's enough to unnerve even a psychopath. Apart from his fake eye, Louie is very classy: shiny brogues, nicely-pressed trousers, vest, white shirt, tie, the works. One-Eyed Louie is what you'd call a low-grade thug. He's been up the river on several occasions - break and enter, armed robbery, car theft, embezzlement - and has never come back home in what you'd call a state of contrition. But he's always come home with an armful of roses for his old flame and, until his next all-expenses-paid trip up the river, he is to be found in the maroon-leather wing chair just inside MaryMary's front door.

24

One-Eyed Louie is not the sort of fellow you'd want to piss off. Check the holster under his left arm. He's a nasty piece of business. One-Eyed Louie was in the vicinity when three men departed this life for the next. Three that I know of. The cops had their suspicions. However, suspicions didn't cut it.

But One-Eyed Louie is another story.

As luck would have it, I didn't drop in to MaryMary's. Garth had to get right home and I didn't feel like going solo. Just as well, since Betsy was waiting at the window - the curtains were fluttering closed as I locked the car and looked up. By the time I got up the stairs, she had the door open. She gave me a hug and a kiss and a sniff. All she got for her trouble was a whiff of machine coffee and stale smoke and a hand on either cheek.

"Ahh," she said, "you came right home to Momma."

I told her it had never crossed my mind to do anything else. She gave me one of her 'don't bullshit me' looks.

How I wound up with Betsy is, I was on the rebound. Never the time to hook up with anyone, as any sap knows and every pal will tell you. The trouble with pals is, you only listen to the advice you want to hear. The rest of it is preachy, cheap and forgettable.

Betsy was a friend of a friend of a friend. We met at a house party. I was out on the back porch having a smoke. Betsy came out for a breath of air. Five six, five seven, streaky blonde hair, built. Hm.

Her first words: 'you shouldn't be doing that'. I asked her what I shouldn't be doing.

"Smoking, for one."

"And for two?"

"Having another beer."

She caught me in a weak moment. Having another mother felt kind of cozy. I flicked the cigarette into the backyard. I finished the beer but, in deference to Betsy's tastes, I switched to coffee. She seemed to sense some kind of victory. She could sense whatever she wanted to sense. I was living, at the time, in a rooming house and was itchy for a change of address ... and a roommate if possible. As my old granny once said, all things are possible.

Sure enough. A week and a half later I was at her doorstep,

garbage bags full of clothes in either hand. We spent our first conjugal evening washing my clothes.

Betsy doesn't mind the poker. But she's death on booze. If she'd been born at the turn of the century, she'd have been the president of the Women's Christian Temperance Union, a thumper in the pulpit, a carrier of placards on the sidewalks outside the roadhouses of town. An uplifter, that's my Betsy.

Like a lot of women, she's constantly patching, sewing, hemming, picking the lint from and otherwise fussing with the moral fabric of her man. I am her mission. Her project. As she has said more times than once, I am the kind of project it would take her two lifetimes to complete. "You got more habits than a convent. And all of them are bad."

Now, this can be endearing or annoying, depending on the circumstances.

And the alternatives.

The alternative in this case was a rented room, a hot plate, a concave mattress and cockroaches the size of mice.

A certain amount of female fidgeting is tolerable.

And some things about me, she does not think require a lot of change or improvement.

"That was terrific," said Betsy, picking her nightie from the floor and pulling it over her head. "We ought to do that more often."

I told her I had no plans for the rest of the morning.

She, however, was in the mood for pizza. Then she had to get it in gear, get dressed, and get to work down at the bank.

Pizza for breakfast?

So, we phoned and placed our order and now we were waiting, seated on the sofa. My toes were on a mission. Betsy slapped my leg. "Huntzie!"

"You started it."

She wanted to know about my night. When I got done telling her about the body and the Mustang and the scene by the riverbank and Mister 'I Sell' she sat for a moment chewing it all over. "What do you think happened to her?"

"It's anybody's guess."

26

"What's your guess?"

I told her it smelled faintly of drugs, or sex. Or maybe both.

"Do you think it's the same wacko who did in the other girl?"

I told her that seemed like a natural leap of logic.

The pizza man arrived. I took the box and told him to keep the change. Betsy was looking at me when I turned around. "Why do you tip a pizza boy?"

I told her: the guy's on minimum wage, he's driving his own car into the ground. Every time he parks his car he's gotta be wondering if someone's lured him into a trap, if they're waiting for him with a knife or a gun. It's what I call a piss-poor way to make a living. If he doesn't deserve a tip, then no one deserves a tip. "But," I said, "I think I've explained my position previously. Like the last time we ordered pizza, which I think was last week."

Betsy smiled. "I know. I just like to hear you explain it again." She was on her feet, wrapped in the blanket, heading for the kitchen. She stopped in front of me and planted one on my cheek.

That's Betsy for you.

In a minute, she was back with two cans of Coke and a pile of napkins. We settled back on the couch with the pizza box between us. "Want to know what I think?"

"Shoot."

Between mouthfuls, this was what Betsy thought: "That weasely I Sell sonofabitch probably did her in."

"Know him?"

"I don't haveta know him. I know his type. Sonofabitch."

I asked for elaboration. I ate, Betsy elaborated.

"When I was in school, I had a friend. Did I ever tell you about Carrie Coghill?"

"Not that I remember."

"She was my best friend from about Grade 9 to the end of high school. We were just like this." Betsy crossed the first two fingers of her left hand. "Like sisters. She had a father just like 'I Sell'. Money, money, money. He had bags of it. And bags were never enough. He was an accountant, or a broker. Something money-grubbing like that.

27

I never could figure men like that. All they think about is money. God, that's boring. I had a cousin like that. Benny Suter. Did I ever tell you about Cousin Benny and his get-rich-quick scheme?"

"One story at a time."

"Remind me to tell you about Benny."

I told her I would.

She went back to her story. "There wasn't anything Carrie didn't have. I mean, nothing. Anything she wanted, she got. And she got lots of things she didn't want and didn't need. And she couldn't care less about any of it. What she didn't have was her father. He was always out there making money."

"And?"

"And what?"

"What happened to her?"

"I'm getting to that."

"Can we take a short-cut? I'm getting tired."

"Short-cut?" She gave me one of those looks. "I never tell you to take a short-cut when you're telling stories."

I told her I always got right to the point. She swatted my leg, and pushed my foot away. "I'll short-cut you, buddy."

"Honest to God, baby, I've gotta go to bed. I'm seeing two of you. Which is, of course, a pleasure. But in about two minutes I'm going to be fast asleep."

She cut to the chase: The bottom line was, Carrie Coghill was starved for affection and the natural result, as anyone could have predicted, was that she started chasing pretty well everything in trousers. It was a miracle she didn't get herself knocked up by Grade 10. Word got around. By Grade 12, she'd graduated to the bars. She'd moved on from the football team to the boys in the bands and the boys at the bar. The worse they treated her, the more she seemed to like it. Now and then, Betsy caught sight of her "and it wasn't a pretty sight." And it was all downhill from there. In the end she was about as far down in the gutter as you could go. And then one of her weasels laid a beating on her.

"End of story?"

"He didn't stop beating her until she was dead."

End of story.

"So, I think probably something like that has happened to Cindy Lou Gilmore."

I told Betsy it was an interesting theory. But since we didn't know zip about Cindy Lou or Wayne Vincent we could hardly ...

"What more do you need to know about him than the licence plate on his Jag?"

Since Betsy had weighed in so eloquently on that side, I put a buck on the fact that I Sell would not be a prime suspect.

"Why not?"

"Just a hunch."

"Details, please."

"For one thing, I don't think a murderer would race down to the crime scene and get into an argument with the cop who's investigating his victim's death."

"People set fires and then come back and watch the fire fighters fight the fire they set."

"You can hide in a crowd at a fire scene. You can't hide when you're in the front seat with the inspector."

"I still say it's him. You said yourself, he looked like a weasely little shit."

"Exactly. Entirely too weasely to be caught at the scene of a murder he'd just committed."

Betsy gave me a little 'hm'. Then she got up off the couch and went over to the sideboard and pulled her wallet from her purse, fished around for some loose change, came back and put four quarters on the table. "Put your money down."

I put down some change of my own. "It's a bet."

Maybe it was the pizza.

I dreamed of Cindy Lou Gilmore six ways from Sunday. I dreamed her dead and her head on a sharpened stake - like something out of Heart Of Darkness - and I dreamed her drowned with her hair like silver moss in the moonlight and I dreamed her buried alive under the Mustang silently screaming and I dreamed her in the

29

freezer of her boyfriend's house and while all this was flashing past on the screen of my brain I could hear her calling out faintly in the distance 'help me' 'help me' 'help me'. Over and over and over. Next thing you know, I'm lying there, eyes open, wide awake, staring at the cracks in the ceiling. I got up and went out to the living room. Half past nine. Two and a half hours sleep and wide awake. This was not promising.

The place was empty. Betsy had gone off to work. So I had a smoke, and a couple of fingers of whiskey from the bottle I keep in the tank of the toilet, and I managed to settle myself down. Then I had another couple of fingers of whiskey and another couple of smokes for good measure and then I went back to bed figuring I'd given dead hookers the dodge. No such luck. Now I was seeing Melissa McBride's face, or what was left of it. And I was seeing her body in the ditch and there I was, wide awake again. Talk about your haunted house.

I gave up, got up, got dressed and got the hell out of there.

What I needed to do was get myself somewhere where it wasn't quiet. What I also needed was to get myself some place where someone would cook me breakfast.

Quarter past ten, the glass was rattling as the front door of The Bandit's Cafe banged closed behind me. I grabbed an early edition from the pile of papers on top of the cigarette machine. When I turned, The Bandit was standing behind the counter with one wrist against his waist. "Whyn't you just break the friggin' glass and be done with it?"

The Bandit is a piece of work: two hundred and seventy pounds if he's an ounce, last had a shower maybe 1954, last changed his apron sometime the following year. The Bandit is a nightmare for the Health Unit. They keep threatening to shut him down. 'On account of my smokin' a fuckin' cigarette while I'm cookin? What the hell harm's a little cigarette ash gonna do to anythin' I cook?'

The Bandit's Cafe is kitty corner to The Spectator. His place, and Jimmy Lee's Bar down the block, are the city's two unofficial press clubs. They're also hangouts for most of the posties in town, and a good many of the cops, most of the business people and shop owners from Ouellette Avenue, the seniors from Terminal Towers. What you can't find out in The Bandit's or in Jimmy Lee's you wouldn't want to know in the first place.

"What'n hell you want?"

"How about a smile and a kiss on the cheek?"

"How about you kiss my cheek?" He turned and half bent over, slapping his ass.

"Well, aren't we in a mood."

The Bandit straightened up and went back to flipping something on the grill. Might've been a burger. Whatever it was landed with a splat. "If you're waitin' for table service, you'll be waitin' until Armadragon."

I went behind the counter and helped myself to some coffee. I gave The Bandit a little slap on the butt with my newspaper and headed for my table. "Don't start nothin' you can't finish."

There were half a dozen conversations on the go: two at the counter, the rest in the wooden booths by the steamed-up windows. The topics ranged from last night's loss for The Tigers ("when the hell're they gonna get some frickin' pitchin'?") to City Council ("If I've told 'em once about them skunks, I've told 'em a thousand times and nobody never comes out and does nothin'. You tell me what I'm paying all those jeazly taxes for? I ask you.") I slipped into the corner booth, the one where you faintly sniff the bathrooms on the other side of the wall, and lit up a smoke.

"I can't read minds, Mister Pulitzer." The Bandit was giving me the stare. He had one hand on his hip. In the other he held a mug. He sipped at his coffee, then put the mug on the counter. "Anyone touches my mug'll lose three fingers." By way of demonstration, he banged the scraper down, sidewise, on the counter. A shower of grease.

"Holy shit, Bandit." A geezer two stools down made as though to wipe off the sleeve of his jacket. "I'm gonna haveta send you the cleanin' bill."

"Whyn't you go back to Terminal Towers? And remember to take your teeth with you this time."

I told The Bandit I'd take the usual.

"The usual what?" But he was already turning to the grill and cracking the eggs.

I opened the paper. Sports. Lifestyles. Classified. Someone had made off with the front section.

I went back to the cigarette machine, rooted through the pile.

Wasn't a single front section anywhere in there.

"Anyone got the front section of The Spec?"

An old queen on the first stool said she had the front section, but she wasn't done with it yet. I asked her if I could have a quick peek. She wasn't sure. She sized me up and you could tell she didn't much like what she saw, or thought she saw. But with the place full of customers, how dangerous could I be? She offered me the paper.

Garth's shot was right there in the middle of Page One: Freddie and his helper humping the bagged body up onto the gurney, the Mustang in the background. Underneath it was a four-column headline:

WOMAN'S BODY FOUND IN WEST END

Just below the headline, there was a two-column shot of Wally the Dog Walker and Leslie Ambrose.

My story ran to the bottom of the page and then turned to Page 2.

The usual shock and horror, a bunch of quotes from the neighbours, who were freaked right out, two bodies in three weeks. I'd quoted Tubby Taylor saying that people shouldn't panic but admitting that, yes, there were a number of similarities between the first slaying and this one, though he wouldn't say just what. And no, he did not think women in general needed to start taking extra precautions. But he did think it would be a good idea for the city's prostitutes to be "extra vigilant" while plying their trade. He did not mention what kind of extra vigilance they should be practicing.

The story also said that anyone with any information about the incident should contact Crimestoppers.

Which told you everything you needed to know about the state of their investigation.

Cold as The Bandit's toast.

"The Spectator's just across the corner, you know," the old babe said. "You could always go over there and buy your own paper."

Whatever happened to all the nice little old ladies?

I gave her back her front section and headed back to my table in the corner.

I turned to sports.

The Tigers were on a streak. Six losses, back to back. Tram and Whitaker had turned another ballet double play. There was a picture of Lou underhanding the ball to Trammell who was straddling the bag waiting for some cement-foot from the Jays to slide headfirst into his waiting glove. From the looks of things, Tram would have had him by two feet. Turn the page, check the stats. The Tigers were now only 16 games out of first place. May 22. Hm.

I was reading, but I was also listening. Useful skill. Especially in a place like The Bandit's Cafe. Like I said, what you can't learn sitting in a corner booth at The Bandit's isn't worth knowing. And most of what you want to learn, you'll learn by keeping your eyes on your paper, your mouth shut and your ears open.

About fifteen minutes after I'd settled in and a couple of minutes before The Bandit finally came through with bacon and eggs and toast, a couple of beat cops came in, one in his twenties, the other in his forties. They helped themselves to coffee and sat down at the two stools across from my booth. Right after The Bandit slid my plate in front of me, he asked the cops what the news was.

The news was the body in Balmy Beach.

"They know who she is?" the Bandit wondered.

"Not yet," said one of the cops. "Except it isn't the broad they thought it was."

"The paper said it was some high class hooker," said the Bandit. He looked over the heads of the cops, directly at me, and winked.

"I don't think you can use hooker and high-class in the same sentence, Bandit." This was the older cop.

"There some kind of war on hookers these days?" This was an old-timer, sitting on a stool down the counter from the cops.

"There's always a war on hookers," said the younger cop. When he said it, he shook his head, a sad little shake of the head.

I put my money on the counter beside the register and headed for the door.

"Where you off to in such a rush?" The Bandit's cigarette butt bobbed as he spoke. An ash fell. On the floor, this time.

"Hotel Dieu. Get my stomach pumped."

"Very funny."

"Can you give me a lift?" This was the geezer at the counter, a few stools down from the cops. "I think I need mine done too."

"The two of youse can just fuck right off."

"Bye, Bandit."

"And don't be callin' me Bandit. These two meatheads might haul me in."

"They'd need a crane, Bandit." This was another geezer, in a booth by the window.

Everyone was laughing as the door banged shut behind me.

-THREE-

The city editor looked at the clock and then at me and then at the clock. The clock said 10:45. "You in a different time zone?"

Norm Wetherall has been city editor longer than I've been alive. The word is, he's nearing retirement. But they said that when I joined the paper and I joined the paper nineteen years ago.

Norm is pretty nondescript: five nine, five ten and a little on the rotund side. What's left of his hair - which isn't much - has gone white. Apart from the friar's fringe, he's got a little wisp up top where his widow's peak used to be. He wets it down in the morning, but half an hour after he sits down to edit stories, the tuft is standing straight up. All in all, he looks like some kind of clerk. Looks are deceiving. Norm Wetherall is a tough-minded no-nonsense sono-fabitch. If the newspaper business had more Norm Wetheralls, the newspaper business wouldn't be in the shitty shape it's in. You can't bullshit Norm Wetherall, and it's best you don't try.

I saw him fire a guy once. First thing on a Monday morning. The guy had been working Sundays. He and the photog had been sent to a local church to cover the dedication ceremony for a new bell. The photog got a shoulder-to-shoulder shot of a bunch of smiling church-goers, with the steeple in the background. The reporter wrote a cut-line to go under the picture. Norm had asked for a story. The reporter had clipped a note to the photo: Sorry, Norm. No story.

Like I say, it's best not to try to bullshit Norm. The guy who'd sold the bell to the church had called Norm to tip him off about the dedi-cation ceremony, hoping to get the name of his bell company in the paper. The guy went on, for quite a while, about his wonderful bell:

where it was made, how much it weighed, the craftsmen who made it. Et cetera and so on. 'That bell sure as hell better ring when they pull the rope, eh?' said Norm. The salesman said that was the worst part, sitting at the back of the church, sweating bullets and waiting for someone to pull the rope. Norm had asked the guy if he always showed up for the dedication ceremonies. Every last one. Always sat in the back, praying like a madman. Norm asked if the bell had ever not worked. 'If one of my bells failed on a Sunday, Mister Wetherall, I'd be selling used cars come Monday.' Which had sounded like a story to Norm. Which he mentioned to the reporter. To which the reporter had replied: 'There was no salesman there, Norm.' Goodbye, asshole.

Another time, Norm fired a guy right over the phone. Norm had sent him out to a construction site. Word on the police scanner was, a guy had fallen from the third storey of a building under construction. Norm dispatched this reporter and a photog. Half an hour later, the guy phones in, says there's no story. 'What?' says Norm. 'The guy wasn't even hurt,' says the reporter. 'What?' says Norm. The reporter repeated himself. Norm told him, 'you find that guy and find him fast and call that story in to rewrite for the final.' The reporter tells Norm he's sorry, but he can't do that. 'Why not,' says Norm. Well says the reporter, 'for one thing, the worker's already left the construction site and for another, I have to pick my kids up from school. The wife's working.' 'Well,' Norm said, 'you just go right ahead and pick your kids up from school and keep right on going and don't bother coming back. This afternoon, or ever.' The reporter wanted to know how come Norm was so pissed off. Every head in the newsroom turned when Norm banged down the receiver.

You've gotta love a guy like Norm.

I told Norm what'd I just overheard at The Bandit's. "So we better play it straight with the Gilmore angle. It was her car, all right, and her I.D. So we're safe to say that. But heads up after that."

"We haven't said it was her body."

"And as long as we don't, we're fine."

I asked Norm what they'd found out about Cindy Lou.

Cindy Lou was a high-grade hooker who'd moved to town shortly after the Casino opened. She had a reputation, but no record. Her reputation was, she worked the third floor of the Casino, exclusively, hitting the high rollers and the big spenders. She was remembered by some anonymous casino workers as "a classy lady" and "a very bright woman" and a very big tipper. She lived in a sprawling ranch in Southland Gardens, a spread worth at least half a million. "Here, see for yourself." Norm shuffled the photos on his desk, and handed me a glossy of a very classy, very sprawling, very expensive house. "Nice." I handed the photo back. "What else?"

Gilmore also maintained a penthouse suite at The Stardust and according to one room cleaner she was a very friendly lady, very pleasant, and tipped like royalty.

"And?" The cops were quite anxious to get together with a guy named Wayne Vincent who, though they weren't saying so, was very likely her pimp. All they were saying was that Vincent was "known to the department". The cops said he wasn't a suspect. "At the present time they said," said Norm. "They said they'd like to have a little chat with him, and they hoped he'd phone, or drop by."

"You know we've got a shot of him, eh?"

"Who's we?"

"We. Garth shot him last night at the scene."

"Guy with a late-model Jag?"

"That's the guy. Gimme the pictures."

Norm handed me the pile. I shuffled through them. The shot wasn't there. "Where are the castoffs?" Norm pulled another pile of photos from a basket on his desk. Seven photos down, there was Wayne Vincent. "That's him there. With the greased down hair."

"You sure?"

"Sure I'm sure. Caused a big stink. Wanted to go down and have a look at the car. Taylor told him if he took another step toward the car, he'd have him arrested. And then the guy got back in the Jag and took off."

Norm flipped the photo and wrote 'Wayne Vincent' on the back. He put it in his top drawer and shut the drawer.

"What else have you got?"

"We got through to Gilmore's father. He runs a dairy bar up in Orillia. He hadn't seen his daughter, or heard from her, in three years.They had some kind of falling out. He hadn't seen her, hadn't talked to her, had no idea what she was up to. Then he hung up."

"He knew why you were calling?"

"Oh yah, he knew. The cops had already talked to him."

"How'd he sound?"

"Let's just say he didn't sound exactly heartbroken."

"So, who's doing what?"

Benny Grant, the police reporter, was down in Balmy Beach, seeing what he could dig up. Karen Hall, one of the feature writers, was piecing together a bio of Cindy Lou Gilmore. Johnny LeBlanc, the rewrite whiz, was backgrounding the McBride murder and writing an update for the final. And that was it, so far.

"Count me in."

"What's your angle?"

"Haven't got one, yet. But I want to work the streets and see what comes up."

Norm looked at his assignment book. So far, there was only one meeting pencilled in for the night shift. Public Utilities Commission. "I guess we wouldn't get a front-pager out of that."

"No," I said, "I guess we wouldn't." I gave him a pat on the back.

"Keep in touch," he said.

"I'll drop you a line."

"Something for the early edition would be nice."

I told him I'd see what I could do, and I rounded his desk, heading for the door.

"Don't trip over too many bodies, Scoop." This was a moron on the editing desk. I gave him the digital salute.

"Whoooo-eee. Prima Donna's a little touchy."

Prima Donna had half a mind to lift the weasel out of his chair and punch his lights out.

Prima Donna thought better of it.

Prima Donna thought he'd go back home, get shaved, get showered, get presentable and hit the streets in search of a story no one else could get.

Just past eleven thirty in the morning, MaryMary's is not exactly a bee-hive of activity. One-Eyed Louie was nowhere to be found.

"What's the matter?" said MaryMary. "The wife throw you out?"

"As a matter of fact, yes she did. But that's an old story."

"Too bad. Hate to see a good marriage go down the toilet."

I told her I didn't think my marriage would have qualified. As least not in its later stages. "They never do, in the later stages. It was the earlier stages I was thinking about." MaryMary gave me what would pass for a motherly smile. Then she turned and led the way through the dining room toward the kitchen.

MaryMary is not a morning person. She was in a bathrobe, hair in rollers. She was wearing slippers that slapped against her heels as she walked. "I was married a few times. Every time I got divorced I'd promise myself never to get married again." She pushed the swinging door leading to the kitchen. I caught the door on the backswing. "Then I'd forget. My problem was, I had a short-term memory when it came to marriage. Show me a ring, I was sunk. I always was a sucker for that happily ever after crap. Which is crazy, eh?" I followed MaryMary into the kitchen. "I never did believe in happy endings," she said.

One of the girls scampered past us, one towel around her head, another wrapping her body. Well, most of it. "Hi, Huntzie."

"Hello Angel."

"Lookin' for a little action?"

"I'm not up for it, just yet Angel."

Angel twittered and vamped across the dining room and out of sight.

"The bar ain't open."

I told MaryMary I'd be grateful for a cup of coffee. "Coffee I can manage. Just made a pot." MaryMary swept past the kitchen table where one of the girls was sitting, doing her nails. "Hi Huntzie." Ecstasy gave me one of her patented smiles. "Cover up the goods, dear. He's not shopping. And scamper along. We've got business to discuss." Ecstasy pulled her robe together and took her goods through the door.

"Cream?"

39

I nodded.

"Have a seat."

I sat down at the kitchen table. It was one of those big harvest tables and, fittingly, there was a large wicker basket filled with fruit - apples, plums, bananas, oranges - in the centre between a pair of candlesticks. All around the table there were hand-woven place mats. Just like going home to grandma's. Depending on your grandmother.

Mary set one mug in front of me and another on the place mat across the table and took a chair. She lit a smoke and squinted at me. "So?"

"I need a little information."

"Library's two blocks down, on the left. Can't miss it. Big white building with 'Library' in big letters right above the door."

"What I need I can't get at the Downtown Library."

"What do you need?"

"All the information you can give me about a woman named Cindy Lou Gilmore. "

"Why?"

She was all ears as I told her what I knew so far. When I was done, she lit another smoke, brought the pot from the stove and refilled our mugs, took the pot back and leaned against the counter. "So, what you got is one dead hooker."

"Two dead hookers. And several questions."

"Beginning with?"

I told MaryMary it seemed there might be some connection between the two dead women, given that their bodies had been dumped within five hundred yards of each other.

"Stands to reason."

I told MaryMary it seemed kind of odd that Wayne Vincent would turn up at the scene, get uppity with Tubby Taylor, get very excited about seeing the car, never mention a word about Cindy Lou and then disappear.

"Not necessarily."

I asked what she meant, 'not necessarily'.

"If Cindy Lou Gilmore were a rock star, this guy Vincent would have been her manager. She wasn't. And he was a pimp."

I asked MaryMary what she knew about Wayne Vincent.

"Not much. Only that I didn't like him and wouldn't trust him. He's a cockroach. And a smart one."

Would he have killed Cindy Lou?

"Not likely. You don't kill the goose that lays the golden egg, so to speak. And definitely not a girl who lays them kind of eggs. From what you're sayin', and I never met her, this Cindy Lou woulda been his prime property. Most likely he wanted to be sure it was her car the cops had found. Maybe he was looking for something else. Something that'd been in her car, or something in the area. And he definitely wanted the cops to know he wasn't the one who offed her. You'd gotta be a moron to turn up at the scene if you knew the cops are about to find a body you just dumped there."

Either a moron, or a very clever killer.

"I've got twenty bucks that says he didn't kill her."

Why would he be making himself scarce?

"Five'll give ya ten he's lookin' for the killer himself. And very much wants to find the creep before the cops do."

"Which brings us back to Cindy Lou, and Melissa McBride. Why do you think someone would want to kill a couple of hookers?"

"They may have knew too much."

"About?"

"Answer that, and you got yourself a killer." MaryMary finished her coffee and set the mug in the sink. She returned to the table and sat down and lit up another smoke. "Maybe they saw somethin'. Or maybe they heard somethin'. And maybe someone figured he hadda shut them up." She tapped her cigarette against the lip of the ashtray. "On the other hand, they were very different types of girls, from the sounds of things. Working different parts of town, different types of johns. Chances of them crossin' paths is slim to none. A girl like this Cindy Lou wouldn't be caught dead in the same place as the other one."

"She was."

MaryMary smiled. Shook her head. "You are a sick one." She

41

drew on her smoke, exhaled. "Then again ..."

Then again, what?

"Maybe they didn't know enough."

"Enough?"

"To spot a sicko when they met him."

Hm.

The kitchen door swung open behind me. I half turned to give Louie a smile. He was giving me the eye. "You writin' Mary's life story?"

MaryMary laughed and coughed and laughed some more. "That ain't exactly a story for your local family newspaper."

Louie grinned - "certainly ain't" - and helped himself to a coffee. "What's up, hotshot?"

"Hotshot here's lookin' for a killer."

Louie turned from the counter, mug in hand. "Yah? Well, nice to meet you." Now he laughed, then he pulled a chair back and spun it around and sat down with his forearms crossed over the chair back. He was curious, but he wasn't about to ask too many questions. Mary filled him in.

"You know this Cindy Lou?" Louie shook his head. "I don't exactly travel in them circles."

Melissa McBride? "Yah. Seen her around."

Wayne Vincent? "Prick."

Which is how things can get interesting, all of a sudden.

As it turned out, One-Eyed Louie and Wayne Vincent - "which ain't his real name, by the way" - had run into each other on a number of occasions, the first being the time they were overnight roommates down at The County Jail. Louie was waiting trial on a charge of burglary - "a trumped-up charge" - while William Van Allen - "which is his real name" - was passing through on his way to The Big House for the first time: aggravated assault, using a weapon in the commission of a crime, and theft. "What he'd done was, he'd pistol-whipped this guy when the guy wouldn't make good on a debt. Then he walked off with this guy's girlfriend's mink coat, by way of a late payment." When she'd objected, he'd decked her. "But just with his fist." William Van Allen struck Louie, first time he laid an eye on the

42

guy, as the type of guy you don't turn your back on. Louie had spent the night flat on his back in the lower bunk, eyes wide open, the good one and the glass one. "You just get a feelin', is all. You don't trust your feelin's, you don't live long. Specially in the joint." Louie tapped a fingernail against the pupil of his glass eye. "I ever tell you what happened to my first eye?" He had, but I lied. I love to hear Louie talk.

"What happened was, I shoulda knew better than to ignore my feelin's. Like I said. I was havin' a little dispute with a guy, eh? I'd knocked him on his ass. I forget just why. Anyways, I coulda put the boots to him. One good kick woulda took care of him. But for some reason, I didn't. Which is another rule, eh? Never give an asshole a break. Anyone else for that matter. None of this hug your enemy shit. Anyway, I didn't put the boots to the guy. I just knocked him on his ass and then turned and started to walk away. Next thing the little sonofabitch is on my back, I mean right on my back like some kind of fuckin' monkey, and he's reaching around and tryin to gouge my eyes out. I got his one hand outta my eye, but I wasn't quick enough with the other one and just like that, the fucker popped my eye out of its socket and yanks the fuckin' thing right off."

I asked Louie what happened to the guy.

"Whaddya think happened to him. I crushed his fuckin' skull." He shook his head. "What I'm tellin' you is, you get a gut feelin', you better pay attention to it."

I asked him what had given him a gut feeling about Willie Van Allen. "When he got to the part about deckin' the guy's girlfriend, he smiled. One thing I can't stand, it's a guy who hits a lady. Ain't no call for that. Never. A guy who likes hittin' girls is some kinda freak."

Next time Louie saw William Van Allen was about five years after the jail encounter. Louie was working as a bouncer down at the British American. "You remember the B.A.?" I told him I did. "You're older'n you look. Which don't seem possible."

The B.A. was a three-storey brick hotel, beer parlour on the ground floor, rooms on the upper two. It was a river-rats kind of joint and it turned at least a couple of guys into millionaires back in the days when the ferries used to run across to Detroit and all those thirsty passengers had to pass right by the front door. Then the ferries stopped running and the B.A. languished and then they tore it down. An old and familiar tune in our town. There aren't two dozen bona fide historic buildings left. And this is one of the oldest towns in the country. But that's another story.

Van Allen had come in to the B.A. looking for trouble. He'd found it. He came in making a lot of noise about how he didn't allow his girls to be wasting their time drinking when they should be out on the street working. He started poking his girl on the shoulder, to punctuate his point, while he was backing her into the corner. Then all of a sudden he slugged her. Louie was never one to tolerate trouble, unless he started it himself. "Business is business, but he had no right to slug her. Like I say, I don't put up with men hittin' ladies. Ain't right." Next thing Van Allen knew, he was being ushered out. His feet weren't touching the ground. Louie had him by the scruff of the neck and the ass of the pants "and I danced him right out the door." Van Allen wasn't amused. "He threatened to kill me. Which is the first sign a guy ain't got the guts to do the job. A guy's gonna kill ya, he ain't about to send you a friggin' telegram, eh? But he hadda say somethin', I guess, bein' as how he was flat on his ass on Ouellette Avenue, where I'd tossed him and there's a whole bunch of guys behind me in the doorway, laughin' their asses off." Van Allen cursed and swore and huffed and puffed and then got up off the pavement and brushed himself off and did some more huffing and puffing and Louie had just stood in the door until he headed up the street. "You can always tell the chickenshits. Big wind, lots of thunder, no rain."

The third and last time Louie had seen him was about four years ago. Four or five. Maybe six. "I ain't so good on dates no more." Louie had been called up by a guy who was having trouble with some muscle. The muscle turned out to be William Van Allen.

The guy owned a coffee shop and variety down on Hookers Alley. "You maybe know the guy. Bill Baker? Real nice guy." Anyway, Baker's coffee shop was filling up with working girls. They were taking the window tables where they could see the johns cruising past on Wendell. It was like they were in a display case. "That's the way they do it in Amsterdam, eh? Sit in a window and wait for the customers."

It was working out fine for the girls. The cars would slow down, the girls would smile, the driver would waggle a finger and the girl could go out and do her chamber-of-commerce routine. Ten minutes later, she'd be back in the window, all smiles and twenty bucks richer.

Great for the girls. Great for the johns. Not so great for Billy Baker.

Parents were telling their kids not to go anywhere near Bill's Variety and Coffee Bar and the parents and other regulars weren't coming in either. The girls were buying one coffee every hour, maybe. And Billie boy's going broke. So he showed them the door.

Next thing he knew, a guy with too much grease in his hair and no taste in suits came strutting in flanked by a pair of guys who maybe used to be linebackers with The Lions. Van Allen told Bill he heard there'd been some kind of misunderstanding. He said his girls told him they'd been given the bum's rush.

Bill told Van Allen there'd been no misunderstanding. He had given the girls the bum's rush. And if they came back in, Bill would call the cops, have the whores charged with loitering, trespassing, whatever. "I don't pay a mortgage to showcase a bunch of sluts."

One of the gorillas hit Billy Baker so hard in the gut that it took Baker about fifteen minutes to unfold himself and stand up. When he got his breath back, he called Louie. Louie told him "I'd like nothing better than to have a little conversation with the creep." It didn't turn out to be a conversation, exactly.

Baker tossed the girls again. Van Allen came back. He made a bee-line from the door to the counter, behind which Bill Baker was standing with his arms crossed. Van Allen didn't know what hit him.

What hit him was Louie, who'd been sitting on the end stool and who was watching Van Allen in the mirror and who'd stood up just when Van Allen got within arm's length. The two thugs were as big as Billy said they were. But they weren't stupid. They could recognize an automatic when Louie pulled it out of his holster. And they could recognize a don't-fuck-with-me stare when they saw one.

"What I'm sayin' is, Van Allen's a gutless little weasel. Loves to knock women around. Shits himself anytime he has to deal with a man. Which is all I know about William Van Allen and all I care to know. Unless you're here to tell me he's dead."

I asked Louie if Van Allen was still running a stable on Wendell Street.

"Last time I heard."

"If Melissa McBride was working Wendell, what're the chances Van Allen would've been her pimp?"

"Nine outta ten."

-Four-

I got back to the Beach just before one in the afternoon.

No more crowds, no more cops.

If you missed all the action first thing this morning, you'd never guess - driving past now - that there'd been any kind of commotion at all.

I parked on the side of Water Street, near Chappus.

There are only two houses left, facing the river.

The first one you come to is surrounded by an eight-foot chain link fence. Partly it's to keep people out, keep them from stealing the cord wood that's cut and stacked out back. And partly it's to keep the horses in - the only three horses grazing on a lot anywhere in the city.

There's a bylaw dealing with this - hell, there's a bylaw dealing with just about everything - but the city has only one bylaw officer and he's not actively looking for things to do. If someone calls, he goes out to investigate. If nobody calls, then as far as the bylaw officer is concerned, there's no infraction. Nobody's ever called about those three horses.

A little free firewood for the neighbours works wonders. The neighbours keep warm all winter, the horses graze to their hearts' delight and the bylaw officer doesn't get stressed out. Everyone's happy.

Up until three years ago, there was another horse in Balmy Beach. He's been bottled and sent to classrooms. What happened was, this horse was grazing in a big backyard and nobody much minded. Every now and then the guy who owned it would saddle it up and take all the neighbourhood kids and grandkids for a ride up and

47

down the road.

How could you call the cops on a guy who takes the kids for a ride on his horse?

Here's how.

This particular horse owner had a swimming pool in his back yard. He was going away for a week so he took his horse down to the woman on the corner and asked if he could board it there for the week. The woman said, three horses, four horses, what's the difference? The guy went back home and got ready for his trip.

Then his neighbour lady said: 'do you mind if we use your pool while you're gone?' Well, he did mind. And he told her so. He said he didn't want anyone drowning in his pool while he was gone and then suing his ass off once he came back.

Fine.

Now, why the neighbour lady bothered to ask in the first place, no one can figure out to this day.

However.

A week later, the guy came back from holiday and collected his horse and walked it home and let it loose in the field. His neighbour lady called the cops. The cops sent out the bylaw officer and the bylaw officer was very apologetic, and very firm. The horse had to go. There'd been a complaint, and once there was a complaint, he had to act. And that was it for the fourth-last horse in the entire city limits. The bylaw officer apparently did not pass by the house at Chappus and Water on his way out of the neighbourhood and so failed to notice the three horses standing there, nibbling hay and swatting flies with their tails.

It's not known, for a fact, whether the bylaw officer heats his house with a wood stove.

The woman who owns that corner house and those three horses is Betty McLean. Her husband Norm runs the firewood business. When I was still married, and living in an old house which had a fireplace, I used to order my wood from Norm. That was a long time ago, but when I waved at Betty and said hello, she smiled and waved. "Long time, no see." I explained my absence. "Well, that's too bad. Especially for the kids, I guess." I told her the kids were doing fine. She looked like she might want to ask another question, but then thought better of it. I nodded in the direction of the crime scene. "Nasty bit of business." I asked her what she'd heard.

"You tell me. The cops won't tell us anything. All I hear is, it's another woman. Probably a hooker. Just as dead as the first one." She told me more stuff that I already knew: that someone had found the car and the body in the middle of the night, that Leslie Ambrose had been the one to call the cops, that everyone in the neighbourhood was freaked, for sure, especially the women who lived alone, or who lived alone with their kids.

"There's a lot of wackos out there in the world."

I told her that seemed to be the case.

She asked me what I was up to.

I told her I wanted to have a little chat with Leslie Ambrose.

"Good luck."

"By which you mean?"

"By which I mean, good luck." By which she meant that depending on the day, and sometimes the hour of the day, Leslie Ambrose could be pleasant and neighbourly, chatty and hospitable. Betty had been in Leslie's house any number of times for coffee in the morning and beer in the afternoon or evening and she'd left thinking she'd found a new friend. And then the next week, or the next day, she'd wave and say hi and Leslie would make like she hadn't heard, would turn her back and carry on about her business. "She's a weird one."

I thanked Betty for the warning and told her I'd be seeing her around.

"Most likely. The universe is expanding, but the world seems to be shrinking."

I smiled, and nodded, and hadn't a clue what she was talking about.

Leslie Ambrose's place had definitely seen better days. Give her marks for trying; she'd planted chrysanthemums in some no-tread whitewalls by the driveway. She'd speared a bunch of whirly-legged Donald Duck and Elmer Fudd and Goofy ornaments into the lawn. Maybe eight or ten years back, she'd painted the place pale yellow. But all the trying in the world didn't mask the facts. One of the walls was bulging outward and the roof had a noticeable sag. The place was a dump. Leslie's only hope would be that the city would buy it before the house fell down around her ears. Faint hope.

Her mutts were barking their asses off as I walked across the lawn.

"I don't want to be interviewed."

Leslie might have been 32, as she'd told me last night. And the moon might be made of blue cheese. Maybe Leslie wanted to think time had stood still but in daylight it was a tough sell. She'd logged a lot of hard miles. She was thin and her hair was dyed a sort of brownish auburn, but not in the last little while. There was half an inch of grey near her scalp. She was wearing blue jeans and a Led Zeppelin T-shirt, over which she'd pulled on a pea-green cardigan. She was standing just inside the screen door of her front porch. It took a few seconds for the dogs to shut up so she could hear what I was saying. She didn't open the door and it didn't look like she was entertaining the notion.

I told her I didn't want to interview her.

What did I want, then?

I told her I just wanted to ask a couple of questions.

"What's the difference between two questions and an interview?"

"About forty questions and half an hour of your time."

She still had her own teeth. "What'd you say your name was?"

I pulled a card from my wallet and held it up for her to see. "You're the guy from last night?" I told her I was. She told the dogs to lie down and shut up. They knew who the boss was. Then she opened the door and told the growling dogs to stay right where they were. "Come on through. Pardon the mess."

The living room was a mess all right: too much heavy furniture, too many newspapers (piles of them on the floor, copies scattered here and there on tables and chairs), a couple of beer bottles upright on an end table, three others on their sides on the carpet nearby, a plastic basket of laundry, an ironing board (but no iron), a couple of dog blankets. We waded on through to the kitchen. More clutter: unwashed dishes on the counter, unwashed dishes in the sink, cereal boxes and empty soup and stew tins on the table, a couple of yawning black plastic trash bags by the back door beside a tower of beer cases.

50

Leslie cuffed a cat off a chair and told me to sit down. "You want a beer?" I checked my watch. When I looked up, she had two bottles by the necks and was kicking the fridge door shut. She set one bottle in front of me and one in front of herself and sat down. "Question number one?"

"You found Melissa McBride's body?"

She nodded.

"What'd the body look like?"

"I don't want to answer that."

"That bad?"

"Worse than that."

"How much worse?"

"Her face was mush."

I twisted the cap from my bottle and took a swallow. "Mind if I smoke?"

"Is that question number two?" Then she smiled and held up her hand. There was a cigarette between the first two fingers. "Aren't we observant." She shook her head. She flicked the ash onto the linoleum.

I lit up. "Tell me about that day."

Well, that day Leslie was going to take her dogs for a walk across the field and down along the river but as soon as she opened her door, the dogs took off straight for the ditch on the far side of the road.

When she caught up with them, it was all she could do to pull them back from the body. "Every time I go past there I think of that poor woman and what they did to her, eh?"

The woman had been wearing a sweater, navy or black or dark brown - hard to tell in that early thin early-morning light. From the waist down she wore nothing, not even nylons. "Somebody had to have wanted her dead in a real bad way to do what they did to her. God." Leslie took another pull on her cigarette and then her beer. "I can't imagine someone doing that to another human being. You know what I mean? I mean, I can see wanting to kill someone. There's a couple of assholes I wouldn't mind knocking off. My former husband, for one. I can imagine shooting that sonofabitch - it's

51

quick, it's arms length. In fact, I'd love to shoot the sonofabitch after what he did to me and the kids. I can see a guy walking out on his wife, eh? But walking out on his kids? Didn't even say goodbye. Just left for work one morning and never came home. How could a guy do that? What the hell was I supposed to tell the kids? If I'd had a gun at the time, I'd have gone looking for him. No problem. Bang, bang, you're dead. But beating someone to a pulp? How could you do that?"

"I guess you could do it if you were angry enough. Or crazy enough."

"Man, this sonofabitch has to be a psycho." She shook her head and took another pull on her smoke and then snuffed it in the ashtray. "I mean when I say mush, I mean all that was left of her was pulp. The only way they identified her was through her prints, eh? Incredible." She lit up another smoke. "And now another one. And from what the fat man said, the guy with the dogs, it was the same kind of thing this time." She shook her head, tipped the bottle up, then put it on the counter beside herself. "Cops got any idea who the wacko is who's doing this?"

"When they're asking people to call Crimestoppers, it's not what you'd call a good sign."

"Well, I'll tell you one thing, I can't get out of this neighbourhood fast enough. Man. Two bodies in one month. I just wish the city would get off its ass and buy us out."

I asked her if she'd noticed anything odd last night.

"Such as?"

"Cars going into the field, cars coming out. People walking around. You know, that sort of thing."

She shook her head.

"Anything weird the night Melissa's body was dumped?"

"Nope. Nothin'."

I flipped my notebook closed and shoved it in my pocket. I took another sip of beer, then set the bottle on the kitchen table.

"That's it?"

"Yup. That's it."

"That wasn't so bad."

52

I thanked her for her help, then stood up.

Then she started talking about life in Balmy Beach and how much it had changed in the years since she'd moved in with her former husband, the one she wouldn't mind knocking off. "There was a time this was a real nice place to live. Hard to believe now. But it was, once." When she and her husband had moved in, and the kids were small - they were all grown and gone now - "there was all kinds of wildlife around here. Skunks, stray cats, rabbits. It was like living out in the country. It wasn't never The Heights or anything, or like living on The Drive, but, hey, we had a good time and no one bothered us. We had campfires down by the river and the kids could run all over - down by the river or over in the woods - and nobody would give two thoughts to it. But that was twenty years ago. Now?"

Now, the world was going to hell in a handcart, if you asked her. Dopeheads all over the place, people knocking off the corner store to buy crack, woman being dumped in the ditches, perverts snatching kids out of schoolyards, wackos everywhere you go.

As for the neighbourhood, it was shot to hell, too. Most of the decent people had either died or moved out. Most of the places were rented out and the renters didn't give two shits for their neighbours. "Apart from Betty over here, I don't even know any of the people around here. And from the looks of them, I wouldn't want to know them."

What ticked her off was, she'd had a chance to sell four, five years back. "I need my head read. Why I didn't grab the cash is beyond me." These days, nobody in their right mind would buy a place in Balmy Beach. "I'm just waiting for the city to write me a cheque." And the sooner the better.

I wished her luck. Then I finished my beer and stood up. I put my card on the table. "If you hear anything you think might make a story, give me a call." She told me she'd do that. I headed for the doorway leading to the living room and I hadn't gone three steps before both the dogs were up and snarling.

"Shut the fuck up, you guys." They did. Leslie shrugged, in an apologetic kind of way. "They look scary, but they're a pair of sucks."

"Did they bark?"

"Bark?"

"During the night, whenever the body was dumped."

"Which body?"

"Either one."

She shook her head. She gave me a funny kind of look, like she was trying to read my mind. And then she started talking a little too fast. "If someone had come on the property, they'd have gone wild. But cars up and down the road? They don't bother. At least they didn't last night."

Leslie's bedroom is at the front of the house. Standing in the living room you can look through the bedroom window and you can see the field where Cindy Lou's body had been found. It wouldn't be more than three or four hundred yards from that spot to Leslie's front door. Even less to the ditch where Leslie had found Melissa's body.

When I turned, Leslie was staring at me.

"I guess we're all sound sleepers."

I thanked her for her time, and for the beer and then I walked across the lawn and chatted with Betty for a few minutes.

Then I turned and walked back along the edge of the road toward Leslie's house. When I got within a couple of feet of her property line, I could hear the dogs. They were barking their asses off.

When I turned, Leslie was on the porch, staring.

It was four minutes past three by the time I got back to my car. I hadn't been counting on the walk down the river or back. I had exactly eleven minutes to make it halfway across town to Hugh Campbell School. In the middle of the night, with no traffic on the expressway and hitting every green light from the expressway exit to the school, you could make the trip in maybe fifteen minutes. In the middle of the afternoon, considering shift changes at Chrysler's and the likelihood of hitting the traffic lights, you'd be looking at twenty five minutes, half an hour. Easy. Which meant Katie would be crying and Ben would be consulting his Authentic Detroit Tigers watch and telling her not to worry, that Dad was sometimes late, but that Dad never forgot to pick them up. To which Katie would reply, 'oh yah?' and would remind him of that Saturday afternoon not so long ago I'd forgotten to pick them up from the movie.

Who could blame her? Being forgotten, even once, even for just the half hour or so it took Jeannie to track me down, yell at me, tell me to haul my ass over to that theatre and hope to God the kids were there or she'd personally turn me into a eunuch - well, no one, least of all an eight-year-old, likes to be forgotten. And an eight-year-old, once forgotten, will never forget.

Ben could 'big brother' all he wanted, but unless I got there within ten minutes of the appointed time, there'd be no way Ben could keep her under control.

Nothing for it but to haul ass.

Eighteen minutes later, there I was, pulling to a stop in front of a very scowly Katie and a very put-upon Ben.

"Hi guys."

I got the silent treatment all the way to McDonalds. Ben relented but Katie was Little Miss Frosty right up to the cash register, passing her request - burger, shake and fries - via Ben while studiously looking in every direction but mine. Like Mother, like Daughter.

We all thawed out during supper.

"So," said Ben.

"Not with your mouth full."

Ben gave me the eye, finished chewing, elaborately, then swallowed, then: "what about that Alan Trammell, eh?"

What about him? "All he need's a cape and he's Superman."

"He's already Superman, as far as I'm concerned," said Ben.

Well, I guess. Another bottom-of-the-ninth one-out two-run home run.

"Why's he even thinking of retiring?"

"Well, he's getting on. He's thirty-seven."

"You're thirty-seven, and you're not retiring."

"I'm not playing 162 games a year."

"It's crazy. I hope he changes his mind."

"We'll see."

"Who's Alan Trammell?" Katie gave Ben the eye, then smiled at me. Ben missed the point.

"Only the greatest shortstop in the history of the American League."

"What's a shortstop?"

Ben rolled his eyes and stuffed his mouth with fries so as not to have to even attempt an answer.

We were on our way to the mall - "you could get them each some summer clothes, unless you're absolutely destitute, in which case my heart bleeds for you Huntzie, and you can still buy them each some summer clothes" - when Ben seemed to remember that I, too, had a life.

"How was your day?"

"Gruesome."

Which was all they needed to hear.

Now, I don't believe in scaring the shit out of little kids, especially my own little kids. On the other hand, I don't believe in shielding them from the truths of the world. Even the ugly truths. Especially the ugly truths. Kids will get all the ugly truths by the time they're eight and ten. If they don't get the story from you, they'll get it from someone else. Who knows how someone else will embroider things? Even if you did want to paint your kids into some Norman Rockwellian corner, there's no way you could pull it off. Kids have got built-in bullshit detectors. At least mine do. Lie to them, or try, and they'll know it as soon as you open your mouth. The only thing you manage to do is teach them never to trust a word you say. There's no way out. All things considered, I'd rather deliver the news myself. I am in the business.

"What's a hooker?"

Hmm.

Another roll of the eyes, as though Ben couldn't quite believe his sister could be that stupid and still breathe. He was also, very definitely, all ears.

It was quarter past four by the time we'd pulled into the parking lot at the mall and by then I'd given the kids a refresher in the facts of life and a crash course on the danger of selling your body or your soul, or both. And I'd reassured Katie that no one was about to come

56

along with a rock and bash her head in.

"Some people are really sick, aren't they Dad?"

Yes, kiddies. Some people are. Truly sick. "Not many, but some. And you should know this about getting through life: always keep your head up. You know what I mean?"

Ben nodded. Sagely. Katie was looking worried.

"What I'm saying, Katie, is ..." What in hell was I saying?

We were holding hands on our way to The Bay, Ben on my left, Katie on my right.

"What I'm saying is, the vast majority of people are very good, very decent, very kind. The world is full of wonderful strangers who'd help you out in an instant. But there are a few wackos out there, and you've got to remember that. And you've got to make sure you don't put yourself in a position where they ...."

"... can bash your head in with a rock."

Thank you Ben.

"... where they can take advantage of you, let's say."

"And if anyone tries, kick 'em in the balls." Ben was smirking. "Right, Dad?"

"Metaphorically speaking."

"What's metamorphickly?" Katie wanted to know.

"What kind of clothes do you guys want?"

"Dad?"

"Yes, Katie."

"Are you sick?"

"Sick?"

"Yah."

"Not that I know of. Why?"

"Mom says you're sick. She says that's why you're not living with us any more."

"Mom said that?"

"She said you're a sick sonofabitch."

"Katie!" Ben punched her in the arm. "Shut up."

57

"When did Mom say that?"

"When she came home from the lawyer meeting."

"I think your Mom was maybe a little upset. I don't think she really meant that."

"She said you were never coming back." Ben was staring at me. "Did she mean that?"

"Well, Ben ..."

"Don't bullshit me, Dad. Are you or aren't you?"

I looked at Ben and then I looked at Katie and then I looked at Ben. And then Ben said, "Fine, that's all the answer I need."

"Ben ..."

"If it's no, it's no. I don't mind. I just want to know that's all. I don't want to get my hopes up and then find out you're not, that's all. If you do, you do. If you don't you don't. I just want to know what's what."

"Well, I guess what's what is the way things are."

"Why don't you love Mom anymore?"

I looked at Katie. "It's a long story, sweetheart."

"Will you stop loving me one day, too?"

"No. Never."

"How do you know?"

"I just know."

"When you married Mom, you said you'd love her forever."

"That was different."

"How was it different?"

"Another time, sweetheart. Listen. I've got to make a phone call. Follow me."

They followed me out through The Bay and down the concourse to the bank of telephones. I dropped a coin in the slot and dialled, then I turned and watched Katie and Ben standing in the centre of the concourse. They were having a heated discussion about something.

"Wetherall."

"It's your favourite Prima Donna."

"Well, aren't you a mind reader."

58

"What's up?"

"They've ID'd the corpse. They're having a press conference at 5:30."

"I'm on my way."

Norm wanted to know what I'd been up to, and what I'd been doing all afternoon. I filled him in and said goodbye and hung up.

"What are you guys so serious about?"

"We were ..."

Ben punched Katie on the shoulder. "Nothing."

The summer clothes - jeans, T-shirts, sneakers, Tigers caps - Jeannie appreciated. Dead hookers she did not. "Huntzie! How could you?"

"How could I?"

How could I not?

Try telling that to Jeannie. Jeannie had passed her Protective Mothers course with straight A's. I would not say that Jeannie was fearful of the world. But she does have an aversion to its more unpleasant aspects. Jeannie sees nothing wrong with a holiday at Disney World. When I suggested a month's tour of Europe, by the seat of our pants, Jeannie was mortified. We went. But we went on a package tour. Fourteen days, seven countries. Taxes, meals, hotels and tips included.

Dead hookers did not enter into Jeannie's scheme of things. She's one of the few wives in the history of the world who did not want to sit down at day's end and hear, chapter and verse, what her husband had done all the day long. "Please," Jeannie would say, holding up a palm, the way cops do to stop traffic.

"You are truly sick, Huntzie. Honest to God. You're going to turn your children into . . ."

"Her face was mush, eh Dad?" Timing is everything, Ben.

Jeannie gathered the children, one under each arm, and gave me one of her no-nonsense stares. She pinched her lips together and held back whatever it was she wanted to say with the greatest effort of will. What she was holding back was something like: "if you ever , and I mean EVER, so much as mention a dead ...."

Then she pinched her eyes half closed in her most threatening fashion and then she reached out for the edge of the door. "GoodBYE Jonathan."

"Bye Daddy."

"Bye Katie."

"Bye Dad."

"Bye .... "

I was waggling my fingers at a closed door.

The press conference began a few minutes late. Normally, a cop named Lloyd Peters does the pressers. Not a bad guy, considering his job is to give you as little information as possible, and only the dull stuff if he can get away with it. But today, Lloyd was sitting at the right hand of one of the gods who had apparently been ordered by The Chief himself to meet with the rabble. Clearly, The Deputy would rather have been down at the morgue, helping out with the post mortem. It became clear within a couple of seconds that The Deputy had been told to slam a lid on this one, and pronto.

He did give us the victim's name. "The deceased person is one Carole Tippet, female Caucasian, seventeen years of age. Ms. Tippet was known to the department."

"Seventeen?" I said.

"Seventeen," The Deputy said.

"When you say she was known to the department, exactly what does that mean?"

The Deputy gave me one of those high-powered 'who rattled your chain' looks, then turned his attention back to the paper in his hands. Lloyd Peters, who was rolling a ballpoint back and forth, fingers and thumb, said "please hold all questions until The Deputy Chief has completed his statement".

Another couple of seconds, and that was it for The Deputy's statement. Apart from the name and age of the deceased, he hadn't told us a stitch about her. I put up my hand.

Lloyd pointed a finger in my direction. "Mister Hunter, you have a question for the Deputy Chief?"

"Is this the work of a serial killer?"

Which is why they'd sent The Deputy. "We are encouraging you not to leap to any conclusions. What we have here is a female

60

deceased person. Her body was found in the same general location as the body of another female deceased person some three weeks ago. As for any connection between the two, the department is unable to say. The investigation continues."

"Should women in our community be concerned for their safety as they walk the streets at night?" This was a Hair-Do from Channel 2. The Deputy applied a linen handkerchief to his brow and patted it around up there for a second or two. "Women in our community should not be any more concerned for their safety than they normally are."

"What's that mean?" wondered the Hair Do.

"What I mean, is ...."

"What The Deputy means, is ... the streets of the city are no less safe than they were yesterday for ordinary citizens of our community."

"And for hookers?" I wondered.

Lloyd looked at The Deputy, The Deputy looked at Lloyd and Lloyd looked at us: "The department is advising those working in the sex trade industry to be especially cautious."

"Was Ms. Tippet a prostitute?"

"She was known to the department."

"So am I. But I'm not a prostitute."

"Want a second opinion?" This was a Deep Throat from AM 7-Something Or Other. I gave him one of my most gracious smiles.

"We can't release any more details at this time, for fear of jeopardizing our investigation."

"What do you say to the women of the city who are now terrified of being alone at night?" Hair-Do, once again.

The Deputy apparently had a thing or two he'd love to say to Hair-Do when the camera wasn't focusing right on him. "I would tell the women of the city, generally speaking, that they have no more to worry about than they did yesterday. As Sergeant Peters says, however ...."

"What can you tell us about this girl?" I said.

"I've told you all we can tell you at this point in time."

"What can you tell us about Cindy Lou Gilmore?"

"We have put out a missing person's report on Ms Gilmore."

"Do you have any idea how Carole Tippet wound up with Gilmore's car and I.D.?"

"That's one of the questions we'll ask her, when we find her."

"Assuming you find her," I said.

"Alive," said Hair-Do.

The Deputy was standing up. The Deputy was heading for the door. I checked my watch. Elapsed time of press conference, including questions and answers: nine minutes. The Deputy Chief preceded everyone out the door, his white shirt clinging pinkly to his back. Then a couple of guys thought they might as well ask Lloyd a question, since they'd come all the way down. Then the TV crews shouldered their stuff down the hall. I was waiting by the door.

"Deputy's going to give you a kiss, next time he sees you."

"I'll make sure to lower my trousers."

"What can I do for you?"

"We've got two dead hookers, right?

"Right."

"Each one had her head crushed, right?"

"Right."

"Their bodies were found within a few dozen yards of each other?"

"Right."

"And you're telling us, there's no connection?"

"I didn't say there wasn't a connection."

"I asked ..."

"You asked if this was the work of a serial killer. I don't know that. But I do know there's some connection. And that's what we're working on. And that's all I can tell you."

"A connection as in, one wacko killing both hookers?"

"There's a connection. That's all we can say without ...."

"... jeopardizing the investigation." I grinned. "One more question."

Peters waited for it.

"What's with the purse, and the car?"

"You find out, you tell us."

"I'll do that."

Peters edged his way past me and started down the hall.

"One more question."

Peters stopped and turned and looked at me. "What is it?"

"What are the chances Cindy Lou Gilmore is dead?"

Peters rolled his eyes toward the ceiling. He gave off one of those exasperated sighs. "Huntzie. C'mon."

"Just wondering."

Peters was heading down the hall.

"One more question."

He stopped, turned: "last one."

"How come a seventeen-year-old kid wound up working the street?"

"Beats me."

"She from around here?"

He nodded.

"Her parents still in town?"

He nodded.

"Address?"

Peters looked to his left, and then to his right, and then at me. "I can't tell you that."

I looked at him.

He looked at me.

He looked to his left, and then his right, and then at me.

"Harry is a name you might want to remember."

I smiled. "I owe you one."

"Yes," he said. "You do."

"Thanks, Lloyd."

"Don't mention it."

"I won't." I headed for the door.

"Huntzie?"

I turned

"Don't let that sonofabitch off the hook."

He turned and headed down the hall.

I headed for the stairway and my car.

-Five-

It's a sorry street, Wendell is, at least that section east of Ouellette where the girls ply their trade. They work the stretch from Ouellette to Parent. It's about a mile and a half of desperation. Most of the buildings are two storeys, cement block sides, brick fronts, apartments up the stairs. A few of the places were houses, once upon a time, but these days there are shops where the living rooms used to be.

All kinds of shops. There are appliance shops (Buy Sell Trade) and donut shops; there are variety stores (No Change For Bus) and alteration shops (We Make Dress's). There are beauty parlours and barber shops with sun-bleached photos taped to the inside of the windows. There's a cosmetic place with bright red bristol board signs advertising cellulite reduction (One Treatment $15) and body piercing (Most Body Parts $50 - Jewellery Included). There's a place that specializes in used refrigerators (All Units Guaranteed One Month) and a place that sells nothing but used tires (Just Like New Five Bucks). There's a laundromat open 24 hours where, for a small extra charge, the attendant will run the clothes through while you go next door and have a few brew. There's a place where you can rent to own - TVs, VCRs, stereos, you name it - (No Long-Term Obligation, No Credit Refused, Best Deals In Town). There are four taverns and one gay hangout (Big Bob's Bar and Grill). There are three used car lots (nothing under the flags and banners newer than 10 years old). There's a furniture store which occupies most of one block, but not for long (After 70 Years Building Sold Everything Must Go). There are bakeries and coffee shops and video shops. There's a Bingo Palace. Curiously, there's also a travel agency with brochures laid neatly out on the windowsill (Florida, Hawaii, Virgin Islands). There are pawn shops with stereo speakers and hockey pads sharing space in the window with toasters and irons and ghetto blasters (Competative Rates On Short-Term Loans).

It's all buy and sell, like any other commercial strip in town. But down on Wendell, nobody really has their heart in it. Breaking even seems to be the name of the game. Profit would be a surprise.

Some of the business owners are starting out and hoping to work their way up to a shop in the high-rent district - a plaza, maybe, The Mall eventually - and a house in the suburbs and a membership in a country club. Some of them have done and had all that and have fallen from grace. The rest have been working Wendell all their lives, as their mothers and fathers worked it before them. Only way out: in through the back door and out through the front door of Marentette Brothers Funeral Home down the street. The business owners are not a great deal different than the girls who ply their trade, sundown to dawn's early light, from the doorways of those same shops. You'd think, given their run of luck, these business types would be a little more tolerant of those one step down on the stairway of life. You'd be wrong.

The business types are tougher than churchgoers when it comes to working girls. The uplifters - most of them women, curiously, and all of them with a straight face - say the hookers are a blight on the neighbourhood. The businessmen couldn't give a rat's ass for morality: they'd flunked out of that course, or switched to Scraping By 101. Their concern was pretty basic. They didn't want the hookers to give the neighbourhood a bad name, chase away any potential customers who might be wandering the street, though what kind of reputation they thought the neighbourhood had and what kind of customers come calling after closing time they would be hard-pressed to explain. It didn't much matter. Once they start bitching loudly enough and to the right people - a couple of right-wing types on city council - about property taxes and business taxes and the fact that small business is the lifeblood of the city and so on, council would rise up righteous and send a message to the Chief of Police and the Chief would dispatch the uniform boys. The uniform boys would slap the girls with a hitchhiking ticket - 80 bucks a pop - and the girls would snap their gum and cross the street and stick out a thumb again and the cops would cross the street and write them another ticket. Takes a lot of blowjobs to pay off a couple of hitchhiking tickets. So it generally worked, at least for a while. The girls would drift to another part of town. And if it didn't work, the chief would send out the decoys and the decoys would collar a few of the girls and a few of the johns and things would settle down for a couple of weeks or a month. The girls who got collared would have a holiday - no beatings, three squares a day - at county expense and the johns would pay their anonymous fines and go home to their wives in the suburbs and the girls who hadn't got caught would work somewhere else and then the girls would get let out of jail and the others would start coming out of the woodwork and things would go back to normal until indignation rose again to an audible whine.

Pretty well any night of the week, any week of the year, you can count a couple of dozen girls working their turf. Sorry sight. Sorriest of all in the dead of winter when the girls are huddling in doorways, fingers and toes numb, noses running, ears red and burning, trying to dodge the wind. They stick their heads out now and then, hoping for traffic, hoping for business, hoping to turn enough tricks to make quota before they turn to ice. Winter is when the girls tend to make stupid mistakes. If you're cold enough, and close enough to quota to think about quitting for the night, you can be fooled into ignoring your better judgement. You can start to think that any warm car at all, even with a questionable john behind the wheel, has got to be better than the goddamn unrelenting west wind knifing through your too-thin clothes.

So winter is generally when we do our break-your-heart feature stories from Hookers Alley: girls beaten up, girls arrested, girls trying to make a living in the freezing cold. Spring, summer, fall or winter, we do an occasional not-in-our-front-yard story. I've done my share of both, the last one just before Thanksgiving.

There's a church about a mile down from Ouellette. It's called Our Lady of Sorrows. It's one of those big old downtown churches which was built and paid for by the Italians who built the neighbourhood. The Italians worked hard, got prosperous and moved a few blocks south and east. They sold their tidy little homes to those who came in the next wave: Poles and Czechs and Slovenians and others with names you'd have a tough time spelling or pronouncing. Then they worked hard and got prosperous and moved on and sold their aging bungalows and cottages to anyone with a down payment and then those people stayed on until they could afford to move up and out. Eventually, most of the houses got bought by people who didn't want to live in the area, only wanted to rent to those who could afford to live nowhere else. A motley crew. The neighbourhood settled and sagged and became known as The Swamps.

Beside Our Lady of Sorrows there's a parking lot. The church owns half of it and Crazy Jack from Crazy Jack's Furniture and Appliances (No Reasonable Offer Ejected) owns the other half and it works out fine. The shoppers use it during the day and the week. The church goers use it on Sundays. The church-hall bingo-goers and the hookers use it at night.

The back part of the lot isn't too well lit which means that things are just about perfect: the girls can see the street, but the cops on the street can't see clearly into the cars parked at the back of the lot. On bingo nights, the cops can't tell a john's car from a bingo-goer's car.

Problem is, the bingo ladies would rather step on dogshit than on a damp condom on their way to the church basement. And they also don't like catching glimpses of what they can catch a glimpse of when they can't help peeking into the parked cars. They tut-tut with each other and trade all the lurid details, then go see the priest and tell him, only in vaguest detail, about what they've had to endure.

The priest played along, acting horrified as they told their shocking little tales. He shrugged them off as long as he could. But complaints are one thing. A drop in bingo profits quite another. Turn The Other Cheek has its limits. In the end, the priest joined the local chamber of commerce types in front of city council. Given his status in the community, Father Martin was the one they shoved front and centre and it was he who wound up on the front page calling for 'an end to this scourge among us'. Zoot, our editorial cartoonist, had a ball with it: he showed all the store-owner sleazoids and blue-rinse matrons in front of city council, Father Martin in the centre of the group with bingo cards and dollar bills stuffed into his pockets. There was a terrified hooker on the floor before him about to get zapped by the bolt of lightning in his hand. The caption read: Christian Charity. No one ever accused Zoot of having a light touch.

The next week, Our Lady of Sorrows held a Candlelight Vigil. It was one of those Take Back Our Street things. Not many people showed up. Maybe forty or fifty. Seven working girls strutted in. You couldn't help but notice. They stuck right out. Their clothes, for one thing: leather jackets or fake minks, mini-skirts and leotards. Plus, they were sitting right up front, the better to hear Father Martin. The rest of the crowd looked like they might be parishioners, or residents of the neighbourhood. The same people who'd bitched and complained about the presence in the parking lot of the women now snapping chewing gum in the front row.

Father Martin got going right on time. He was at the front with his back to the altar, surrounded by potted plants and dying flowers. He was wearing a white robe with red trim. Attached to the collar, there was a little microphone so those of us in the back could hear. A good thing because, except for Father Martin and the whores, everyone was in the back.

"Dearly Beloved." He had a nice sermony kind of voice, the kind I remember from when I was a kid and my mother used to drag me to church. "We are gathered here tonight to pray for the troubled souls of women who are victimized night after night after ...." He rattled on for ten or fifteen minutes, saying how sorry he was these troubled women had had to make their living the way they did.

"But wasn't it inevitable?"

Then he then launched into a bit of a tirade about the lack of morals in today's society and what a shame it was that young girls aren't getting more direction from their parents. And that got him going about the fact that so many people in our society are not blessed with two caring parents as was once the case almost universally. In fact, many people in society today are not even blessed with one caring parent, which is how so many of these young women wind up on the street in the first place.

Then he went on for a bit about how sad and tragic it was that people out there on the street preyed on these young women. Enslaved them, he said. That certainly was a crime, and it was his fervent and urgent hope that whoever did those dark deeds would be dealt with as severely as the law would allow.

Which got him off on a tangent about the law, and how ineffective it often seemed to be in containing and preventing the crimes which seemed to be rampant in our society. And that got him going on all the crimes that were committed daily on the sidewalks in front of this very House of God and how could our society have sunk to such a low and abysmal state? and wasn't it high time all of society began looking to its moral health and welfare? and wasn't it time that people in authority did something to bring a sense of values back into play? Et cetera and so forth.

Pretty predictable stuff. But Father Martin really got rolling and his deep sermony voice seemed to expand and fill the entire church and the audience was certainly lapping it up. At least most of the audience. They especially seemed to like it - lots of murmuring - when he got around to the part about decent people taking back the night. He said, wasn't it high time the decent people took back their neighbourhoods? He said, wasn't it high time decent people took back the sidewalks in front of their homes and their businesses and their churches. Wasn't it high time that ....

That was about as much as one of the hookers could stand. She jumped to her feet and hollered out: "Isn't it high time you shut the fuck up?" Father Martin was startled. He looked down into the body of the church. He cocked his head a little to the side, the way a dog does when it's not quite sure it heard what it heard. He was squinting, trying to pick out the person who'd done the talking. The place was buzzing with whispers.

Then the hooker who'd jumped up was in the main aisle, about ten feet in front of Father Martin. "You talk about taking back the night? For who?" She turned and looked at the congregation. "For this bunch of hypocrites?" She turned and stared at Father Martin. "Very fucking Christian of you, Father. I'm sure Christ would be impressed." Then she turned on her heel and headed for the door. And then all the other working girls were on their feet and heading for the door, too. The last of them paused in the aisle just long enough to give Father Martin the finger. "What a bunch of bullshit."

The place was in an uproar: people sucking in their breath in horror, people exclaiming what an outrage it was for people 'like that' to be in God's House in the first place. And wasn't this all the proof anyone needed that someone ought to clean up the streets, and clean them up in a hurry?

Father Martin didn't know what to do. He was staring at the doors as the doors slammed shut. Then he was staring at the people in the crowd, who were staring back at him. Then people started getting to their feet and, for lack of anything better to do, they started heading out the door.

Finally, Father Martin pulled the microphone off and set it on the

70

altar and came down the steps into the main aisle of the church - perfect spot for Garth to grab a shot.

"You can't take a photograph in the church." The guy doing the talking was a bit of a doughboy, a little pasty, a halo of hair sweated to his scalp. "Well," said Garth, "apparently you're wrong about that. Because I just did take a photograph. The way you can tell is ...." he fired off another frame, blinding the old guy with his flash. Then he turned to me. "What do you say we get out of here?" I was all for that. I wanted to catch the girls before they scuttled out of sight.

"If you publish that picture, I'll ...."

Garth spun around. "You'll what?" He glared at the old guy. The old guy shut right up.

The girls were out on the sidewalk right in front of the church. They'd stopped to light up their cigarettes and then they'd found themselves surrounded by the good folk from the congregation. The good folk were in a state of what you'd call indignation. The girls were what you'd call pissed off.

"Whyn't you take your holier than thou bullshit and stick it up your rosy red ass, madam."

And so on.

Then a couple of beat cops waded in to separate the combatants. Garth and I were still up on the steps, just outside the church. A perfect vantage point from which to witness the proceedings. And a perfect vantage point from which to fire off half a roll of film.

On the front lawn of the church there's a statue of Our Lady. It looks like she's praying; she's holding her hands together just under her chin, palms pressed together, fingertips pointed upwards. Her head is bowed. She seems to be focussing on the grass near her feet. You can't blame her.

Garth fired off a few shots with Our Lady to one side and the fist-shaking hollering congregation to the other. Page One, guaranteed. It was just about then one of the churchgoers tried to grab his camera and, just like that, the churchgoer was howling from the pain of having his arm jammed up behind his back. "You touch me again, I'll snap your fucking arm right off. Am I making myself understood?" Garth jammed the guy's arm up a notch higher, then let go. Then he turned and fired off another half roll of the wahoos down on the sidewalk.

Page One, indeed. Letters to the Editor for a couple of weeks running.

'How dare you publish....'

I parked in the church lot. No bingo tonight, and only a couple of cars at the back of the lot. I got out and locked the doors and took a stroll.

I was looking for a girl named Sue. I'd interviewed her right after Father Martin's annual uplifter clean-up campaign. After Sue read the story she called the paper. She got through to city desk. Midnight Eddie had clapped his hand over the receiver. 'Hey Huntzie. A lady on the line wants to talk to the asshole who's doing the bullshit stories about the church ladies trying to clean up Wendell Street.' He gave me one of his 'this is your lucky day' smiles, put Sue on hold and transferred the call. Sue wanted to know whether I knew what balanced news coverage was all about. I told her I'd gone to the School of Balanced News Coverage. 'Then why'n fuck don't you give our side of the fucking story?' Half an hour later, Sue and I were talking in the front seat of the staff car. She gave me some great quotes, none of which would make it in the pages of a family newspaper, most of them having to do with the backseat antics of the husbands of the women doing most of the bitching about the whores in the church parking lot. I cleaned up her comments and the story made the front page. The Letters To The Editor column went wonky for days.

Sue had staked out the corner across from the Wendell Hotel. The street is like any other workplace; seniority has its perks. Sue had been working Wendell longer than anyone. As other girls quit or retired or OD'd and died or gave up and moved on, Sue moved closer and closer to the Wendell Hotel corner. When the last tenant got a pistol shoved in her mouth and decided enough was finally enough, Sue inherited the corner. Only a newcomer or an out-of-towner would set up shop on Sue's corner if Sue was out with a john or feeling lazy and taking the day off. No one else was that stupid. Sue had been known to rip the earrings off any other hooker who moved in on her turf. And if she wasn't up to the task, her 'Man' certainly was. I'd seen him around: a no-neck former football player, six something, two hundred and thirty or forty pounds. 'Mean' only half describes him.

When I got to her corner, Sue wasn't around. I wasn't in any kind of hurry. I leaned against the wall of the bank and waited. I'd been waiting about ten minutes when a Cadillac pulled to a stop and the door opened. Sue stepped out, giving me a clear view of the driver. The driver was a lawyer named Joey Brewer, although on his business card he was known as W. Joseph Brewer Junior. Joey Brewer had been born with a silver spoon up his ass. He'd worked exactly as hard as he had to work in order to maintain his standing in the community, his membership at Wood Grove and his partnership in his father's firm. Which wasn't very hard at all. I gave him my best shit-eating grin. "How's tricks, Joey?" Joey scowled and, as soon as Sue had slammed the door, hit the accelerator.

"Friend of yours?" she wanted to know.

"Not exactly."

"Good. He's an asshole."

I told her I concurred.

"He's also a cheap asshole."

"He's a lawyer, what do you expect?"

"He's a greaseball."

"That's what I said. He's a lawyer."

Sue wondered what I was doing in the neighbourhood. I told her I'd come down on business. "This is my lucky day. Things keep going like this, I can book off early, go play the ponies." I told her it was another kind of business I was thinking of. "Jeez, just when you get my heart going pitter-patter." I asked her if we could go somewhere and have a coffee and talk. "Talkin' don't pay the rent, sweetheart. And it don't keep The Man happy, either." I gathered it was mostly 'The Man' she was worried about.

"You payin' for information?"

"I can pay for the coffee."

She laughed.

"Okay," I said, "coffee and a donut."

She laughed again, but this time the edge was gone. She grabbed my arm and pulled me toward the street. "C'mon Mister
73

Rockyfeller." We went into Donut Heaven. We took a booth at the back. She sat with her back to the window. "So?"

I asked her what she knew about Carole Tippet.

"Why you want to know?"

"She's the one who got whacked."

"Carole?" Sue recoiled, just slightly. Furrowed her brows. Glanced at me, sort of sideways.

"I just came from the press conference."

"Fuck."

Sue just sat there for a few minutes, working through her cigarette and her coffee and her thoughts. She lit a new cigarette from the stub of the old and then exhaled and shook her head. "Not like it's any fuckin' surprise, or anything. She'd been working on being dead for quite a while." Sue ran her forefinger around the rim of her mug. "I'm actually kinda surprised it took her this long to get it done. I guess she's happy now. Hell of a lot happier than workin' this fuckin' street, anyway."

Sue thought about that for another minute or two, then she looked at me.

I asked her what Carole had looked like.

"You maybe seen her around. She worked down near Parent, north side. Brunette. Five two, five-three. Skinny little thing. She went missin' a couple days ago. One of the girls saw her gettin' into a car night before last, and she never come back."

"What kind of car?"

"Something fancy. Mercedes, maybe. Somethin' like that."

"Anyone report her missing?"

"Yah, we told the cops. They made a report."

I told Sue I hadn't heard anything about her having gone missing.

"Cops don't exactly advertise when it comes to missing hookers. And they don't bust their ass tryin' to find them, either." And you can't blame them. Girls come, girls go. They don't have much in the way of roots. The whim comes over them, they're gone. They don't usually leave a forwarding address. They just hit the bus stop and the road.

74

I asked her what she could tell me about Carole Tippet. "Apart from the fact that she's dead?"

"Yah," I said, "apart from that."

Carole Tippet was nasty as a nail in a board. And she'd been a weird one, right from the start. She'd started working The Alley a couple of years earlier, without a Man. The pimps had noticed, right away. The way things work is, it's finder's keepers. First Man to notice a new broad working the street, that Man walks up and introduces himself and informs her that she's working his particular stretch of The Alley, which must mean that she's now his property. He outlines the terms and conditions and that's that. Everyone knows it and everyone plays by the rules. Except Carole Tippet.

Carole Tippet told the first Man to fuck right off and she told the next one the same thing and they were all a little taken aback, figuring a girl - especially a little kid like Carole - wouldn't talk to a Man like that unless she had another Man somewhere in the background. So they were all a little edgy at first, kept their distance, figuring this invisible Man, whoever he was, was muscling in on their territory and they waited to see who he might be but they never saw Carole with anyone except the johns. They left her alone for a week or so, seeing what would shake down, then one of the Men moved in again and laid down the law: either she was working for him or she wasn't working at all, at least not this stretch of The Alley. She told him the same thing she'd told him the first time around. He went to grab her. Next thing he knew, he was on his knees, hands cupping his crotch, and when he looked up Carole was lighting a smoke. "You lift a hand against me again, I'll cut your guts out." She broke his nose with one kick.

"What I'm tellin' you is, she was one tough little bitch." And the word on the street was she'd been in the slammer at least three times - not bad for a kid who was, what?, all of fifteen at the time, fourteen or fifteen?

I asked Sue what Carole had been sent up for. "Nickel and dime stuff, the first couple of times. Boosting stuff out of Sears. B and E. But the last time she got a year in juvenile detention. Hard time. "What for?" "For slicing a pimp from the navel to the breastbone."

"Like you said, nasty."

Sue nodded. "She had everything you need if you're gonna sur-

75

vive on the street. And the one thing that guaranteed she wouldn't."

"Which was?"

"A nasty habit." Everything she earned she stuck directly into a vein. She was so fried most days she couldn't tell a cop from a post-man.

"Why would a nice girl like Carole Tippet do a thing like that?"

"You ever had fifteen or twenty guys stick their dicks in your mouth? A day?"

"How did a nice girl like Carole Tippet wind up doing things like that?"

"Same reason all us nice girls wound up doing things like that."

Which was?

"We were all fucked up by the time we were three."

Details?

"Never asked her." Sue set her mug down. "But take your pick. Any sad story will do. One's as good as the next. You got a light?" I picked up her lighter from the table and held the flame to the tip of her cigarette. She was looking right at me. She exhaled. "And why would you care, anyway?"

"I'm paid to care."

"A professional peepin' tom."

"Yah. I guess you could say that."

"How'd a nice guy like you wind up doin' things like that?"

"All fucked up by the time I was three."

She laughed.

"Another coffee?"

"If you're still buying."

I bought the coffee and a couple of muffins and then I asked her if she knew of a hooker named Cindy Lou Gilmore. She shook her head and made a frown. "Don't know the name. Which don't mean I wouldn't know her if I seen her. Girls tend to change names like they change clothes. Where'd she work?" I told her. "If she was workin' that trade, she'd wouldn't be caught dead down here."

"She won't be now."

76

"She the one whose car they found down at The Beach"

I nodded.

"And she worked for Van Allen?"

I nodded again. "What connection do you think there might have been between Cindy Lou Gilmore and Carole Tippet."

"Smells like drugs."

I asked her what she knew about Melissa McBride. "Not a whole hell of a lot." But fifteen minutes later, she was still talking.

Melissa McBride was early thirties. Until she reached her late twenties all she knew about prostitution was what she'd read in cheap thrillers and in the court columns of The Spectator.

She'd been a nice girl. Grew up in a nice neighbourhood. Married one of the nice boys she went steady with all through high school. They settled down in a townhouse and later bought themselves a house and had a couple of kids and everything was going along fine until Melissa discovered her husband was sleeping with the babysitter. Well, not sleeping, exactly.

Thus ended the storybook romance and the marriage. She tossed the bum out and she and the kids made do on the wages she pulled down at Zellers. And then Zellers cut back on her hours and she and the kids suddenly weren't 'making do' anymore. The husband wasn't coming through with child support, or alimony, and he also didn't see any reason to continue paying mortgage payments on a house he wasn't living in.

The For Sale sign went up and Melissa and the kids moved out and for a while they stretched it out in a one-bedroom right downtown and when they had to run out on the landlord in the middle of the night she found another place - a little smaller, a little dumpier - and when she had to run from that one in the middle of the night there was no place left to go but the bus depot where they slept sitting up. Next morning there they were, back of the line at the Welfare Office. Which was how she and the kids had wound up in a townhouse in The Projects, which was a ten-minute drive and a world away from the place where she'd started out in life not that many years before.

One day, Melissa was walking on Ouellette and saw an old school friend coming toward her and she smiled and waved and she knew damn well the friend had seen her but the friend did a quick left turn into a clothing store and by the time Melissa got to the store the friend was fingering the dresses on the sale rack, her back to the door. And Melissa thought, as she told Sue over far too much beer later that night, 'that smug bitch is a divorce away from welfare herself.' Which, as Sue had said, may have been the reason the friend ducked out of sight, there being some truths in this world which are a little too tough to stare at, unexpectedly. Melissa had been in no mood for Sue's philosophy class.

Never mind what the finger-pointers in the suburbs think - and what the hell would most of them know, anyway? - it's not a lot of fun trying to raise two kids on a welfare cheque, plus whatever cash you can earn working midnights in the corner store. Melissa McBride thought she deserved something better than hand-me-down clothes and Kraft dinners and an empty fridge the week before the cheque came in. And she thought her kids deserved better too. And she knew a high-school diploma was not going to cut it in this new and scaled-down part-time minimum-wage I'm-okay-screw-you world.

Thinking about that is sometimes more than a person can bear, especially late in the night, listening through too-thin walls as your scummy neighbours scream and swear and throw things at each other.

The first trick had been the hardest. But it was all downhill from there, gravity and gin doing most of the work.

"After the first few dozen, it gets a little easier." Sue tamped her smoke out in the ashtray, then used the butt to move the ashes around. "You just switch off your brain." She glanced at a passing car. "And your emotions." She looked back at me. "And?"

"And what?"

"And what else do you want to know?"

I asked if Melissa had been Van Allen's property.

"She used to be. But that changed. She was workin' for another guy, most recently."

"Who?"

"Luther Cross."

"Sounds greasy."

78

"Yah, that just about describes him perfect. About as greasy as William Van Allen."

"What can you tell me about Van Allen?"

"Apart from the fact that he's a vicious little prick and a thief and a con-artist and beats his girls and screws them out of their money, not a lot. He's one of my favourite people."

Melissa had worked for another guy at first. Jerome something or other. He'd spotted her the first night she started working The Alley. He'd approached her and offered her protection, for a price. She got the message. At first things had been fine. "But at first, things are always fine." Then he started taking bigger and bigger cuts of her earnings and when she started holding out on him he put a beating on her and when she held out on him again he put her in the hospital.

Van Allen heard about it. "There ain't much he don't hear." And next thing you know, he shows up in the hospital with a dozen roses and that was it for Melissa and Jerome something or other. Melissa couldn't recall the last time anyone had brought her flowers.

"Sounds like one of those Barry Manilow songs"

"Yah," said Sue. "Actually, it was worse than a Barry Manilow song and anyone in her right mind would have sniffed him out in a second. But when you're in the hospital with a concussion and a broken arm and four cracked ribs and one eye's bruised shut, you can mistake Manilow for Pavarotti."

Van Allen had left the hospital with a 'contract'. And at first, when Melissa got back on the street, everything was going fine. She got to keep more money than she'd ever kept before and Van Allen was buying her nice clothes and taking her to nice restaurants and she was happier than she'd been since she was married. So happy, in fact, that she started skimming her earnings so she could save up and buy him a nice ring, maybe, or a fur coat, or something that would let him know how special he was and how much she loved him. Which was just about exactly when he grabbed her by the throat and told her that nobody, 'least of all some little truck-stop slut' was going to rob him blind. He was a little more subtle than Jerome what'shisname, but she didn't walk right for the next three weeks. "It took that long for the cigarette burns to heal." And walk she did, because he was watching and he was waiting at the end of every shift and he was taking all her money now, until she paid off her shortfall.

"Why didn't she just tell him to fuck right off?"

Sue smiled and shook her head. "You never been a hooker, have you?"

"Not in this life."

"Well, let me tell you. You don't work this street unless you have a Man. You don't have a Man and you'll get screwed more ways than one. You don't have a Man, you can wind up dead."

"You can wind up dead anyway."

"Yah, well, try it with no Man and you'll wind up dead even sooner."

"Anyway, next thing you know, they're all chummy again. Everything's prime and pretty. She's hangin' on his arm and givin' him the look. Looked like they were going to be living happily ever after. Then, the next thing you know, she's over working with Luther Cross."

"Why?"

"Beats me."

"How long had she been working for him, before she got killed?"

"About a week."

I asked Sue what the chances were that Van Allen had knocked her off, or had someone else knock her off.

"You're not really that stupid, are you?"

She lit another smoke and thought about things for a minute or two. She was looking out the window and then she looked back at me. "Then again, eh?, it could just be some fuckin' wacko."

I asked her what she'd been thinking about, a moment earlier when she'd been staring out the window. She drew on her cigarette and then exhaled and then stamped the cigarette out in the ashtray. "I was just thinking a girl can't be too careful." I asked her how the girls protected themselves. "You can't. Completely. Some asshole wants to whack you, you'll get whacked. All you can do is use your sixth sense and hope it's workin' right. You get vibes, sometimes, and you just pay attention to them. You say no to the creeps and you keep your wits about you even with the ones who don't seem like creeps right off the bat and you always keep yourself between the john and the door so you can get the hell out when you need to. And you carry a little help." She patted her handbag.

"Gun?"

She shook her head. "Blade."

"What else?"

She made a shrugging gesture. "That's about it. You just keep your eyes and ears open and you don't take foolish risks and you tell the girls where you're goin' so if you're not back at least someone knows you're missin', though fat lot of good that'd do. But in the end, eh?, some perv wants to kill you, he'll kill you. And if your Man wants to kill you, then he'll kill you. Either way, you're dead meat. You got two bodies in a ditch, by way of proof. And maybe another one, somewhere."

"You worried?"

Sue finished her coffee and slid out from behind the table and shouldered her bag. "I don't lose sleep over it, if that's what you're askin'. You get whacked, you get whacked."

Out on the sidewalk, she looked one way, then the other. "Only thing that pisses me off is, there could be some wacko out there and nobody seems to get too excited about it. Half the so-called pillars of society are down here getting blowjobs right after their chamber of commerce meetings. You think you'll hear one of them stand up and start hollering for the cops to do something to protect us working girls? That'll be the day hell freezes over. The only time they ever stand up is when they want to make pious speeches about cleaning up the streets and keepin' them safe for decent law-abiding folks. For all I know it's one of those pot-bellied bald-headed bastards who's getting his rocks off killing the girls he's screwing." She shook her head. "Fuckin' men." Then she smiled: "present company excluded." She took my arm and we crossed the street. She ducked into the doorway of the bank.

"You know anyone else who knew Carole. Could tell me a little about her?"

"Might try The Haven. She spent some time there after she got out of jail."

I thanked Sue for her help and wished her luck.

"Sure you don't want a quick blow-job? I got a sale on."

81

I called Garth from a phone booth a couple of blocks west of Sue's corner. Ten minutes later, we were on the street and for the next couple of hours we worked Hookers Alley. Up one side and down the other. Garth kept his distance, shooting with a long lens from half a block back. It was perfect: the streetlights were on and the traffic was heavy and the girls kept getting whistled over to the curb to talk to would-be johns and Garth just kept firing away and firing away and I kept talking and writing.

The girls were scared shitless and they didn't mind saying so and they said so in all kinds of vivid detail. They talked about what it was like to work the street and what kind of crazies they ran into night after night and how it felt when they got into some loser's car and started heading for some back alley, wondering if they'd ever see the light of the street again. They talked about the beatings they'd endured and the beatings they'd fled and the friends that were no longer around to talk to reporters or anyone else. They talked about how angry they were that they had to make a living like this in the first place and how unfair it was when people started getting on their cases, trying to drive them from one part of town to another and how the cops could give two shits if they got mugged or knifed or worse.

The last story was the best. The girl said her name was Helen, although it took her a second or two to remember that. She said she'd grown up in Northern Ontario and had worked the streets of her hometown until her old man found out and came after her and drove her down the road eight or ten miles and stopped the car and told her to get out and start walking and to keep walking and never come back. "He told me if I ever showed up in town again, he'd have me killed." She got the feeling he meant what he said. So she walked and walked and finally got a ride and wound up in Toronto and worked the streets there for a year or so, until the night a guy put a knife to her neck and told her to do something she had no intention of doing, in this life or the next. "I mean, there are sick guys out there, but I'd never run into one this sick. Tongues are made for a lot of things, but they sure as hell ain't made for that". But a man with a knife is a man you take seriously and she'd made as though to do what he demanded and then, when he was in no position to do much about it, she kneed him where it hurts the most and bolted from the car and just kept running until she couldn't run anymore.

She'd quit the streets after that and took any kind of work she could take but the kind of jobs you can do with Grade 10 are not the kind of jobs that put a lot of food in your belly or much in the way of clothes on your back and by then she had three kids and no men to help her support them and so it was back to the streets. "I come down here, figurin' it was safer, eh?, in a smaller place. Plus I had friends here and we could take turns takin' care of each other's kids." But safer wasn't an adjective she would use any more. She pulled up her shirt. The scar went from her waist to just under her right breast. "A fuckin' screwdriver. Guy come at me with a screwdriver." The cops had met her at the hospital. "I had the asshole's licence plate and everything. They said they'd track him down and get back to me. And that was the end of that." So she, like Sue, now kept what she needed in her purse. And she said she wouldn't hesitate for a minute to cut a guy's throat if she had to, even if it meant she'd be spending half her life in the joint.

"One thing you learn on the street is, there ain't no-one gonna protect you and there ain't a soul except the other girls and your own kids who'll miss you if you're gone. It's a lonely scary fuckin' life, and it just got a whole lot lonelier and a whole lot scarier and you can write that down."

Garth and I high-fived each other all the way back to the office.

Three in the morning, my story was done and the night editor, Midnight Eddie Brown, was pissing himself as he was reading it. "Fanfuckingtastic, Huntzie." I was reading over his shoulder. "Yah, just this once, I have to agree." He finished the piece and then turned in his chair. "Who helped you write it? The copy boy?"

A few minutes later, Garth came out of the darkroom with a pile of black-and-whites and he laid them out on the desk and then he stood back and admired his own handiwork and who wouldn't? He had every kind of shot you'd want: shots of the girls leaning down and talking to the johns; shots of the girls leaning against lightpoles, leaning in doorways, standing at curbside with a hand on a hip. He even got a shot, nice and grainy, of a hooker and a john in a car at the back of Our Lady of Sorrows parking lot. Now you see two heads. Next frame you see one.

We left the gnomes to do the things gnomes do best: fuck up a brilliant story and crop the shit out of some award-winning photos.

We headed for the coffee machine and were just coming out of the cafeteria when Broom hove in to view behind his janitor's trolley - mop upended in the garbage bin like a mast on a listing ship. Broom seemed to be listing a little himself. "Youse guys want a little sumpin' in yer coffees?"

"No," said Garth.

"I'm off the stuff myself," said I.

"Yah. An' I'm Brad Pitt." Broom jerked his head to the left in a 'follow me' kind of way and we followed him down the corridor and around the corner to the publisher's office. He closed the door behind us and fished a bottle from the depths of the garbage bin on his cart. "This'll put some lead in yer pencil."

We pulled some chairs up by the window and put our feet up on the sill and toasted ourselves. Broom was all ears. When our coffee was a little low, he filled the cups again. He'd filled them once more - now we were drinking pure high-test - by the time we'd finished the story of the day's events.

"Now, I got the IQ of a muffin, I'll admit, but explain one thing for me, will ya Scoop?"

"Shoot."

"This broad, this dead one ..."

"Carole Tippet?"

"Yah," said Broom. "She's what, seventeen?"

"She was."

"And she'd been workin' the streets for how long, a year? Two years?"

"Longer than that, from the sounds of things."

"Which means she started hookin' when she was fourteen, fifteen?"

"Sounds like it."

"You tell me how that can happen."

"How what can happen?"

"How somebody's little girl, somebody's daughter, can wind up a hooker when she's fourteen years old. I'd like to know that."

Garth looked at me.

I looked at Garth.

84

-Six-

One-Eyed Louie was chewing on the burnt-out stub of a White Owl. MaryMary's no-cigar rule was still in effect. As she has said on more than one occasion: 'You should flush those suckers, not light 'em. And you sure's hell don't light 'em in my house. This is a whore-house, not an outhouse'.

We were seated around the table in MaryMary's kitchen; Louie and Mary and Angel and Garth and I. Angel was working on a dou-ble screwdriver, on the house. Mary'd done the pouring and when she was done she set the bottle in front of Angel and told her to help herself. "You're a peach, Mary. Honest to God."

It is, as Betty McLean had observed, an ever-contracting world.

Angel and Carole Tippet had roomed together when Angel had first come to town. This was two years earlier. It had been one of your coincidences. Angel was a farm girl. By the time she was sixteen, she'd seen all of farm life she'd wanted to see, this lifetime and the next. So she'd packed up a few of her personals in a duffle bag, hiked down the road to town and hopped a bus for the city. She was hav-ing a coffee in the bus station cafe when this very cool-looking young man plunked himself down on the next stool. A couple of hours later, they were laughing and drinking beer in a beerhall on Wendell, swapping biographies. Then it got on for closing time. The guy won-dered where Angel was going to be staying. Angel said she was going to find a room, somewhere. The guy said he had a room she could use for a couple of days, until she got herself squared away.

Talk about luck, eh? Angel had her duffle bag over her shoulder and was headed for the door with this guy when she got spun around and found herself face to face with Carole Tippet, very tiny, very tough.

'You know this piece of shit?' Angel hadn't had time to answer. 'You know what a pimp is?' The guy tried to get Carole's hand off Angel's duffle bag. Just like that, he was on his knees. And Angel was being half-dragged across the room, toward the door.

"She'd just saved my ass. That guy was one of the scummiest bastards you'll ever meet. Another ten minutes, I'd have been his piece of meat. And five'll get you ten I'd be dead by now."

Carole had taken Angel under her wing, taught her the tricks of the trade, watched her back until she'd learned to see out the back of her head. "Which is funny, eh? Considering she was about as old as my kid sister. She was probably only about fifteen. Fifteen, the most. But what she knew, it was amazing. It was like she was born on the street."

I told Angel what Sue had said about Carole. Angel had to agree. But she had to add this, as well: "If you went through what she went through, you'd be nasty as a nail yourself."

"What'd she go through?"

"I don't know the details. All I know is, she got hard as a hammer every time you mentioned her family. What they did to her, I don't know. But it musta been awful. She hated them. I mean with a passion. If she said once she wished they were all dead and rotting in hell, she must've said it a dozen times. I'm surprised she never killed them herself. The way she felt."

"Where was she from?"

"Here in town. She grew up ten minutes from here." She told me the street. Described the house.

"You've seen it? Her house?"

"Yah, we drove by it one night."

"Why?"

"I dunno. She was doin' the drivin'. We were just out toolin' around, havin' a smoke. Next thing you know she pulls up to the curb on the far side of the street and says, 'there it is'. I says, 'there what is?' 'The house from hell,' she says. 'Whaddya mean, 'the house from hell?' I says. 'The house where I grew up. So called,' she says.

Her exact words." She just sat there for a minute or two and then put the car in drive and off we went."

"She say much, after that? About her parents?"

Angel shook her head. She was looking down at her drink. Her hair curtained her face.

"One last question?"

"Shoot."

"If Carole was so tough and so shrewd, how come she wound up dead?"

Angel stirred her drink with her finger, then licked the finger and shook her hair out of her eyes and looked at me. "She had a habit that just wouldn't quit."

"You get a habit like that," said MaryMary, "you start forgetting all the things you need to remember if you want to stay alive."

"Such as?"

"You forget to trust your instincts," said MaryMary.

"Give me a for instance."

"For instance," said Angel, "you meet some scummy bastard and your instincts tell you to put some quick miles between you'n him. But your arm's tellin' you to get what it needs. And your arm always wins. So you follow him and sure enough, he's a piece of shit and he beats you up, or screws you out've your pay, whatever. And you knew it all along, only you can't think straight anymore. And then one day you wind up dead, a piece of meat someone dumps in a ditch."

Mary nodded in agreement: "I'm always telling the girls, 'girls,' I say, 'you can smoke and you can drink, but them better be the only two habits you got. Because you got another habit, and I find out about it, I put the vanishing cream on you'. Ain't that right, Angel?"

"That's right. "

"Exactly," said MaryMary.

"Can I bum one of your smokes?" Angel reached for my pack. I told her to help herself. She thanked me and lit up. "Weird thing is, eh?, of all the girls you'd never expect that to happen to, it happens to Carole. She used to be so savvy. But man, I seen her a few times the last year or so, it was pathetic. She was so skinny and wasted, I hard-

87

ly recognized her. It was scary. The last time, this would've been six months ago, five six months, I asked her what the matter was. 'Nothin' serious', she said. 'It's only a broken heart'."

Angel reached for the Kleenex.

"I told her come with me, I said. Come and work at Mary's. I told her we'd help her go straight, get herself cleaned up. She knew she should've. She told me, 'Angel,' she said, 'I know you're right'. But she couldn't. She said to me, 'Angel,' she said, 'I need the shit more than I need to live'."

"Truer words was never spoken," said MaryMary.

Angel shook her head and turned her glass on the table. "How do you figure, eh?"

"You don't figure," said MaryMary. "There ain't no figurin' when it comes to a habit like that. A habit like that is a death wish. That's all it is. And there ain't no cure for something like that."

I looked at Louie. "What do you think happened to her?"

"You got me," said Louie. "Drivin' another broad's car, carryin' that broad's ID. Type of car, type of broad, this Cindy Lou could've been Carole's supplier. Maybe. Maybe Carole whacked her for the drugs and the cash and the car. You get crazy, sometimes, if you get enough of that shit in your veins. So maybe she whacks the Gilmore broad, and then Gilmore's Man whacks her, eh? Or, coulda been some dealer. Who knows? Very fuckin' peculiar."

"Very," said Mary.

Which wasn't the only peculiar thing. I told them about my conversation with Leslie Ambrose, and I told them about the dogs and how they barked like crazy when I stood out front of the house. "And she says she didn't hear a thing during the night. There's no way some strangers could have been out front of that house and those dogs didn't hear them."

"Well, obviously," said Louie, "she was lyin'."

That much I knew. Why she was lying was what I didn't know.

"Because she was scared."

Scared of what?, I asked Mary.

"Scared that whoever dumped the body would come back and get her if she opened her mouth."

"Obviously," said Louie, "she seen whoever it was that dumped the body. And if them dogs were barkin' their asses off, like you said, then they'd of looked over at her house and they'd of knew she was lookin' at them and maybe they even come over and told her to keep her mouth shut, told her that whatever she seen, forget it, she never seen nothin'."

Which didn't make much sense to me.

"If she saw whoever it was who dumped the body, and they saw her, then wouldn't it stand to reason that they'd have whacked her, too, just to shut her up for certain?"

"Maybe," said Louie. "And maybe not."

"Why not."

"Not if they knew her."

What are the chances that a woman would look out her window at four or five in the morning and recognize the guy or the guys who were dumping a body in the field across the road?

"We're hypothesizing," said Louie.

"There's another maybe," said MaryMary.

"Which is?"

"Maybe she saw the killer dumping the body, but the guy didn't see her. If she saw him, and could identify him, she wouldn't exactly want you to advertise that fact on the front page of The Spec and have this guy come and pay her a little visit."

"Or maybe," said One-Eye, "she dumped the body." He laughed and gave MaryMary the look.

"You're tirin' my brain out." I finished my drink and set the glass down and stood up.

MaryMary had the glass in her hand in a flash. "Whyn't you just have another drink and then go home and sleep on it. Maybe it'll come to you in a dream." She held the glass up. "Double?"

I nodded.

Garth nodded too.

We sat around another half hour and hypothesized some more. But we were going in circles. And so was my head.

I had one last question: "What about Melissa McBride, the first girl? What connection could there be between her and Carole?"

"Apart from the fact that they're hookers, and they're dead?"

"Apart from that."

"There's two people who know that. And neither of them's speakin' just now."

We sat around for another few minutes, considering the angles, but we weren't getting very far.

"You want a single or a double?" MaryMary was on her feet.

"Neither, Mary. Time to get back to work."

"All work and no booze makes Jack a dull little shit."

"He's already dull as church service," said Garth.

"Thanks." I gave Garth one of my best shit-eating grins. "Let's go, cowboy."

It was half-past eight, light and bright, by the time I got home. Betsy was long gone, which was fine by me. If your head is thrumming with questions and the questions are taking you in circles, then the last thing you need is to come home to someone else's questions. Especially when all those questions were rhetorical. Nothing worse than 'where you been?', 'who were you with?', 'you been drinkin' again?' Especially at four or five in the morning. Especially when it's four or five in the morning and you've got a buzz on. If you've got a buzz on, you are at a definite disadvantage when it comes to confrontations. All things considered, I like my confrontations in the evening.

There was a note on the table.

Betsy and her notes.

I have to admit, I never thought I'd wind up with another note-writer. But the Fates like to play around with you, from time to time. Just for the sport of it.

My mother was a note-writer. Used to drive my father crazy. There'd be notes taped everywhere: on the kitchen door and the bathroom mirror and the lamp shade beside their bed. Whenever something jumped into her mind, she'd jot it down on a scrap of paper and tape it up. There were notes reminding him to pick things up at the hardware, or the grocery store or the variety store. There were notes

90

reminding him to do the chores he was always promising to get around to. There were notes telling him to go the liquor store, the bank, the garage. What drove him crazy was, she also told him to pick these things up or get them or do them. Often times she'd be telling him what to do while writing a note telling him to do the very same thing. She'd no sooner remind him to get a haircut after work than she'd tape a note to that effect to the door so he'd see it on his way out. Sometimes she wrote notes referring him to notes she'd written him earlier. 'Don't forget the hardware list'. It was an amazing paper trail.

As I got older, I got my share of notes as well. She was usually quite careful to address the notes to one or the other of us, although on occasion she'd forget and I'd go up to her with a big smirk on my face and say 'Ma, I'd love to go to the beer store for you, but I don't think they'd let me buy anything'. She'd grab the note and pencil in my father's name and stick it back up on the door. 'Yours is the bread and milk note, you nut.' I never thought much about the notes - they were probably some of the first things I saw when I was brought home from the hospital: 'Al, remember to put the diapers in the wash' - until I got older and some of my pals came home with me after high school and remarked on them. 'Whatsamatter? Can't your old lady talk?'

It was probably inevitable. When I moved from the town where I grew up to the city where I got my first big-time big-city big-newspaper job, I moved into a rooming house run by a woman named Mrs. Stout. She put my mother to shame. Notes everywhere. Doorframes, tables, lamp shades, mirrors, walls. She even had notes on the underside of the toilet seat (Put Me Down When You're Done. There's Ladys in The House). Every scrap of paper bore a Rule Of The House. No Long Distance Calls Without Permission. No Visitors After Eight PM. No Female Visitors At All. No Liquor On Premises. No Smoking In Bed. Shower Limit: Ten Minutes (Hot Water Costs). No Drugs Consumed On Premises. Front Door Will Be Locked and Chained at 1 a.m.

And it did not take me by surprise to wake up on my first full day of married life and see a note taped to the alarm clock beside our bed. "Love You." The content and tone of Jeannie's notes changed, however. And not for the better: 'Don't worry about the light bulb. I changed it.' 'Forget earlier note, I got the groceries.' And so on.

My memory is not what it used to be. No, that's not true. My memory never was up to much. I probably never developed much memory because I never had to. Everywhere I turned, all my life, there was a note telling me what to do, where to go, what to buy, what to bring home, what to take with me. It was like having a personal secretary. You get spoiled. Problem is, when you're surrounded by notes, you eventually stop seeing them. They're just part of the background. It's like living with someone who talks all the time. Eventually you tune out. With notes, you get forgetful. Jeannie would make grocery lists and I'd forget where I'd put them. She'd tape a 'honey-do' list to the fridge and I'd put it in my pocket and then next thing you know, it had been through the wash, in the pocket where I'd put it so I wouldn't forget to do everything on the list. Hopeless.

Which was, ultimately, Jeannie's judgement. And not just about my memory. End of story.

Then I met Betsy.

"Dear Huntzie. (I include the 'dear' only out of habit). Where the hell have you been?"

I won't bore you with the details, but the gist of the note was this: if I enjoyed hanging around whorehouses so much, and spending all my time drinking and smoking and joking around with hookers, why didn't I just move into Mary's? It would be perfectly all right with Betsy. In fact, the longer she sat by the window waiting to see me, the more convinced she became that her life would be a whole lot easier and a whole lot simpler and a whole lot happier if I just became a whore's companion. And she presumed my life would too.

"So," she said in an elaborately flourishing finish, "be my guest. Pack up and ship out. I guarantee you I won't shed any tears. It won't bother me one little bit to get my life back to normal."

And so on. Another page and a half of so on.

"Cordially yours ...."

Cordially?

I crumpled the note. I attempted a three-pointer into the trash basket in the corner. One bank off the wall. Missed.

I lit a smoke and looked out the window. A caravan of sedans and station wagons and mini-vans heading downtown. An army of suits and ties, tailgating their way toward look-alike office-tower cubicles.

Very depressing.

I punched the numbers, cradled the receiver between shoulder and ear. "Hi," I said, mustering all the cheer I could. "It's your favourite vagabond."

"I hope you're calling from a phone booth."

"How you doin'?"

"You sound pissed."

"I've had a couple."

"Huntzie, you promised."

"Promised what?"

"You'd stop drinking."

"I never promised any such thing."

"You did too."

"I couldn't have. I'd remember a foolish promise like that."

"You were near death at the time."

"Well, death-bed conversions shouldn't be held against a fellow."

"Huntzie?"

"Yes, my love."

"There's something I want to ask you."

"Shoot."

"Pack up and get out of my apartment before I get off work. Lock the door after yourself and slide the key under the door."

"Betsy . . . "

Betsy had turned into a dial tone.

"Betsy?"

Well.

I sat there for a few minutes in Betsy's favourite chair, the one by the window, and looked down at the street, the way she must've been sitting there looking down at the street, waiting for me. Tick tock. Tick tock. Tick tock. Half past nine. And I started to feel bad. She was a pretty good sort, Betsy was. I'm not sure I'm in love with Betsy. I'm not sure I'm up to loving anyone just now, except the kids, but if I was to love someone, it would probably be Betsy. Just that picture of her sitting by the window is enough to do you in.

On the other hand, life was seeming a little on the crowded side. I could see what she meant. A little space might not be such a bad thing. For a time. Wouldn't have to be permanent. We could have a cooling-off period, then get together for dinner and see how things were shaking out.

In fact, that might be a very good idea.

On the down side, it would mean finding a place to live. That would mean coming up with the first and last and a security deposit and money for hydro and the phone. It would mean going to K-Mart and buying some cutlery and dishes and towels and sheets. And a bed. And some chairs.

Becoming a bachelor, again, would not be as simple as it seemed. I know. I've been through it. It was definitely not something you'd want to rush into. Definitely something that needed a little mulling over.

I went to the bathroom and lifted the lid of the tank. The bottle was gone. Taped to the inside of the tank, at the back, just above the water level, one of Betsy's notes. Pink paper, blue ink: 'Only a hopeless lush would hide his whiskey in a toilet tank.'

I left the note right where Betsy had stuck it. I would not give her the satisfaction of thinking that I went looking for the jug. I replaced the lid and went down the hall to the dining room, grabbed a chair and went to the linen closet. Standing on the chair you can reach up, move the trap door which leads to the attic, get up on your tiptoes, reach to the right and ... voila.

I replaced the trap door, returned the chair to the dining room and took the bottle to the kitchen. I poured myself a couple of fingers of whiskey and went back to Betsy's chair by the window. I sat down and began mulling. I was still mulling when the glass was empty. I filled the glass with ice and brought the bottle back with me, plunked myself down by the window.

Goodbye Betsy?

Hm.

There was the phone. I smiled and shook my head and took a sip and let it ring for the third time. I was still smiling when I picked up the receiver. "Hi honey."

"I may be somebody's honey, but I sure as hell ain't yours." It was Norm Wetherall.

"That's just as well. You're not my type. What's up?"

"Where in hell you been?"

"Doin' a little research."

"Research, in a bottle?"

"That's where you find notes, sometimes, you know."

"I been tryin' to get you for hours."

"What's happening?"

"In your story, you got a broad named Sue."

"Yah."

"And you also got a broad named Suzie. We got two broads here, one Sue and one Suzie? Or we got one broad? And if it's one broad, which name is it?"

"She goes by both."

"Well, pick one. Because I sure as hell can't make sense of the story if we got one broad and two names and the reader's sure as hell not going to figure it out either."

"Sue."

"And it wouldn't be a bad idea if you started reading your stories before you turn them in. You know, like you used to do before you became such a fucking prima donna."

"You done?"

"I'll tell you when I'm done."

"Norm, it's been a long night. What I need right now, more than a lecture, is a little shuteye."

"You need the lecture, first. Then the shuteye. The lecture's over. Just don't get lazy and sloppy on me, Huntzie."

"I thought you said the lecture was over."

"It is. Almost. One more thing."

"Yah?"

"You pissed?"

"Moderately."

"Want some fatherly advice?"

"No."

"Pour the rest of your drink down the sink and go to bed."

"Thanks Dad."

You try sleeping when you've got two dead hookers and one missing hooker running around in your head. Toss in a couple of thieving, women-beating pimps, a car on a riverbank, a purse beside a body ... and half a bottle of Hiram Walker's finest, and there's no way you can keep your eyes shut.

I tossed and turned and tried to shut off my brain, but I couldn't find the switch.

To hell with that.

Garth answered on the second ring. "You still got that nice couch in the basement?"

Twenty minutes later, I was lugging all my earthlies - one battered black leather suitcase, two duffle bags, one portable Olympia typewriter, one 12-string guitar, one ghetto-blaster, six cardboard boxes of books - down the stairs and into Garth's furnace room.

Garth had been helping with the move and he now stood back and surveyed the pile, then looked at me. Pure Basset Hound. "This is only temporary, right?"

"Yah. Right. Soon as I find a place, I'm outta here."

"Promise?"

"Absolutely." I put my hand over my heart. "You can trust me, buddy. A day, two days, I'm gone."

"I'm only askin' because of the last time."

"The last time was exceptional circumstances."

"That last time was six weeks."

"Like I said, exceptional circumstances. This is what? Thursday?"

"This is Wednesday."

"Alright. Wednesday. By next Wednesday, I'll be gone. You got my word on it."

Garth clearly had his doubts. When Garth has his doubts, there is only one thing to do. Get his mind off the subject. I told him I was falling asleep on my feet. I told him he didn't look too perky either. I suggested we both have a snooze and then when we woke up, we could head back down to The Alley and see what we could scare up, by way of front page stories and pictures. Mention front page to Garth and it's like giving a bone to a dog.

"Wake me up at one. I got a call to make. Then I got to take the kids to dinner. Then I'll meet you at the office."

I hit the couch.

I was out like a light.

-SEVEN-

Ten past two in the afternoon, I was banging on the door of Kenny Koster's suburban bungalow.

How in hell a guy like Kenny Koster wound up in a bungalow in a place called Forest Lawn - capital MIDDLE, capital CLASS - was beyond me.

Kenny Koster should be living in a walkup downtown. Or on a houseboat downriver. Or on a farm out in the county.

But here he was at his front door, in his jockey shorts, trying to get the sleep out of his eyes, finger and thumb.

"This better be fucking good."

Kenny used to be a cop. A very good one. Too good, as a matter of fact. Which is why he used to be a cop and now spends his days doing who knows what out here in the burbs.

I met Kenny when he was in his prime. This would take us back seven, eight years. Kenny was working homicide. I covered half a dozen murder cases he solved, including the case that drove him off the force.

Kenny was the kind of guy, there's a murder, he's on the job. Didn't matter if he was on his day off or his vacation or what. A good shooting, good knifing, whatever, next thing you know Kenny would be ducking under the yellow tape and getting to work, no matter who else had been assigned to the job. This did not endear him to the grunts on the death squad, nor did it especially endear him to the dicks who were good at their job. He made them all look like slackers. Which wasn't his intention. Or at least I don't think it was his

98

intention. But it was the inevitable result of Kenny barging in on the case. He was so keen, so tireless, so relentless, the other guys didn't stand a chance. There wasn't another cop on the force who would spend all his waking hours wondering about a case, wondering who'd made the hit, working it through, working it through, working it through until - in the middle of the night, in the middle of a supper, in the middle of a haircut, in the middle of a piece of ass - he'd suddenly jump up and head out the door, chasing down a clue that finally clicked into place.

Kenny's last case was one of those knock-knock you're dead deals.

A doctor answered the door, a kid asked if he could use the phone, and while the doctor was wondering whether he ought to let the kid in, two other kids barged past him. They wanted drugs and money, in that order. When the doctor's wife started screaming, one of the kids slugged her with the butt end of a pistol. When the doctor went for the kid with the pistol, another of the kids whacked him with another pistol. Then the first kid pumped three shots into the doctor's head. Point blank range. Then they shot the doctor's wife in the head. Then they ransacked the place and took off in the doctor's Lincoln Continental.

Their mistake was, they didn't kill the doctor's wife. She managed to crawl to the phone and dial 911. She described the kids and gave the dispatcher the licence number of the car. Then she passed out.

Within five minutes, every cruiser within ten miles was converging on the area and it wasn't a couple of minutes after that the kids ditched the Continental and scattered, cutting through backyards, vaulting fences, ducking through alleys. Two of them ran smack into cops. The third got away.

Or so he thought.

Kenny had spotted him, followed him down an alley, and lost him. Unhappily for the kid, Kenny never lost anyone for long. One time he spent six hours chasing a kid who'd shot out a street light with a pellet gun. As he told me, when I'd heard about that and didn't believe it and asked him if that was true, 'I couldn't stand the thought that little shithead would think he could get away with something like that'. The little shithead hadn't.

So the kid who'd killed the doctor really didn't stand a chance.

He only thought he did.

Every loser's large mistake.

As soon as Kenny lost sight of the kid, he stopped, and looked around. 'What I thought was, if I was a kid, if I'd just shot and killed a doctor and every cop in town was within eight blocks of me, what would I do?'

What he thought he'd do was get in something, or under something, and stay there as long as it took for the cops to lose interest. Hours, if need be. Days, maybe.

There was no way the kid had gone out on the streets either side of the alley: too many cops. So he'd either broken into one of the houses or he was hiding under a porch or in a garage. Kenny thought it was unlikely the kid would try breaking into another house. But he would definitely want to hide under a porch or in a garage if he could find one fast enough. And twenty feet down the alley, there was a garage on the left and one of the doors was open. It was like a Cavin Atkins painting: mostly darkness - blacks and purples and bluish greens - and shadows and the faintest hint of light.

Kenny had kicked off his shoes and crept up to the garage in his stocking feet. Then he got his flashlight in one hand and his revolver in the other and he got down on his belly and started working himself along the pavement, elbows and knees.

When he flicked on the flashlight, the kid was so surprised he banged his head on the undercarriage of the car and it took him a second to orient himself and aim his gun at the light. Which had been exactly one second too long. Kenny's bullet went right through the kid's forehead and brain and out the back of his head. There wasn't a lot left of the back of the kid's head and most of his brains were splattered on the back of his T-shirt and the underside of the car.

The furore which followed - Cop Kills Twelve Year Old - was too much for Kenny to take. The Chief suspended him, with pay, that very same night and told reporters he would personally take a hand in the investigation to ensure that all procedures had been followed to the letter and that the rights of the juvenile in question had not been violated. The Chief had gone on to say that he would not allow trigger-happy cops to be a part of his proud force. And he assured one and all that if Detective Koster was in any way culpable, he would face criminal as well as internal charges. "And that," as Kenny had said at the time, and on many occasions thereafter, "was before we even wrote the fucking report."

Kenny spent almost a year shuffling paper in a back room in the property department while the internal investigation dragged on and while civil rights types did their best to smear him and get him fired. He was eventually cleared of any wrongdoing. He was reinstated and assigned to a desk in records. When Kenny asked his inspector how long he'd be riding the desk, the Inspector had just looked at him like he was stupid or something. Kenny took the stairs two at a time, walked into the Chief's office without knocking, dumped his badge and service revolver on the Chief's desk and told him where he could put them. Something to do with a place the fish don't swim and the light don't shine.

End of story.

End of career.

I'd kept in touch. You'd be nuts not to. What Kenny didn't know about criminals wasn't worth asking about.

Kenny turned from his door and waved for me to follow. We went through the living room - one sofa, one chair, one coffee table - and the kitchen - table, chairs, a clutter of dishes - and down the stairs to what, in most cases, would be a family room. In this case, it was a combination weight room and bar.

"Beer?"

Rhetorical question.

While he was leaning down to fetch the bottles out of the bar fridge, Kenny wanted to know what it was I was after. He mentioned again, kicking the fridge door shut, that it had better be good, after the night he'd had.

I told him I wanted to know anything he could tell me about Cindy Lou Gilmore.

"The dead hooker, who turned out to be not so dead?"

"How'd you know that?"

"I got my spies." He grinned one of his famous lop-sided grins.

"What do you know about her?"

"Never heard of her, until they found her car and her purse. But that don't necessarily mean I don't know her. These broads, they come and they go, eh? They change names the way normal people change their shorts." He looked down at his own, then looked up. "Normal people, I said." He set his beer down on the coffee table and sat on the sofa. "But that car, and that purse, and that body, that kinda piqued my interest."

"I kinda thought they would."

"As it turns out, she was workin' the casino, high end of the trade. Definitely not your street-corner blow-job artist. And she maybe had some interesting connections."

"Such as?"

"She may have been fronting the drug-trade. People come for a weekend, they want a little action, a little ass and a little something extra. What I hear, she was the broad to get in touch with."

"You're doing pretty good, for someone who just rolled his ass outta bed."

"I was in some interesting places before I rolled my ass into bed."

"So I see. What else do you know?"

"I know she was a looker, and a dresser. Wasn't much to her, five feet, five two, weighed maybe a hundred soaking wet. But she was a head-turner. Always wore the best, always looked the best."

"You think she's dead?"

"Could be, but personally, I'm not so sure."

"Why?"

"We'll get to that in a minute. But first, tell me what you know about the other one, Melissa McBride."

I told him what I knew: that Melissa had been working for Willie Van Allen, then crossed the street to work for a pimp named Luther Cross. I told him what I knew about Van Allen and his connection with Cindy Lou.

"You got pretty good sources."

"I thought so."

"And what are they saying?"

"About?"

"About why Melissa got whacked."

"They're saying it smells like Van Allen getting even. They say he

102

wouldn't think twice about having her whacked. A, he's got to let his girls know they can't get out of line. B, he's got to let the competition know he's not about to lose anyone, even a lowgrade hooker. "

"Sounds reasonable," said Kenny. "But I got my doubts."

"Because?"

"I'll get to that in a minute." He took another swallow of beer. "This new dead hooker, Carole Tippet. Whaddya hear about her?" I told him what I knew so far.

"What are your people saying?"

I told him: could be a drug deal gone sour. Could be she whacked Cindy Lou Gilmore, took the dope and tried to peddle it herself, and got whacked for her trouble. And if she had whacked Cindy Lou, maybe Van Allen had whacked her in return.

"Who in hell came up with that?"

"A couple of friends."

Kenny fired up a Camel and took another swallow of his beer and leaned back on the sofa. He was wearing that grin again. "Well, your friends are either smoking some very bad shit, or they been watching too many cop flicks."

"You don't buy it?"

"Impossible."

"Why?"

"Tippet had so much shit in her veins she couldn't think straight, much less point a gun. Plus, she's five one, five two and weighs maybe eighty pounds."

And Melissa?

"Van Allen might want to take her out, if she crossed him. But any idiot could put one and two together and next thing you know the cops would be knocking at his door. Last thing Van Allen would want is the cops sniffing at his door. Too much at stake."

Like?

"Like a corner on a good chunk of the drug trade in town. He and his people have half the bars in town locked up. They've also got the biggest escort service in town, running under four or five names. And he's selling protection to fifteen or twenty very frightened little mom and pop operations in the nicer neighbourhoods. Definitely, he would not want to get the cops any more interested in him than they already are and risk all that just to whack a hooker who'd turned on him." He leaned forward and stubbed out his cigarette. Lit another. Leaned back. "There's only one reason he'd take out Melissa McBride."

Which would be ...

"If maybe he found out she was about to part with some interesting information."

Such as?

"Names and places, dates and times, buyers and sellers. If she worked for him, she might have known enough to cut herself a good deal."

"What kind of deal?"

"New name, new town, and a nice retirement package."

"With whom?"

"The cops, and the prosecutor."

"Why would she want to sing a song like that?"

"Anyone ever burn holes in the soles of your feet?" He aimed a smoke ring at the ceiling. Then another. Then he sat up. "She might've already started singing. Or she might just've threatened to. Which would've been very stupid on her part. But then again, I never met a hooker who was practicing rocket science on the side. If she was a threat, or he thought she was a threat, it would explain why he'd risk his empire in order to drop her in the ditch. And it might also explain why he's suddenly made himself scarce. Himself and Cindy Lou." He raised his bottle and emptied it. "Know how to work a fridge?"

I got us a couple of refills, and sat down again, across from him.

"Or, there might be another reason."

Which would be?

"Him and Cindy Lou could've got themselves into some serious shit and decided to effect a change of address. Another country, perhaps."

"It'd have to be pretty serious for him to walk out on that little empire of his."

"Saving your own ass can be pretty serious."

"Who'd want to ice him?"

"Half the assholes in town. He's a prick. Pricks make enemies. He's made a lot of them. Take your pick. Or, maybe he's been living a little too high, spending a little too much, not paying attention to business. If he hasn't been paying his bills, some very serious gentlemen from south of the border would have a definite interest in talking to him." He looked at me, exhaled, stubbed his smoke. "The Colombian border."

"He was dealing with them?"

"You don't grow cocaine in cornfields."

"Try this again."

"Let's say he's got some debts he can't pay. What a fellow wants to do in a situation like that is disappear. So he fakes Cindy Lou's death, and then he and Cindy disappear. He's hoping everyone is thinking he's gone underground in search of the first pimp. And while everyone's waiting for him to pop up soon, down The Alley somewhere, he's like a groundhog ... popping up out of another hole in the other direction."

"So maybe he and Cindy Lou have taken a little vacation?"

"Could be."

"Somewhere warm?"

"If they haven't been making their payments, they wouldn't be short of cash."

Hm.

Kenny looked at me, then down at the ashtray, then back at me. "Leave it with me. I'll make some calls, see what I can find out."

We spent another little while talking about the weather, the Tigers, the state of the force these days, the state of the paper and our love lives. We were about a minute on our love lives, total. Then he stood up and headed for the stairs. He stopped in the kitchen and told me I could let myself out. "Call me tomorrow. But don't make it first thing in the morning, all right?"

I told him I didn't think two in the afternoon would qualify as first thing in the morning.

"If you don't get home until seven a.m., then it qualifies."

I told him I'd call him at supper time. He was rooting around in the fridge.

"Thanks for the help."

"Anytime." He'd come up with a piece of pizza. "G'bye." He'd bitten off more than he could chew. Half the slice was hanging from his mouth.

I never did like school very much, and every time I park outside the schoolyard fence, waiting for Katie and Ben, I remember why. I get claustrophobic just looking at the yard and the building and the kids. Autumn and spring were the worst: the sky so blue and the breezes so warm and whispery it would break your heart. And there you were, stuck in some classroom that smelled like a locker room, your eyes darting from the window to the clock and back again, barely listening to the drone from the front of the room. It was like being teased in the worst possible way, the way I imagine prisoners are teased by their half hour out in the exercise yard staring up at that rectangular chunk of blue sky they can see above and beyond the mortar and blocks. That close to freedom, that close to life. It's enough to drive you crazy.

And as if that wasn't bad enough, it was a day filled with 'do this', 'do that', 'write this', 'read that', 'I told you I didn't want anyone talking'. Yak yak yak. Rules and regulations and more rules. Left, right, left right. Worse than being in the army. At least in the army, you get paid.

A little bit of power is probably the most dangerous thing you can give anyone, especially someone standing at the front of a classroom, someone who probably goes home and gets yelled at by her mother, or her husband or her father. Give someone like that the power to rap a kid's knuckles with a ruler and she'll turn into Attila The Hen. Meet Miss Henderson, my homeroom teacher. God, I hated that woman. And the feeling was mutual. I think teachers can sniff out the anarchists on Day One. She certainly sniffed me out. I went from the back of the room to the front row before recess of my first day in Grade One. I became her Example. I became the living embodiment of The Bad Student. I was exactly what all the other good little children in the class should work desperately hard to avoid becoming. I was a Plague on her house.

Word had got around.

All the way to Grade 8 I got marched out of class by my ear. I got sent to the principal's office so often that the chair by the door was Little Mister Hunter's Chair. I held the record for most strappings by any child, not just in Eastwood Elementary, but in the entire system (as my mortified parents were told by Mister Elgin, The Principal). And finally, I got the boot. Which was a badge I wore proudly, but which was a kind of Scarlet Letter my mother never quite got over. High school wasn't much better. I remember . . .

Jeannie?

I looked in the rear view mirror. I turned in my seat and looked out through the back window.

It was Jeannie all right.

What was she doing here? Checking up on me? Making sure I hadn't forgotten to pick up the kids? Jeannie waved. Jeannie smiled. Jeannie shook her head. Was Jeannie laughing? She seemed to be laughing. She was definitely laughing.

What the hell was so funny?

I turned around and checked my face in the mirror, checked my hair. Everything normal there, everything shipshape.

Hm.

I got out and walked back to Jeannie's Olds. My Olds, actually, if monthly payments accounted for anything. At least she was keeping it clean. She purred the driver-side window down about half way.

"What's so funny?"

"Do you know what day this is?"

"As a matter of fact, I do. It's Tuesday."

She laughed again.

Say this about Jeannie, she's got one of the world's most engaging laughs. Hear her laugh, even if it's a little twitter of a laugh, and next thing you find yourself smiling and then laughing too. I was doing my best to keep a straight face.

"Only if this particular Tuesday has 48 hours."

Hm.

"It's Wednesday?"

"Has been since midnight," she said.

"Which means it's your turn to pick them . . ." "Hi Dad!" Ben was coming on the run and, three giant steps, had landed in my arms. "Heeeyyyy! Whatcha doin' here?"

"Hi Daddy!" Ben dropped to the ground and Katie nuzzled up for a hug. "You coming home?" I was hugging Katie, but it was Jeannie I was looking at. God, I hate it when she bites her lower lip like that.I ruffed Katie's hair. "No, honey. I'm not. I was just passing by on my way to work. Thought I'd come around and say hello."

"Huh?" Ben had wrinkled his nose. He was giving me the eye. Say this for Ben. He was a hard one to bullshit. "Say hello?"

"Yah. You know, say hi. Keep in touch?"

"Since when?" He was smiling. And he was waiting for me to dig myself a little deeper into the hole I'd already dug. "It's a new tradition. Starting now."

"You're losin' it, Dad."

"Yah, well, it's what happens when you get to be an old fart like me."

"Daddy!" Katie furrowed her brow. Exactly the way her mother furrowed her brow.

I shrugged and smiled. "Sorry sweetheart. An old geezer."

"That's better."

"We're going for pizza." Ben looked at his mother and then at me. "Wanna come?"

"Love to champ. But I've got to get back to work. I'm working on a story for tomorrow's front page. The world is holding its breath for the deathless prose of Jonathan William Hunter IV."

"Another dead hooker story?"

"Ben!" Man, those eyebrows. And that forehead. Jeannie could say more with her eyebrows and her forehead than most people could say in a speech.

"Bye Daddy." Katie gave me another hug, then headed for Jeannie's car. "I'm starving. Can we eat now?"

Ben looked up at me. "Is that a no?"

"I'm afraid so, buddy. Work calls."

Ben looked at his mother and then at me, then back at his mother. "Whyn't you two just grow up?" He jumped in the car and slammed the door. He made a point of not looking in my direction.

I shrugged my shoulders.

Jeannie shrugged her eyebrows.

Her window purred shut. She turned the key. The engine turned once, then quit. Jeannie turned the key and tried again. Fourth time, it caught. I rapped on the window. Jeannie opened it.

"Been doing that often?"

She shook her head. "Once yesterday."

"Take it in to Johnny's. Have him take a look."

She nodded. But it was one of those 'you live your life, I'll live my life' nods.

I smiled. I shrugged my eyebrows.

Jeannie put the Olds in reverse, then into forward and swung out into the street. Katie waggled her fingers as she went by. Ben was still looking any which way but at me.

I was still waving as the Olds rounded the corner.

The house from hell turned out to be pretty unassuming. Nice normal-looking storey-and-a-half, verandah across the front, white wicker love seat, two matching chairs, two potted droopy-leaf plants, some hanging baskets of pinkish flowers. Inner-city lot, maybe forty or forty five feet across and ninety feet deep. Late model Chevy Cavalier nosed up to the garage, year-old Taurus right behind it. Whatever problems the Tippets were having, money apparently didn't figure among them. The city directory listed Harry Tippet as an engineer who worked with one of the local tool and die companies. His wife, Suzanne, was listed as a teacher.

It was Suzanne who answered my knock on the door. Dyed black hair, too much eye-liner, contact lenses that turned her eyes green, forced smile, capped teeth, fake fingernails the colour of dried blood. She shook hands like a man; grip and squeeze. Those green eyes never let up. She invited me to step into the foyer. Persian carpet, grandfather clock, brass-hook clothes-tree, cherry-wood telephone table with a mirror above it. Looked like one of those displays at Coulter's Furniture.

"Harry!" She directed the call up the stairs and a few seconds later you could hear Harry's footsteps and then a few seconds after that he came down the stairs. Right out of a Freed's ad: a vision in brown - slip-ons, slacks, cardigan, button-down. Not a brown hair out of place. Grip and squeeze. "What can we do to help?"

We adjourned to the living room. Another furniture-store display: navy blue leather recliner, matching blue and white striped wing-back chairs, flower-patterned love seat, glass-topped coffee table, all resting on glistening hardwood floors. There was a Bible - a big display model - beside a vase filled with silk flowers.

Harry indicated I should take one of the wing backs. He sat in the leather recliner, Suzanne sat on the love seat.

"I'm very sorry to bother you at a time like this," I said.

"That's quite all right," said Suzanne.

"We understand," said Harry. "Yours can't be an easy job." I told them it had its unpleasant moments.

"I can imagine," said Suzanne. "Would you care for a cup of coffee?"

"No. Thanks. I'm all coffee-ed out."

"What can we do to help you?" said Harry, for the second time.

I told him I was in need of a little background information about their daughter. I asked if they minded if I taped our conversation. "I hate misquoting people. I know tape recorders bother people, but I always tell them it's better to get things right."

"Go right ahead," said Harry.

I started the recorder and put it on the coffee table and got out my notebook and pen.

"Do you always use a fountain pen?" Suzanne wondered.

"Dinosaur," I said.

She smiled right back at me.

"Where would you like us to start?"

When I left, just over an hour later, I'd learned the following: Carole Tippet had been a troubled child, almost from the moment she'd arrived kicking and screaming in this world at Hotel Dieu Hospital nearly eighteen years previous. She'd been a charming girl, but a scheming and trouble-causing one too. At first, Suzanne and Harry thought it was just a troubled early childhood, that she'd grow out of it. But the older she got, the more 'obstreperous' she became.

"Wouldn't you agree, Suzanne?"

Suzanne agreed wholeheartedly.

By the time Carole entered school - Queen Victoria Elementary - "she was decidedly a behaviour problem. Wouldn't you say, Harry?"

That's exactly how Harry would have described her. "And Suzanne certainly knows what she's speaking of here," said Harry. "She's a teacher herself."

From that point on, it seemed to be all downhill. The Tippets had tried, with some success, to get their daughter "into treatment", but no matter how many programs she was enrolled in, Carole seemed only to get wilder and worse. "Finally, when she started getting into trouble, serious trouble, it was out of our hands," said Harry.

"I wouldn't want to blame anyone, specifically," said Suzanne, "but . . ."

Twenty or so minutes later, they had specifically blamed their daughter's troubles, and eventual death, on the Children's Aid Society, The Haven, and The Jail. If the Children's Aid had found appropriate foster facilities; if The Haven had kept her off the street; if the staff at the jail had provided the treatment she needed.

And so forth.

Standing on the verandah, I shook their hands and thanked them for their time and turned to go. Then I turned to face them. "One more question, if I might."

"Certainly," said Suzanne.

"When did you last see your daughter?"

The question took them by surprise. Suzanne looked at Harry. Harry looked at me, then at the tree on the front lawn, then at Suzanne.

"Oh," he said, "it was ..."

"It was a while ago," said Suzanne. "A couple of months, maybe."

"Yes," said Harry. "That'd be about right. Within the last couple of months. Why do you ask?"

"What kind of spirits did she seem to be in. When you saw her last?"

"Fine," said Suzanne. "Pretty happy, actually."

"Yes," said Harry. "I'd say she seemed very happy, actually."

I wrote their answers in my notebook, and thanked them again and went down the steps and down the walk to my car. When I looked over the roof of the car at the house, they were still standing there, in the open door, still smiling their forced smiles. Suzanne waved as I opened the car door.

I drove a block south, then pulled to the curb and opened my notebook, uncapped my pen and made an asterisk and beside it made this notation:

'Whites of their eyes are white.'

-Eight-

"What's your problem?" Garth was loading his camera bag and checking it twice. When it comes to bags full of stuff, Garth is worse than Santa Claus. He checks it and then checks it again and half way to the door realizes there's another something he really should stuff into it, just in case.

"Me?" I said. "Nothing's wrong. Why?"

"You look like shit is all."

"Thank you."

"Honesty is the best policy."

I was looking down at my clothes. I ran my hands through my hair. I straightened my jacket.

"Not your clothes," said Garth. "Your face. You look like you just got the bad news from your doctor."

Truth was, I was feeling like shit. All the way back to the office I couldn't shake Ben's cold shoulder. I kept seeing him looking the other way as the Jeannie drove off. And then I realized it wasn't the cold shoulder that bothered me so much. It was his angry little outburst that bothered me most.

Ben oughta be a dentist. He can put the drill in, exactly where it'll hit the nerve.

'Whyn't you two just grow up?'

Well, Ben, as the old song says, growing up is hard to do. Especially when you never spend much time trying. Or even thinking about it. Harder still when you actively set out never to grow up

113

at all, resolve to be a kind of Peter Pan all your life.I'm still a big fan of Peter Pan.

Say this about that: tough to be Peter Pan and a husband and a father at the same time. Once you learn how to fly, it's tough to keep your feet on the ground.

We've all got our weaknesses. Me? I'm a dope. I'm one of those guys who usually wants to be where he isn't; wants to be with someone who isn't around; wants to have something just out of his reach. Hard to look at the grass under your feet and the grass on the far side of the fence at the same time.

Plus I'm addicted to adrenalin. I hear a siren, I'm like a firehouse dog. If there's a good story breaking, and I'm not on it, I'm in a funk.

The miracle is that the marriage lasted as long as it did. If it hadn't been for Jeannie's perseverance, her determination, her 'never say die', the marriage would have been over half a dozen years earlier. Our friends all jokingly called her Saint Jeannie. Many a truth is spoken in jest.

Say this about a dozen years of marriage. When all is said and done and you find yourself on the outside looking in - as the car heads off down the street and that little face is in the back window and that little hand is waving goodbye - it certainly leaves you feeling lonely. Not an emotion I was expecting. When I was on the inside, I spent a lot of my time straining on the leash: wanting to be out on the job, out with the boys playing poker, out with the boys having a few beers. Out, period.

Then I was. Unceremoniously; all my earthlies in cartons and suitcases and black plastic bags on the verandah and the lawn where Jeannie had fired them in one of her famous bouts of temper.

And then - wouldn't you know it? - as soon as you're on the outside, you're thinking about how nice it would be to be on the inside. I've heard cons talk about The Big House the same way. But cons don't have to stand in the middle of the road and watch a small face in the back window of the Olds as the Olds recedes into the distance and the future; they don't have to watch a little hand waving until the little hand is too small to be seen.

Yah, well. You make your bed ....

"Give me about fifteen minutes. I've gotta make some calls."

114

"Who to?"

"To whom?"

"Right. Whom to?"

"None of your business, actually. But if you have to know, I've got to get some reaction to some things the dead kid's parents had to say."

"When'd you talk to them?"

"This afternoon."

"Who was the shooter?"

"No shooter. I went solo."

"There isn't anything you could write that could stand up with no photos. You oughta know that by now."

"I didn't know I was going to get a story out of them. I thought I was just going to get some background."

"And the story is?"

"They're blaming the death of their daughter on just about the entire city."

"So?"

"So, I've got to give the Children's Aid and several others equal time."

"I'll be in the cafeteria. Come fetch me when you're done making all your calls."

I said I would.

"Good luck."

Good luck indeed.

Eight phone calls later, tracked down the head of the children's aid who had exactly this to say: "I can't comment, except to say that The Children's Aid Society did everything in its power to help the victim." The executive director of The Haven said she had no comment for my story, but if I wished to come down and see her, she'd like to have 'a little chat'. And the director of the jail said not only couldn't he comment on Carole Tippet, he couldn't even tell me whether or not she was ever in the place at all.

Garth was curled up on the cafeteria couch, hugging his camera bag.

"Hey you." I poked him on the shoulder. "Party time."

Ten minutes later, we were down in The Alley.

The rumour mill was working overtime and the girls were definitely getting jittery.

Within twenty minutes of parking the car and hitting Wendell Street, we'd heard four versions of what had happened to the two girls whose bodies had been found down in the Beach. Each of these versions was gospel. Very Reliable Sources. And so forth.

Version One. There was a crazed wacko out there, a kind of Jack the Ripper character. He'd killed two girls and he'd kidnapped Cindy Lou Gilmore and he was probably torturing her right now in some warehouse somewhere and would go on torturing her, like he'd tortured the other two, until she died and then he'd dump her body in the west end just like he'd dumped the other two bodies and then he'd be coming down to The Alley to pick up another hooker. The Yorkshire Ripper had killed, what?, thirteen girls? I told the girl who was telling me this that I hadn't heard anything about anyone being tortured. "The cops never tell you the whole story. They told the whole story, the entire city would be going nuts. Women would be going crazy. There'd be a general panic." According to the cops, and the girl telling me this had got it straight from the cops, this wacko operated just like that Yorkshire wacko.

Version Two. It was the cops doing the killing. One of the girls had overheard a couple of cops talking about the murders. The one cop had referred to the murderer as "the clean-up crew" and the other cop had laughed, out loud. The girl who was telling me this hadn't overheard the cops herself, but she'd talked to the girl who'd been talking to the girl who had overheard the cops talking like that. The hooker who told me all this said that it made sense, when you thought about it. It was no secret the cops didn't much like the trade on the street, no secret they thought of the girls as loners and losers and nobody's loss. The girl I was talking to had heard it, directly from a friend, that a cop had been overheard saying in one of the coffee shops that as far as he and the department were concerned, it was good riddance to every hooker they found in a ditch. "How do you think that makes us feel?" I told her I could imagine how she felt.

116

"You haven't got the first clue how I feel. Me or any other woman, for that matter."

Version Three. There was a very good chance the killer wasn't a man at all. There was a very good chance it was one of the girls working The Alley. And the girl who told me this said she had a pretty good idea who the killer might be. I asked for a name. "You think I'm crazy?" All she would tell me was: "All you gotta do is look at her and you know she could kill her own mother."

Version Four: It was pimps doing the killing. "Any idiot could have told you that." And any idiot could also tell you exactly who the pimps were who were going around bashing girls' heads in and dumping the bodies in the ditches down the west end. "It's the war of the pimps."

Midnight Eddie had his headline. I could see those exact words in 72-point type the moment I wrote them down in my notebook.

"The war of the pimps?"

"Yah, they break out now and then. Couple of assholes fighting over their turf. And we're the turf. Life is cheap on this street. And our lives are the cheapest there is. A hooker ain't worth a pinch of coonshit. And you can quote me."

Twenty minutes of paranoia is about all you can take in one stretch. I closed my notebook and went looking for Sue. The corner was vacant. I stood in the doorway of Sue's bank, watching the comings and goings at the Wendell Hotel across the street. The comings and goings weren't unusual. Guys going in, drunks wobbling out. It was early hours. No falldowns yet. Give it another couple of hours.

I waited twenty minutes, then half an hour. I told myself I'd give it another five minutes, and I did. No Sue.

I followed Garth around for half an hour while he got some more shots, then we both went back to Sue's corner and waited some more. We'd been there about ten minutes when one of the girls came flouncing down the street toward us. "Youse boys lookin' for a good time?" I told her we were looking for Sue. "I can give you a better ride than Sue. And cheaper, too." I told her a ride wasn't what we were looking for. She looked at me, then at Garth. "Youse guys faggots?" I told her we were from The Spectator. "I gathered that. But what I asked was ..."

117

"No, we're not faggots. We're working."

"Now and then you gotta take a break." She was smiling, now. I told her that we were looking for Sue, that I wanted to interview her. "You'll be waitin' out here a while if you're waitin' for Sue." I asked why. "She ain't workin'." I asked why. "You work for the paper and you're askin' why?"

"Know where I can find her?"

She nodded in the direction of The Wendell Hotel. "Last I seen her, she was headed that way."

I thanked her. Then I asked if she had any thoughts about what had happened to Melissa McBride and Carole Tippet. "I got a lot of thoughts." I flipped open my notebook. "But there ain't many of them you can put in your family newspaper." I asked her for them anyway.

"What I think they oughta do, they catch this guy, is they oughta get a nice dull knife and turn him into a soprano. That's what I think." I asked her who she thought was responsible.

"Some nut case. There ain't no shortage of them. Not down here, anyway. Last week, I had this guy who wanted me to pretend to be his mother. While he was screwin' me. His mother! A guy does that, he could do anything. You know what I mean?"

I nodded, and kept writing.

"You can't put that in the paper, can you?"

"I do the writing. I leave the cutting to someone else."

She shook her head. "I'll be buyin' the paper tomorrow, just to see if you get that one in there."

I asked her what the other girls were saying, about the killings.

"I don't know. I don't talk much to anyone. But what I'm sayin' is, this guy's nuts. You gotta be nuts, killin' broads who belong to the guys these broads belonged to. These guys would kill you just for lookin' at them the wrong way. I'd hate to think what they'd do if they knew you killed one of their broads."

I asked her what she knew about Van Allen. "Nothin' I'd tell you." And Luther Cross? She laughed. "How dumb do you think I am?"

"I don't have to put your name in the paper."

"You wouldn't have to. He'd know I been talkin' to you."
"How would he know."

"One of his boys is watchin' us, right now."

"You work for Luther?"

She nodded. Then she cracked her gum and turned and spit it out into the street. "Nice talkin' to you, boys." She took a step and then stopped, and looked over her shoulder. "Sure you don't want a quick ride. Two for the price of one."

It was Garth's turn to laugh.

"You guys are faggots, aren't ya?"

Sue was at a table near the bar, her back to the corner. Cigarette smoke was lazing up from a bent butt in the ashtray. I took her by surprise. She was focusing on the smoke. I apologized for spooking her. "That's alright." She smiled. It was a half-hearted smile.

"Mind if we join you?"

"We?"

I introduced Garth. He extended a hand. Sue looked at it, the way a palm reader might, sizing it up. Then she looked up at him. Then she looked at me. "As long as you're buyin'."

She was drinking whiskey, and she'd have a double. The bartender was already pouring when I walked up the bar. "Youse guys?" he said.

"Couple of draft."

"Glasses or mugs?"

I carried Sue's drink to the table, then went back for the mugs. I put the bill on the bar and told the barkeep to keep the change. He looked at the bill, then at me. "Outta that bill, there ain't no change. Put down another five dollar bill, and that's change. And a decent tip." I did as I was told.

We did a little small talk. Sue asked Garth about photography and whether he'd ever done any fashion work and whether he thought she could model anything nice for him next time he did a spread for the women's pages. "Something nice and slutty." He told her he'd keep her in mind. "If I had you in the back seat for ten minutes, you'd keep me in mind, all right." She smiled one of her wicked smiles, and lit another cigarette. She exhaled, in Garth's direction.

My turn. She sipped her drink and was looking over the rim of the glass at me. "I don't suppose this is an entirely social visit."

"Not entirely. I've got a question."

"Ask away."

"What's the connection between Cindy Lou Gilmore and Carole Tippet?"

"Pretty good question."

"And the answer?"

Sue turned her glass and turned it again, then lifted it and sipped the whiskey. She placed the glass in its own watermark and turned it again. "What I hear, and this ain't necessarily the gospel, eh? but what I hear is, they had kind of a business relationship."

"Which would have been ...?"

"Cindy is in sales, let's say. And Carole's what you might call a compulsive shopper."

"Was a compulsive shopper."

"Right. Was."

"Why do you think Cindy's purse would be beside Carole's body, and Cindy's car a few hundred yards away?"

"You're full of good questions." She smiled at me and then snuck a glance at Garth and then rummaged in her bag for her smokes. Garth was holding the lighter by the time she'd pulled a cigarette from her pack. "The last of the old-time gentlemen."

"And the answer?"

"What I hear, and again, this ain't gospel, eh?, but what I hear, there was bad blood between them. When it came to payments, Carole was always a dime short and a day late. Sometimes more than that. What I hear is, she was into Cindy for a couple of grand, and she wasn't exactly hustling her ass off to make up the shortfall. Some people say Cindy was getting a little impatient."

"And?"

"Maybe a little too impatient. Maybe a little pushy."

"And?"

"The talk is, they maybe oughta be lookin' for a third body."

120

"You think Carole knocked off Cindy?"

"I don't think nothin'. I'm tellin' you what the street thinks. The street's sayin' maybe Carole whacked Cindy."

"In which case, who whacked Carole?"

"Two guesses, and the first guess don't count, unless it's Willie Van Allen."

I flipped my notebook closed, finished my beer and looked at Garth. "You ready?" Garth put his empty mug beside mine and stood up.

"There's one question you didn't ask."

"What's that?"

"What's the connection between Cindy Lou Gilmore and Melissa McBride?"

"And the answer would be?"

"I dunno. But you find out, I think you'll have yourself a killer."

"What makes you think that?"

"I'm not thinkin' it. I'm just tellin' you what I'm hearin'."

The shutter made about the same sound as a fingernail being clipped. It was Garth's funeral camera, a Leica. He'd shot from the waist.

"What the fuck you think you're doin'?"

Garth affected surprise, as though the camera had gone off by itself.

"Who'n hell told you you could take my picture?"

"I ..."

"You fuckin' guys."

Sue was on her feet, now. She finished her drink and plunked the glass down. "You wanna take my picture, you ask me if you can take my picture. I say yes, you take it. I say no, you keep your fuckin' hands off the fuckin' camera. You use that picture, I'll sue your ass."

She brushed past him, then turned to look at me. "Nice class of asshole you're hangin' around with. Next time you come lookin' for me, you come alone." Then she glared at Garth. "Fuckin' peeping tom."

She took a few steps toward the door and then turned to face us. "Fuckin' vultures." She turned and crossed the room and went out the door to the street.

I gave Garth the look. "Nice move, asshole."

Garth shrugged his eyebrows, then his shoulders. He gave me one of his puppydog looks. "Hey. How'n fuck was I supposed to ..."

"Garth. Just shut the fuck up, will you?"

The bartender had watched Sue leave. Now he was looking at us. "There's a nice little whore for ya. Clean her up, you could almost take her home to mother." He shook his head and went back to wiping down the bar. "You gotta wonder, eh? Nice broad like that in the business she's in? Some of them, you couldn't care less. But Suzie? Shit. Musta broke her parents' hearts, eh?, when she took to the streets."

Sue had broken no hearts when she'd left home. She'd told me the whole story the first time I interviewed her. A pretty short story. When she'd left home, no one noticed. Her mother had been busy with a customer in the front bedroom and her mother's boyfriend had been busy with a needle in the living room and one of the boyfriend's customers, fresh tracks in his forearm, was about to make a move on Sue. Sue had sidestepped the loser and hit the stairs. She took with her what she had on her back and, tapping her head, 'what was in here.' The first time I interviewed Sue she'd been gone from home ten years. 'For all I know, my old lady still don't know I'm gone. And if she does know, she sure as shit don't care.' The feeling was mutual. Sue couldn't get away from her mother fast enough.

As she'd told me then, 'I didn't mind being a slut. Like mother, like daughter, eh? But I figured if I was going to slut around, I wasn't going to do it to keep some moron high on smack. I was going to keep the profits for myself. Or so I thought.'

Things hadn't worked out quite that way. A good part of the money she made went into her pimp's pocket. But she was making, as she'd put it 'a decent living' and life on the street was a far cry from life in her mother's walkup. For one thing, her mother's boyfriend wasn't hitting on her in the middle of the night, or slapping her around any time she did something he didn't like. And at least on the street she got to choose her own customers.

Sue was 13 when she started working Wendell. I remember shaking my head when she'd told me that, and remarking that she'd been on her own for a long time. 'I been on my own since the day I was born, practically.' I'd asked her how she'd survived, that first year or so.

'Survivin' wasn't no trouble. I'm a survivor from way back. When your father pulls a disappearing act on you, and your mother spends most of her days and nights on her back, you learn in a hurry. If you don't learn, you don't survive. Simple. And the thing you learn is, ain't nobody goin' to be takin' care of you in this life, so you'd better learn to take care of yourself. And you learn the Golden Rule.'

Sue's Golden Rule: 'Never ask nobody for nothin', never take nothin' from no-one, never trust a fuckin' soul.'

I'd told her at the time that it didn't seem like much of a way to go through life.

'You're right. It ain't much of a way to go through life.' She'd smirked. 'But it's the only way to get through life.'

"Sorry, buddy" Garth was riding shotgun. We were driving back down Wendell toward the office. He'd been looking at the hookers looking at us. "That was dumb."

"You're right. It was dumb."

"I apologize."

"You should apologize. You're a fucking dummy."

"That's what I just said."

"I know. And it bears repeating. You're a fucking dummy. Someone oughta shove that camera where the birds don't chirp."

"I think she already did that."

"And good for her."

Garth was silent for a couple of blocks. He was staring out the passenger-side window. "You think she's right?"

"About?"

"About us. Being vultures."

"Us? I only heard her talking about one vulture. And that was

123

you. And yes, I agree. You are a fucking vulture. And a very clumsy one."

"There's two of us on this particular branch."

We went another couple of blocks in silence.

"Huntzie?"

"What?"

"You feel like a peeping tom?"

"Most days, yah. But it pays well."

Garth was looking out the window, again. We were just about downtown and there was a girl on every corner. Sometimes more than one. They were looking kind of forlorn. He turned and looked at me. "She's right."

"About?

"We should be ashamed of ourselves. Taking advantage of people like her. The only time we give a shit about the hookers down here is when one of them winds up dead in a ditch, or frozen to death under a fire escape."

"You need a Kleenex? I think we got some in the back seat."

"I'm just saying, she has a point."

"And?"

"That's all. She's got a point. Something we should think about."

"Well, thank you Pastor Garth."

I pulled to a stop in front of the cop shop.

"What're we doing here?"

"I'm going to turn myself in." I held out my arms, wrists close together. 'Officer, you're looking at a peeping tom. Clamp the cuffs on me. Lock me up. Throw away the key'."

Garth was not smiling. He nodded in the direction of the building. "Seriously."

"I'm gonna see what we can find out about a dead hooker. You sit tight and make yourself feel bad. I'll only be ten minutes. And don't leave without me."

I was back in less than ten.

"So?"

Carole Tippet had a rap sheet four pages long. Single spaced.

"Anything interesting?"

"Not unless you find prostitution interesting."

"And?"

"Possession of a variety of drugs. Possession of stolen goods. Break and enter. Theft under. Theft over. A couple of assaults."

"A minor leaguer."

"Definitely."

Garth was staring straight ahead all the way back to the parking lot behind the office. I parked and pocketed the keys. He shut his door and looked at me across the top of the car. "If she was such a bush leaguer, how come someone wanted her dead so bad?"

"Maybe it was because she was a bush leaguer," I said.

"Now there's an interesting thought."

"Something we can chew on during supper."

"Dead hooker. How tasty."

"Now, that's sensitive."

"Huntzie." Midnight Eddie is the only newspaperman still in existence who actually wears an eyeshade and those little metal sleeve suspenders. He looks like an extra in an Ed Woods movie. He swivelled around as soon as he spotted Garth and me coming in.

He consulted his watch. He was always doing that, as though his watch was about to tell him something more than the time. Then he looked up at me. "Very fortuitous."

"Very is redundant. If something is fortuitous, it's fortuitous. It's not a matter of degree."

"One of these days, we'll get you on the editing desk." He paused and regarded me with one of his famously superior looks. "Which is, of course, where you belong. Eddie swivelled around again. "There was a broad in here looking for you."

"How long ago?"

"Fifteen, twenty minutes."

"What'd she look like?"

"Very classy. In a low-grade way. If you know what I mean."

"Like Wendell Street?"

"Approximately." He nodded in the direction of the reception area. "Go over and have a sniff. You can probably still smell her perfume." Eddie jerked one of his eyebrows up, then did it again, in case I'd missed the innuendo. "Eau de Lilac, I think."

"Leave her name?"

"No name. No number. Just a message."

"Which was?"

"She'll be back"

"When?"

"Didn't say."

"I don't suppose you asked?"

"That would have been impertinent."

Impertinent.

Hm.

I started toward my desk.

"And Betsy called."

Betsy?

"She leave a message?"

He handed me the message slip. In the box marked Return Call he'd made a little tick mark. At the bottom of the sheet, he'd written the time the call had come in. She'd phoned just after my mystery guest had come calling. My lucky night. Women crawling out of the woodwork.

I tossed my note pad on my desk and sat down. I picked up the receiver. I dialled the first three numbers, then hung up. I wasn't up for a Betsy confrontation. At least not on an empty stomach. I shoved the message in my pocket.

I went into Photography. Garth was already in the darkroom. "Hey. You hungry?"

"Starving."

"Wanna grab a burger before you get to work?"

"Love to." He turned from the trays. "But the front page calls."

I told him I was heading down to the corner. "If Midnight's looking for me, tell him I'll be back in half an hour."

"Tell him yourself, chickenshit."

"It's easier to tell him after I get back."

"He'll be dancing on the desk, waiting for your deathless prose."

"Tell him I was about to faint from hunger."

Garth said he'd do that. For a fee.

"What fee?"

"A burger and fries. Hold the onion."

"Hold the onion?"

"You never know. This could be my lucky night. Maybe when we go to Mary's I'll meet the love of my life."

I told him I didn't think any of Mary's girls could care less if he had his burger with onions, or garlic. As long as he paid.

"Bring me a mug of beer."

I told him that takeout service had its limitations. But, as we were friends, I'd drink a beer for him.

"What are friends for?"

I smiled. "Exactly."

Jimmy Lee's has been around for years and years. At one time it was a mariner's bar. This was back in the days when the river was alive with steamers and ferries and passenger boats and tugboats. Nowadays, the only tugboat tied to the wharf is a restaurant. Now and then, a navy ship will tie up for a day or two. And some big American cruisers. And that's about it. The river traffic died right out.

Back at the turn of the century, Jimmy's was called The Harbour Light. The first owner was a retired sailor named John Lindblad. Lindblad had somehow got his hands on a big buoy, a channel marker, and rigged it up above the front door, facing the wharves. The red light flashed night and day. There's an old photo in The Spec Library, a shot of Lindblad taken the day the buoy was hoisted into place. In the picture, Lindblad's looking up at the buoy, smiling around a big stogey. The cutline quotes him as saying he hoped the buoy would 'beckon the weary and the buffeted' and that his Harbour Light would provide 'a place of quiet and reflection in the midst of life's storms.' His hopes were apparently dashed. In its heyday, which was long before my time, The Harbour Light was a real bucket of blood. As one old timer told me, 'you hadda puke twice and show your gun before they'd let you in.' There was a long bar, front of the place to the back, and a few tables and chairs and spittoons every few feet. Of all the bars in town - and there used to be dozens and dozens of them - The Harbour Light held the record for gallonage of beer sold and for murders committed on, or adjacent to, the premises. Jimmy is proud to say that since he took over from his dad - Jimmy Senior - there have been just two knifings, only one of them fatal. His father's record was four. And his father had owned the joint since Prohibition ended. But back in the twenties, and before that, sixteen souls had departed this life on the floor of The Harbour Light or in the alley out back. The alley was a favourite spot for settling scores.

The most famous killing of all, though, occurred just inside the door. A sailor had been minding his own business, beer after beer. Then a noisy party descended on the table adjacent. Remarks were passed back and forth, leading the sailor to warn the guy doing most of the yapping to shut his trap and drink his beer. Advice is cheap, and rarely acted upon. Which was unfortunate for the man with the runaway mouth. Two or three pointed remarks later, the sailor reached down to his left, grabbed the spittoon and, in one graceful sweeping motion, he swung it over his own head and slammed it onto the head of the man who had been annoying him, a man who, in an instant, was dead on the floor, his head split open, back to front. The sailor had then put the spittoon back on the floor and went back to his beer.

Life, these days, is not nearly so interesting. And Jimmy Lee's was as quiet as a dentist's waiting room.

"Where the hell is everyone?"

"Not here," said Jimmy Lee. He set a beer on the bar and held out his hand, palm up.

"You're such a trusting soul, Jimmy Lee."

"I trust them who pay. I am not often disappointed."

I put some coins in his palm, placed our order for burgers and fries, and raised a glass to his health. He brought out his own glass - whiskey, neat - from beneath the bar and raised it in return. "Here's lookin' at ya."

Jimmy had been working on a cigar and had set it down in the ashtray near the beer taps. It had died a natural death. Jimmy picked it up and examined it, knocked half an inch of ash from the business end then examined it once more, as though contemplating whether it was worth lighting it up for the few remaining puffs it contained. Then he stuck it between his teeth and struck a match, jutting out his chin so as not to burn his nose. "So," he said, "I see you're writing mysteries these days."

"So it seems."

"So what's the word on the street?" The cigar bobbed as Jimmy spoke.

"I was just going to ask you the same thing."

"Some people say it's the pimps. Hitting each other where it hurts."

"Other people?"

"Drug wars."

I sipped on my beer and stared at myself in the mirror behind the bar. Not a pretty sight. I looked at Jimmy. "Could be."

"This last broad, the kid ..."

"Carole Tippet."

"They say she was heavy into heroin. Nasty habit. A girl can rack up some major-league debts doing shit like that. And she wasn't exactly making major-league wages. Word is she got whacked by her drug man."

I took another sip of my beer and lit up a cigarette. "Doesn't explain a couple of key things, Jimmy. There was another whore's purse beside her body, and that other whore's car was nose first in the river a few yards away."

"Maybe you got another dead whore out there somewhere. Maybe this one, the kid, maybe she killed the other broad. Some kind of squabble. Over drugs maybe." Jimmy sucked on his cigar. It had died again. He pulled it from his mouth and had a look at it. He dumped the butt in the garbage. "Maybe the other hooker was the kid's drug connection. Maybe the kid killed her and took off with her money and her car."

"Possible. But if so, then who killed her?"

"The other broad's pimp. Or partner. A guy wouldn't like it if a high-grade hooker like that got knocked off by some H-head."

Hm.

"All right. While we're solving mysteries, solve this: What's the connection between Carole Tippet and Melissa McBride. Two bodies, same field.

"Maybe there ain't no connection." Jimmy unwrapped a new stogey, chewed the end off and spit it out. He fired up the cigar.

"A little unusual, to find the next body in the same neighbourhood as hers, wouldn't you say?"

Jimmy thought about that for a moment or two, during which he replenished his whiskey. "Not necessarily." He tapped his stogey against the rim of the ashtray. "Let's say you're the pimp in question. You've just knocked off a tramp who'd knocked off one of your girls. What you'd want to do is cover your tracks. In a hurry. Make it look like there's some kind of serial killer out there. What's the best place to dump the body? Right where the first body was found."

"You weren't a cop in a previous life, were you?"

"Didn't haveta be. Stand back here and listen to cops talk all night and you start to think like them. Which is not always a healthy thing." He set the cigar in the ashtray, then lifted the hinged section of counter near the wall and headed for the kitchen.

I finished my beer and put the empty on the bar, checked my pocket for change, pulled a quarter out of Jimmy's tips jar and went to the payphone beside the bar.

Betsy grabbed the receiver before the second ring. "Where are you?" I told her I was in Las Vegas, that I'd just hit the jackpot and I was leaving for the South Seas on the first available flight.

"Seriously."

"I'm in jail, and this is my only call. Get through to my lawyer and tell him to get his ass down here, pronto. With bail money."

"Huntzie! Seriously."

"Where do you think I am? I'm at the office."

"When'd they put the jukebox in?

"Just this week. Help boost morale.

"Where's your clothes?"

"The essential ones are on my back."

"The rest of your clothes. Where are they?"

"Whaddya mean, where's my clothes. You told me to take my stuff and shove off. I took it, and shoved."

"You should know me by now."

"Whaddya mean, I should know you by now."

"I was upset. But I didn't mean for you to take your stuff and ..."

"You were joking?"

"Not joking, exactly. But I wasn't serious. You should know ..."

"Huntzie!" Jimmy was holding my empty draft glass. He was pointing at it. I shook my head. "Sure," I said.

"Sure what?"

"No, not you Betsy."

"One or two?" said Jimmy Lee.

I held up two fingers.

"One or two what?" said Betsy.

"Nothing."

"What are you talking about Huntzie?"

"Betsy, I gotta make tracks. I'm on deadline."

"When are you coming home?"

"I'm not."

"What do you mean, you're not?"

"I'm not. I've moved out and I'm staying out. You were right."

"Right about what?"

"Right about me not being the guy for you."

"I never said that."

"You said something to that effect." Jimmy Lee slid a pair of draft onto the bar in front of me. "Thanks."

"Thanks for what?"

"Thanks for the good times. I gotta go. Bye bye."

"Huntzie?"

"Seriously. I gotta go."

Betsy didn't say anything. She just held the phone right where it was and waited for me to say something. God, I hate it when people do that to you. It's like blackmail. You hate to be the first one to hang up. On the other hand.

"Bye, Betsy." I hung up.

Jimmy had the bag of burgers on the bar. "Little problem with the little lady?" I told him it was nothing that wouldn't resolve itself.

"Yah, I could tell."

"You always eavesdrop on all your customers?"

"If I didn't eavesdrop, I wouldn't know nothin', then guys like you wouldn't come in here wonderin' what I knew. Then I'd be outta business." He was studying the remains of his cigar. "Want my advice?"

"Not particularly. How much I owe you for the burgers?"

Jimmy slipped the bill across the bar. "My advice is, go home and give the little lady a little hug and say you're sorry and that you won't let it happen again."

"Won't let what happen again?"

"Whatever it was you done that pissed her off."

"What I did, as if it's any of your fucking business, I moved out."

"Why'd you go and do something like that?"

"Because she told me to."

"And you believed her?"

"Of course I believed her. She told me to pack my shit together and hit the road. The message doesn't get a whole lot clearer, Jimmy."

"Broads. They never say what they mean, and they never mean what they say. You're how old and you don't know that yet? A broad tells you to move out, what she's really sayin' is, she's sayin' send me flowers, tell me you love me, let's go out to dinner."

"Kind of a funny way to ask a guy out on a dinner date."

"She's not askin', you moron. She's askin' you to ask. Fuck, are you thick."

I paid, waited for my change, grabbed the bag. Jimmy slid the change across the bar. I scooped it. "You're taking that puny little bit of change?"

I smiled.

"You oughta tip me twice as much for the advice."

"Thanks, Jimmy. Thanks a million."

Quarter past two in the morning, I'd finished the story. Quarter past three, Page One was laid out and proofed. Love that headline:

'IT'S THE WAR OF THE PIMPS'

Right under that, Midnight had penned a subhead:

STREETWALKERS TERRIFIED AFTER SECOND BODY FOUND

My story was wrapped around a six-column photo. Garth had stood in the middle of Wendell, right on the white line. There were headlights coming toward him and tail lights heading into the distance and, with a wide angle lens, he'd caught the hookers huddling in doorways on both sides of the street.

Brilliant.

My story quoted all the girls we'd been talking to earlier in the night, plus some of the girls we'd talked to right after Carole's body had been found. Eddie had run a box around the whole package, 2-point, black. It was a grabber. He stood up and looked down at the page proof. Smug wouldn't quite encompass it. He looked like the cat who'd swallowed the canary.

Garth was in the mood for a couple of drinks at Mary's.

I was in the mood to pull the covers over my head and sleep for ten hours. After Garth headed out, I proofed the front page, and then proofed it again. I took the proof back to Midnight. "Another winner, Midnight. One of these days, they're going to give you a medal."

"I'd prefer a raise, actually."

"I'll have a chat with the publisher, on your behalf."

"I'll be rolling in dough in no time."

The manila envelope was sitting on my typewriter. Inside, there
133

was an eight-by-ten of Sue, sitting at the table. Paper clipped to the photo there was a note. "Couldn't help myself." I could see why.

The bar - bottles lined up in front of the mirror - was slightly out of focus in the background, but the light was like a halo around Sue. Her head was tilted slightly to the right and there was just the trace of a smile on her lips. She looked like a kid: a little sad, a little bewildered, a little vulnerable. She was looking off to the left, as though she might be waiting for someone to come and take her away.

A picture like that, you look at it long enough, it'll break your heart.

Twenty minutes later, I was lying on my back on the sofa in Garth's basement, my hands clasped behind my head, staring at that photograph taped to the ceiling: Sue staring off into the distance with that sorrowful hopeful heartbreaker look on her face.

-Nine-

Donna Russell lives in a neat little flowers-bordered one-storey in the west end. It would take you about four minutes to drive from her house on Prince Road to the ditch in Balmy Beach where her sister's body was found. Donna has made the drive any number of times. She can't quite explain why, other than to say "it's the only place I can go where I can feel close to her. Weird, eh?"

Well, yes, and no.

Donna's twenty-nine years old. She's married and has two daughters, six and four. Now that Melissa's two daughters, who are nine and seven, are living with her, the house is a little on the crowded side. There are only two bedrooms, so Donna's husband went out and bought two sets of bunk beds and the four girls now share a room that wasn't really big enough for two. "Randy's thinking maybe come summer he'll put an addition on the back. Or maybe we'll move to a place with three bedrooms. That way we could have one room for the older girls and one room for the younger girls and one for us."

Right now, however, an extra bedroom is not high on Donna Russell's list of priorities. Top of her list is just getting through the day and making it to the next without going to pieces. She's been having moderate success. "There are times during the day when I just start crying. It's weird, eh? I'll be fixing the meal, or just sitting having a tea, and all of a sudden I'm crying. No warning, no nothing, just tears all over the place. I try not to do it when the girls are around, especially Mel's girls. That's all they need, to see me bawling my eyes out. Then all of us are into the Kleenex. But sometimes, you just can't

135

help yourself. You know what I mean?"

I told her I did.

But I hadn't a clue.

If you didn't know Melissa and Donna were sisters, you'd never guess as much looking at the framed photo of the two of them which Donna has hung on the living room wall. Melissa's face was narrow and her cheekbones prominent. She'd bleached her hair and, despite the smile, there was a toughness in that face, in the eyes especially, as though they'd seen more than they deserved or wanted to. Donna's face is round and girlish. When she smiles, she looks like a teenager. There were three years between them. But three years doesn't begin to account for the difference.

"That was took at Christmas time. It's the last one where we're together." Donna rooted around in bureau drawer clutter and came up with the most recent one before that which showed them side by side. It was taken at Melissa's wedding, thirteen years previous. If you asked Donna to put her finger on the moment when her sister had taken the fork in the road which would lead, ultimately, to a ditch in Balmy Beach, Donna would have put her finger at exactly that spot on the map of her life. "Why she ever married that guy is beyond me. My parents told her he was a jerk. I told her he was a jerk. Her friends told her he was a jerk. But she was in love, eh? She couldn't see it. She thought he was Prince Charming."

"Until the incident with the babysitter?"

Donna looked at me, a little surprised.

"A friend told me about it."

"Oh."

The babysitter, as it turns out, had been the least of Melissa's problems. It was the beatings which had come to rule her life. And the beatings had begun on their honeymoon. It was one sick spiral from there on down. It had taken Melissa six years to admit what everyone knew from the start: that her husband was worse than a loser. Vastly worse. Give her credit, she'd somehow found the will and the courage to take her girls and flee. What she'd fled to, unhappily, was nearly as grim.

What she'd fled to was poverty and despair. It's a familiar tune and there's a whole choir of bruised and battered souls out there singing it.

When Melissa left her husband, she wound up in a little apartment and found a couple of part-time jobs to help her make ends meet. Then she met a guy she kind of liked and a few months later they moved into a little house, not far from Donna's place. "It looked like she was getting things back together." But things didn't work out with the new boyfriend and when he left, she couldn't afford the house anymore and so it was back to apartment life.

And then Donna picked up the story right about where she'd left it the first time we'd talked, right after Melissa's body had been found: Melissa losing hours at Zellers where she had a part-time cashier's job, getting more in debt as the months passed until she was making interest payments when she could afford to make payments at all and skipping out on one landlord after another. And then she'd decided to make use of the one talent she thought she had left.

"Hard to imagine, eh? A beautiful person like Mel having to do that, just to keep food on the table and clothes on her girls backs. When I first found out, I was furious. I went over to her place and we wound up yelling and screaming. I told her she didn't have to stoop to that to get by. I told her I could help her out until she found other work. But she was proud, eh? She was always proud and independent. She never wanted to be beholden to anyone. The way she figured it, she was on her own, making her own money, calling her own shots. I told her, 'you call working for some pimp being independent? I told her, 'if you're not beholden to a pimp, then what the hell are you?' I told her, 'you're so proud? You're not too proud to going around screwing strangers in the back seat of a car'. We really had it out. But that was it, that one time. I wasn't about to change her mind and she wasn't about to change her ways. And so we just agreed not to talk about it.

"After that, we didn't see much of each other. She'd call now and then, and I'd call her, but with her hours I mostly ended up talking with the babysitter. I wasn't judging her, but I think she thought I was." Donna was looking at her sister's picture. "To be honest, I guess I was. I was disgusted by her doing that. I couldn't stand thinking about it. I didn't want those thoughts in my head. I didn't want to picture her doing that with all those strange men. It would have driven me crazy. But every time I saw her, I couldn't help it. I started imagining what she had to do. I couldn't take it. So we just drifted

137

apart."

Donna saw her sister twice in the month before the murder.

"What was strange was, the first time - this would've been a month before the murder - she was so happy, eh? I hadn't seen her that happy in a long time. She said everything was going fine. Going great was how she put it. 'Things are going great, Don'. That's what she said. I didn't know what to ask, after that. Like I said, I didn't want to know the particulars. So I just told her I was happy for her. She said she knew I didn't approve of what she was doing. But she said I wouldn't have to worry about it too much longer. She said she was working her way into a different part of the business. Kind of supervisory is what she indicated. Supervising the other girls, I guess. She said she and her Man, that's what she called him, eh?, not her pimp, but her Man, she said she and him had worked out a kind of partnership. There'd been some other girl doing that kind of thing, but now the Man was edging that girl out and Mel was taking over. 'I'm movin' up in the world, Don. You wait. Things are turning around for me'.

I'd stopped writing and I guess I was staring. Donna stopped talking and just looked at me.

"She said the Man was edging out another woman?"

"That's what she said."

"Did she mention any names?"

"The pimp was a guy named Willie."

"Van Allen?"

"She never mentioned a last name. Willie was the only name she used."

"And the other woman?"

"I think it's the one who's missing. Cindy."

"Gilmore?"

Donna nodded. "Early on, she talked about this Cindy a fair bit. It sounded like she'd kind of taken Mel under her wing. I know Mel liked her. But lately, things had cooled off between them. I think maybe this Cindy thought Mel was cutting in on her or something. And maybe she was.

"Then, I saw her again. This would've been a couple of weeks before she was murdered. It was like she was a whole different person. She was on edge, real twitchy. No more smiles, no more high hopes. It was like all of a sudden she had to look over her shoulder all the time. I asked her what was going on. All she said was 'everything's changed'. She said she'd left her Man, this Willie guy, and she was workin' for someone else. She wouldn't say who. But you could tell she was in some kind of trouble. It was like all of a sudden, in the space of those two weeks, her whole world had collapsed. And you know what the last thing was she said to me? She said, 'somethin' happens to me, Don, make sure you take care of my girls'. That's the last thing she said before she left. Gave me the shivers. It was like she had some kind of premonition, eh?"

Donna looked over my shoulder, again, at the photo on the wall.

And just like she said, the tears started. No warning, no nothing. One minute she was fine, the next minute she was up out of her chair and heading for the kitchen and the Kleenex box.

I got held up by a train. Trains are the bane of our existence. There are level crossings all over town and the trains take their own sweet time shunting back and forth across the road. Now and then you'll see the engineers smirking down from their perches high in the cab as they drift past you. Then four or five minutes later, just as the last of the freight cars is about to clear the crossing, the train stops and you know you're in for it. The train just sits there for a minute and, sure enough, it starts backing up and there's the engineer, smirking as he goes the other way.

One time, out by the mall, the crew stopped the train right on the Howard Avenue crossing and climbed down and crossed the field and went into McDonald's. Five or six minutes later, they came back out with their bags in their hands. The drivers were going crazy. I'll bet you could have heard the horns five miles away. But the crew just sauntered back to the train, taking their own swaggering fuck-you time and clambered back up into the cab and then got that baby slowly rolling down the track, eating while they went. One of these days, a crazed motorist is going to scramble up the ladder into the cab of one of those idling trains and he's going to cork an engineer right between the eyes. You can bet that story will make the front page. And you can bet the letter writers will be cheering for weeks on end.

Anyway, a train spent exactly eight minutes shunting back and forth across Sandwich Street near the pollution control plant and so it took me twelve minutes, rather than four, to get from Donna's house to Water Street. I parked on the shoulder and walked the few dozen yards to the spot where they'd found Melissa's body, three weeks before. A hundred or so yards across the field was the spot where they'd found Carole's body.

There was a dog barking, somewhere. Maybe one of Leslie's dogs. And the birds were looping from tree to tree. Just another nice quiet west-wind spring day. Look down into the ditch and there's no sign anything untoward ever happened in this particular spot. No sign that a woman's body had been dumped there like so much trash.

You've got to wonder, eh?, how someone could do that, kill someone and dump the body like that. Murder you can comprehend, in a vague sort of way. People will do the damnedest things in a moment of passion: hate and anger. That's why the cops hate getting called to a domestic. A domestic is just about the worst kind of situation you can imagine. Knock knock, walk in, anything can happen. A cop told me one time he walked in the front door and just froze. For some reason, he hadn't pulled his revolver. Why, he couldn't explain. He always pulled his revolver when he walked into a situation like that. Anyway, his gun was in its holster and he was in the living room and he looked to his right and there was a wild-eyed man standing there with a shotgun in his hands, the butt end resting against his shoulder, one of those wild eyes taking aim at whatever was down the barrel. Then my cop friend turned to his left and there was a woman with a pot of steaming water in her hand, ready to heave it at the guy with the shotgun. Both of them quiet as cobras. And then the guy says to my cop pal, he says, "officer, I'd suggest you take a couple of steps forward or a couple of steps back because I am about to kill this bitch and I'd hate for an innocent man to get in the way." My pal, his brain is working like crazy now, but in the end, he decided to back up and he was no sooner back in the doorway than the steaming water went flying one way and the buckshot the other and there was a thump as the woman and the pot hit the ground and a screaming as the water hit its target. A bad marriage is like a keg of gunpowder with a lit fuse stuck into it. You can hope that common sense licks its finger and thumb and snuffs that fuse. But common sense is usually somewhere else at the time. Which keeps us and the cops and the ambulance

140

boys and the emergency room nurses and Fred The Body Man and the undertakers on the run.

So, killing you can imagine in a vague sort of way. But dumping the body, that would be something entirely different. You'd have run right out of passion. You'd have cooled down, and you'd be left with a cooling, bloodied corpse sprawled at your feet. You'd have to manhandle that body into the trunk of a car and then drive across town, knowing that body was back there in the trunk, knowing that up until a few moments ago, that body was capable of walking and talking and breathing and laughing and crying and imagining and dreaming and fearing. And once you'd arrived at the ditch, you'd have to manhandle the corpse out of the trunk and get your hands under its arms and drag it over to the side of the road and then roll it down to the bottom of the ditch. Then you'd have to climb down there and try to cover it up a little bit with leaves and whatever else was handy and then you'd have to stand there for a minute and look at it, seeing what kind of a job you'd done.

Exactly what kind of thoughts would you be thinking while you looked down at the body? What kind of thoughts would you be thinking as you scrambled up the ditch bank and got into the car and drove away? That's the part I couldn't imagine. Would the guy feel guilt? Would he feel remorse? Wiping the blood from his hands, would he feel disgusted with himself? Looking in the mirror over the sink, towel in his hands, would he feel loathing rising up like bile in his own throat?

What would you do next?

Toss the towel on the floor, comb your hair, walk down to the corner tavern and order a couple of draughts and watch the end of the ball game on the TV above the bar?

How could you take another step?

How could your life even begin to unfold in any normal kind of way, once you'd done that, once you'd beaten the life out of another human being?

You could wash and scrub all you wanted, but you'd never get your hands clean. You'd never get that smell out of your nose. You'd never get that sight out of your brain. That body, lying there bruised and bloodied and going grey. That would be something you'd take to the grave with you.

If you were any kind of normal human being.

Which was probably my first lapse of logic.

I looked down at the spot where Melissa's body had been discovered.

"So, how'd a nice girl like you wind up in a spot like this?"

Sorrowful thing, when you think about it, eh?

Drive down Hookers Alley and it's hard not to think about it.

You see those girls huddled in the doorways and you can't help but think that once upon a time, a long time ago, they were all little kids like Katie, all in school in their sweaters and skirts, all laughing and joking and jumping rope, knobbly knees and rolled-down socks. Once upon a time, they were all some daddy's little girl.

And even if those fathers were jerks and assholes, there must have been a moment when they cradled those little babies in their arms and sang them lullabies, crooned them to sleep against the warmth and heartbeat of their chests. They must have whispered to themselves, even one time, I will love this little child and keep her from harm.

Yah, well.

Maybe yes.

Maybe no.

Maybe Love got distracted, turned its back for a couple of minutes. You know how quick things can happen. Next thing you know, it's Little Girl Lost, little girl on her back in the backseat of some family sedan, a sweating grunting stranger writhing on top of her.

Then again, maybe Love never entered into the equation in the first place.

I looked across the field at the stacks and the plumes of Zug Island and then up at the cloud-drifting sky and then back down at the ditch.

'I'm movin' up in the world, Don. You wait. Things are turning around for me'.

There are some mistakes you just don't want to make. Some very serious errors in judgement. Apparently, Melissa McBride had made one.

Life on the street is never easy. But The Street has a way of equipping you for the task. If you're smart and you watch and you listen, The Street teaches you a lot of things. It teaches you to smell danger the instant it comes around the corner or into the room. It teaches you to figure out odds in precisely the number of seconds it takes you to shove your hand into your pocket and get a grip on your knife or your gun. In this particular school, there are no As and Bs and Cs. You either pass or you fail. You survive or you wind up in the bottom of a ditch in Balmy Beach with last fall's leaves scattered all over what's left of your face.

"I'm movin' up in the world ...."

Either Melissa hadn't been smart enough to smell an enemy when she made one, or she hadn't been smart enough to care. Either way, she'd paid a big price. But you had to wonder about a girl like Carole Tippet.

Carole Tippet knew the streets better than the rats know the alleys. So what was her fatal mistake?

The Haven is an old three-storey house down in the west end. It was built by a fellow named Oliver Harrison. Oliver Harrison owned a couple of roadhouses down Sandwich Street. He was a gambler, a crook and a sonofabitch. Which made him a very wealthy man. His son, Tyler, ran the biggest bootlegging operation anywhere along the border during Prohibition years. He wound up even richer than his old man. And like his old man, he didn't live long enough to enjoy the cash. The last thing Oliver Harrison ever saw was a double flash of flame coming from the business end of a .12 gauge sawed-off shotgun. The last thing Tyler Harrison saw was an ocean liner receding in the distance, the ocean liner from whose deck he had been tossed. As my grandmother used to remind me, from time to time, 'be mindful of the company you keep'. You should also be mindful of the people you screw. Oliver and Tyler weren't quite mindful enough, on either count. Old Ollie was gunned down by the thugs of a thug whose territory he was trying to take over. Tyler was pitched over the rail by the thugs of a scar-faced thug from Chicago whom he'd tried to screw on a liquor shipment. Further proof that the only thing you should try screwing is a light bulb. But that's another story.

When old Ollie Harrison built The Haven, it was the biggest

house in town. Its back lawn extended all the way to the river. They say he had docks down there, and gazebos and tennis courts, fountains and a pool. The works.

The back lawn still extends to the river, but where once there was elegance, these days there's just grass. The dock and the gazebo are long gone. The pool's been filled in. Elegance is no longer a word you'd use to describe the house. The chandeliers are gone, so too the heavy furniture and thick-framed paintings that you can see in the photograph in The Spectator's morgue. Samuel Harrison, Tyler's son, auctioned off everything in the place before he turned it over to the nuns who have transformed it into a home for what they still refer to as 'wayward girls'. The standing joke at the time was that Tyler had created enough wayward girls to keep the nuns busy for quite some time.

Back in the 60s, we used to call up and when a nun would answer, we'd ask 'do you save wayward girls?' and when she said 'yes, we do' - and they always said 'yes, we do' - we'd holler 'well, then, save one for me, I'm on my way down' and slam down the phone as all the rest of the guys were pissing themselves in the background.

I probably slammed down the phone on Sister Mary Joseph once or twice. She's been at The Haven since the day it opened. She met me at the front door and led me up the half dozen linoleum steps, waited for me at the top and then, extending her arm, indicated that I should enter the sitting room. More linoleum, some 1950s leatherette chairs, an unremarkable coffee table at the centre of which, on a doily, was a plastic jug of plastic flowers. Sister Mary Joseph sat on one maroon leatherette chair and indicated I should take the one beside it, to the right. "This is my good one," she said, tapping her right ear. "Even so, I might have to ask you to speak up." She smiled. I smiled right back. I was already feeling badly about all those years-ago late-night telephone calls.

"How may I help you?"

"Well," I said. I told her how Carole Tippet's sad and short life story had ended."What I'm trying to do now," I said, "is work my way back to the beginning."

"Why do you want to do that, if I may ask."

"Well," I said. "It seems kind of tragic to me that a 17-year-old can end up dead in a ditch and I'd like to know exactly how that could have happened."

"To what end?"

"Pardon?"

"I'm the deaf one." Sister Mary Joseph smiled. But her eyes weren't smiling. Her eyes were giving me the third degree. "What will you do with all this information, once you have it?"

"Write a story, Sister."

"What will that accomplish?"

"It will let people know the truth."

"And what will that accomplish?"

"Who knows? Maybe it will cause some changes to be made in the way the system works. So that another kid can be spared the same fate."

"Perhaps it will do no such thing. Perhaps it wasn't the fault of the system at all. Perhaps it was simply the fault of some ordinary people. People who cared. People who didn't. Then what?"

"Then I tell that story."

"Apportion blame?"

"If there's blame to be apportioned."

"And who designated you the Avenging Angel?"

"I'm kind of self-assigning, when it comes to that."

"Don Quixote, with a pen?"

"You might say."

" 'Vengeance is mine, saith The Lord'."

"He can wreak the vengeance. I'll be happy just to finger the suspects."

"And if the suspects were to include me?"

"You?"

"Me." Sister Mary Joseph's icy blues were locked right on me.

"Well, you could count on me to spell your name correctly."

She smiled. Then she laughed. A chirpy little laugh. Then she leaned over and patted me on the knee and started talking. When she had said all she wanted to say she stood up and when I stood up she approached me and hugged me. "God bless you."

What do you say to that? 'God bless you, too?' A tad presumptuous, under the circumstances. I smiled and followed her out of the lounge and down the stairs and passed through the door which she had opened for me. "I'll be waiting, with some interest, to see what you write." I told her I'd get her a copy of the story. "There's no need. I subscribe."

Say this for Sister Mary Joseph, once she decided to talk, she had no qualms about talking: Carole Tippet had come to The Haven when she was thirteen. She'd been in and out of foster homes one after the other, each stay shorter than the stay which preceded it. The cops had found her down on Hooker's Alley, too much make-up, not enough clothes. They returned her to the Children's Aid. But the Children's Aid had just about run out of patience and foster parents. "She was a troubled soul, certainly." After a boisterous beginning - a couple of chairs flying across rooms, dishes shattering against walls, nuns being told to fuck right off - Carole seemed to settle in. "She was with us for almost seven months." During that seven months, she warmed up to the nuns a little, but she never opened up to anyone. "She was always wary, always guarded, always skeptical of anyone's attention. But, then, after what she'd been through, who wouldn't be wary and guarded and skeptical of anyone's attention." I asked Sister Mary Joseph what Carole had gone through. "Everything you could imagine, and then some."

I asked her for details. "You know I can't give you details."

"You know I have to ask, anyway."

Our conversation drifted from the specific to the general, from Carole to all the kids who had passed through The Haven on their way to something better, something worse. I asked Sister Mary Joseph what she thought about when she thought about all these kids.

"I wonder why they fail," she said. "Was it because they didn't have enough love to begin with? Some of them will tell you they've never had it so good as they have it in here. Food on the table every day. Clean clothes. No one yelling at them, or hitting them, or frightening them. They'll tell you 'I never had it like this at home'.

"When people ask me what's wrong with these girls, I say it's mostly a lack of love and attention. Many parents do love their children and from the best of homes girls can go wayward. But I think basically these kids want a different kind of attention than they got at home, a different kind of care. That's why they get in with their gangs. They get from their gang something they never got at home. They won't tell you that, they won't admit it, but basically there's a yearning in them to feel wanted, to feel accepted for what they are. So many of them are promiscuous and, to me, there's no secret there at all. With sex, what they're really looking for is happiness and joy. They have a hunger for happiness. They turn to sex because they feel lonely. They turn to drugs to blot out whatever haunts them. They turn to crime to pay for drugs. It's pitiful. Really, it is.

"My heart aches for these children," Sister Mary Joseph had said, standing up. "I feel like taking them in my arms and hugging them."

She hugged me, instead.

The death notice said visiting from two until five in the afternoon, seven to nine in the evening. I thought the evening might be more interesting than the afternoon.

I was right.

I sat in the car and listened to the 7:30 news. There was nothing on the news that we hadn't had in the paper the last couple of days. The only item of interest was a brief clip of Suzanne Tippet. She was spreading blame like farmers spread manure in the springtime. As far and wide as possible. Read between the lines and you could read 'lawsuit' in capital letters.

I locked the car and went inside.

Henderson Brothers Funeral Home was having a good week. Four of the six salons were in use. Carole's room was down the hall, last room on the right.

The Tippets hadn't picked the model covered in grey cloth, but they were only a couple of hundred dollars up from it on the price list. There were three arrangements of flowers to the left of the casket and two to the right. There was a bouquet of roses lying on the lid of the casket.

Suzanne and Harry Tippet were standing at the foot of the casket. She was nicely done up: a kind of dark blue business suit - skirt and jacket - and a white shirt with a frilly collar. Harry was in pinstripes, dark grey. There was a young man beside them. One of the sons, pre-

147

sumably.

They were all smiling and talking with an elderly couple whose backs were to me. Suzanne stopped smiling when she looked over the elderly woman's shoulder and caught a glimpse of me. I didn't nod or smile. I just looked right at her. She turned to her left and said something to Harry. He lost his smile, too. Then he excused himself to the old folks and headed right for me.

"Is there something I can do for you?"

"No," I said. I told him I was just dropping in to have a quick look, then I was heading on my way. I told him I hoped he didn't mind the intrusion. I knew that it was an intensely emotional time for him and his family. I told him that this was one of the more unpleasant aspects of my job, as he might imagine. I told him I hoped he didn't think I was some kind of vulture.

Put them on the defensive. It works most of the time.

Next thing you know, Harry was apologizing and telling me to stay as long as I needed to. He and Suzanne didn't mind a bit. They'd just been startled to see me, that was all.

I told him I could understand that. I told him I'd be as unobtrusive as possible, then I'd disappear. We stood looking at each other for a couple of uncomfortable seconds. It looked like he was about to excuse himself to me and head back across the room.

"Do you mind if I ask you a question?"

"Not at all," he said. "Go right ahead."

"I've got a couple of kids of my own. A daughter and a son. Just before you came over, I was wondering what on earth would be going on in my head if I had to do what you're about to do: bury my daughter. I was just wondering what goes through your mind as you're standing there, beside Carole's casket."

"Oh," he said. "Many things."

"Such as?"

"I try to think back to the happy times we had."
I fixed on his eyes.

He was looking for an answer. But, apparently there was nothing written up there on the ceiling, or on the far wall, or down on the carpet.

He looked back at me. "Just a lot of little happy moments." He forced a small smile. "If you'll excuse me. I should be getting back to my wife."

"Is that your son?"

Harry looked at the boy and then at me. "Yes," he said. "That's Harry Junior."

"You have another boy?"

"Yes," he said.

"Is he here?"

"Yes," he said. "James." He looked over my shoulder. "That's him there."

James was sitting on a sofa at the back of the room. He was staring at his sister's casket.

"He's taking his sister's death very hard. Very hard," said Harry. Then he excused himself and went back to his wife's side. He whispered a few words to her, which got her staring in my direction. Then they both turned, with their sad smiles, to greet the next of the mourners.

Next thing you know, they lost their smiles in a hurry.

Sue and three of her pals came strutting in the door and across the room and up to the front. They silenced the room in a hurry. Everyone was looking from them to the Tippets and back to them. The tension was as thick as the girls' perfume. The Tippets looked just about as uncomfortable as a middle-class couple can look.

"You the parents?" Leave it to Sue to barge right in.

"Yes," said Suzanne. "Yes, we are. I'm Suzanne and this is my hus...."

"You're a real pair of fuckin' assholes, from what I hear. And since it was Carole who told me, then I guess I got the goods. I don't know what you did to her, and I don't want to know. But whatever it was, you fucked her up pretty good. I hope you're proud of yourselves. And I hope you rot in hell."

Then Sue made a hard right turn and marched for the door, her three pals bringing up the rear.

She winked as she passed me.

I turned to watch her go. Then I just stood there, like the rest of the people in the room. We were all waiting for someone to make the first move, the first comment.

Then someone up front drew in her breath and someone whispered something to someone else and a few minutes later, little conversations had broken out here and there.

James Tippet was still sitting on a sofa at the back of the room. He was leaning forward, elbows on his knees, supporting his forehead with the tips of his fingers. He sat there like that for another minute, maybe more. Then looked up at his parents and his brother and it was the look in his pale blue eyes that told me he was the key to the story. All I had to do was get him alone.

All I had to do was wait.

A few minutes later, he left the room. I followed him down the hall and into the main lobby. When he went out through the front doors and stood on the step and lit a smoke.

I stood a couple of feet away. Pulled my smokes from my pocket. Faked a search for matches, then turned to him: "Got a light?"

He flipped the lid of his Zippo and cupped it in his hands.

"Thanks."

He nodded, then went back to staring at the traffic passing by on Ouellette Avenue. I told him who I was.

He kept looking at the traffic. "Why'd you come here?"

I told him. And I told him what it was that I wanted to know.

"You should know that," he said. "You wrote the story."

"No," I told him. "I want to know what happened to her. Back at the beginning."

"Nothing much," he said.

And then, in the time it took him to smoke a cigarette, he told me.

I asked him if he'd tell me that again, when I had a tape recorder rolling.

He nodded.

I got out the recorder, pressed Play and Record.

Kenny Koster was standing at the bar, watching in the mirror as I came up behind him. I edged in, to his right. He didn't turn. He kept looking at me in the mirror behind the bar. "Where the hell you been?"

"Snooping."

"Me too. But I was on time." Kenny checked the clock behind the bar against his own watch. "I sure's hell hate buyin' my own beer, and I just drank two of them."

I apologized. I told Kenny where I'd been.

"Must've been fun."

"Let's just say it was interesting, in a weird sort of way."

"How were the parents?"

"Not exactly beside themselves with grief. If you ask me, and you are, I'd say they were busy playing the part. And that was about it." I ordered a couple more draft and Kenny led the way to a table in the far corner. He took the inside chair so he could keep his back to the wall. He was probably born sitting in a chair with his back to the wall.

"So?"

I told Kenny I thought we could dispense with the theory that Melissa McBride had been about to sing a song about Willie Van Allen.

"What makes you think that?"

I told him where I'd been, what Donna had said about her sister. He was all ears, especially when I got to the part about Melissa heading up in the world.

"Hell hath no fury," said Kenny. "There are some broads you just don't cross. And this Cindy Gilmore was one of them."

"You think Cindy whacked Melissa?"

"I'd say you can take that to the bank."

"Why're you so sure?"

"Willie Van Allen is not easily separated from his money. But he put out the call: he's willing to separate himself from ten grand if someone brings him Cindy Lou's head on a platter."

"Sounds like he's a little upset."

"Sounds like he's a lot upset. And I presume it's because his former Number One Bimbo just knocked off his new Number One Bimbo."

"Which tells us what about Carole Tippet?"

"The word is, Cindy Lou set her up. Van Allen apparently tried to lure Gilmore into a trap - offered to buy some serious drugs off her. Gilmore smelled a rat, gave Tippet her I.D. and her car and sent off with the stash to make the sell. Bye bye."

"Who do you think did the job?"

"Good luck trying to find out. There'd be fifty or sixty shitheads in this town who'd knock off their grannies for that kind of cash."

"But they got the wrong broad."

"Yah."

"Which means?"

"Which means, Van Allen won't pay. Yet."

"Which accounts for Miss Gilmore's timely disappearance."

"If Miss Gilmore is as smart as it sounds she is, she'll be a hell of a long way away from here by now. Or ...." Kenny finished his draft, set the glass aside and started on the fresh one. "...she could be right here in town. Waiting."

"Waiting for what?"

"Waiting to return the favour."

"Waiting to whack Van Allen?"

"What I hear is, she was getting a little too big for her britches. She was running more and more of the action for Van Allen. And she may have been running some of her own business as well. She ain't stupid. Once she started getting the message, started getting shoved aside, she started to set things up for herself. A little drug action here. A couple of girls there. When Van Allen put the hit out, she'd have taken that personal."

"If you were a betting man, where would you put your nickel?"

"I'd put it on the slot that says Cindy's still in town. I think these two are gonna duke it out."

"Cindy and Van Allen?"

"Yah." Kenny set his bottle down and scratched his head and then looked up at the ceiling. "They got a nice little business here. They're

152

makin' a killin'. I wouldn't be surprised they're bringin' in six, eight hundred thousand a year. All cash. That's tough to walk away from. Van Allen sure as hell isn't walkin'. And from what I hear about Cindy Lou Gilmore, it don't sound like she's the walkin' type either. I'd say we got a battle brewin'."

"If you had another nickel, would you put it on the Cindy Wins square or the Willie Wins square."

"I'm bettin' Cindy all the way."

"Why?"

"I think they're both dogshit. But Willie Van Allen has been lookin' for it for a long time. And I'd say his number's about to get flipped."

"Any time soon?"

"I'd say real soon. The drug boys hear there's a sizable deal comin' down. Couple hundred thousand. There are maybe five or six people in town who could handle that kind of action. Cindy Lou and Van Allen are two of them. The way it works is, Cindy lines up the buyers. Van Allen brings in the goods. Cindy makes the sale. They split the cash. At least, that's the way it used to work, before Melissa McBride started movin' in. So I'd say there's a thirty or forty percent chance that Cindy Lou and Van Allen are involved in this deal."

"You think they're together?"

"Someone puts a hit out on you, safest place to be is the other half of the bed. Cindy Lou Gilmore's probably closer to Willie Van Allen than his own shorts."

"What'd you find out about Luther Cross?"

"He's one mean mother. He's been up a couple of times. First time for armed robbery. Beat up a variety store clerk and made off with a couple of hundred bucks. She was pregnant at the time. Which didn't seem to trouble him. Next time, it was attempt murder. Shot a guy in the gut"

"How come?"

"Guy owed him some money. Didn't pay when he was supposed to."

"Nice."

"He runs a little stable. Runs a card game here and there. Deals in

153

whatever drugs he can get his hands on. Mostly, he's a small timer. But the boys say he's getting a higher profile these days. I'll see what else I can find out." Kenny finished his beer and pushed his chair back. "Gotta run." He stood up. "Keep in touch. And I'll let you know what I hear." And he was gone.

-TEN-

Every twenty-fourth of May, we go to the cottage. One year I take the kids, the next year, Jeannie takes them. When we were married, we used to go together. It was one of the highlights of the year. The kids love the cottage. It's an old lake-facing place in Southampton, on the Lake Huron shore. The place has been in my family since the turn of the century. My grandfather built it and when he died he willed it to my father and when my father died, he willed it to my brother and me. By that time, my brother had moved to the west coast and had no need of the cottage. He did have need of some cash, however. So I bought him out. Which was fine by me. That way, no hassles figuring out who got the place on which weekends, and who took which month in the summer.

When Jeannie and I split up, I kept the cottage, Jeannie kept everything else: house, car, savings account, stocks, bonds, the works. Plus, her lawyer now wants me to pay her half my weekly salary in alimony, on top of child support. She'll probably get it, too. It's what passes for a fair settlement in divorce court these days. But that's another story.

This twenty-fourth of May, it was Jeannie's turn to head north for the weekend. I told Jeannie I'd be around, about supper time, to say goodbye. They weren't leaving until tomorrow, but with the way my life works these days, better say goodbye a day early, just in case.

I knocked a couple of times and then turned my back to the door and looked out across the park to the lake. Lovely view, especially on a full-moon night when there's a moonpath from the beach to the far horizon. But that lake haunted me, the first couple of years after we'd moved into the house. Jeannie couldn't see anything wrong with the kids wandering over to the park to play on the swings and slides. All I could think of was two tiny bodies, being pulled out of the lake. 'God, you're morbid.' Well, yes and no.

Not surprising, I guess, given the business I'm in, but I'm always nagged by the feeling something terrible will befall my children. It's not paranoia. God knows, given the state of the world, there's ample chance for anyone to meet with disaster these days. But it really does drive me crazy. I'll be lying awake at night, staring at the ceiling - even before I'd put Sue's picture up there - and find myself wondering about the kids growing up, and then going out into the world on their own, and then Jeannie and me dying and the kids being on their own. And I wonder, what happens if they need someone to help them. What happens if they need someone to shelter them. What happens if they're in desperate need of help and they're alone in the world and there's no one there to help them at that moment when they need it most? And I just want to somehow guarantee them that at that moment, someone will be there for them. Someone will be able to wrap them in his arms and guide them out of danger and if they're hungry, feed them, or if they're homeless, shelter them, or if they need to talk, listen to them.

The usual maudlin middle-of-the-night crap.

Still.

I thought the older the kids got and the older I got, I'd get over this vague sense of dread, but if anything it seems ....

"Hey, Dad!"

I turned and leaned down and Katie was in my arms. "How's Daddy's little girl?"

"Hi Dad."

I had one arm around Katie and the other around Ben.

"What're you doin' here?"

"Doing." I gave Ben the look.

"What are you doing here?"

"I just came to say goodbye."

"Where are you going?" Katie was looking up at me.

"I'm not going anywhere."

156

"Why are you saying goodbye then?"

"You're going to the cottage."

"That's not until tomorrow."

"I know. But tomorrow, you never know. I may not be able to get around before you leave."

And there was Jeannie, wearing a nice tight pair of jeans and a nice loose T-shirt and a weird little half smile. "Hello, Jonathan."

God, I hate it when she calls me Jonathan. She never called me Jonathan, even when we first met. It was always Huntzie, right from the start. Or Hunter, when she was angry. But never ....

"To what do we owe this pleasure?"

"I just came around to ...

" ... he's saying goodbye."

"Goodbye?" Jeannie has a way with her eyebrows. The left one. She can hold the right one dead still and arch the left one. Looks like a female Robertson Davies. Without the beard. "You going on a trip?"

"No. Saying goodbye to you guys. I don't know whether I'll be able to get around tomorrow. Before you leave. For the cottage. So, I thought I'd ...."

"Well, isn't that thoughtful."

And what did she mean by that? That's the thing about Jeannie. She could be saying one thing and meaning another, or she could be saying one thing and meaning exactly what she said. Impossible to know. Even if you'd been living with her for a dozen years. Trust me.

"While you're here ...."

Twenty minutes later, the four of us sitting around the dining room table, just like old times - well, almost like old times - I'd gone through all the cottage-opening instructions: turning on the water, turning on the electricity; turning on the fridge and the stove. The whole thing gave my heart a little squeeze.

Opening the cottage had always been a neat time for the four of us. It was like the beginning of the best part of the year. Right after she finished teaching for the year, Jeannie and the kids would move north for the summer. Every Friday night, I'd hightail it up the highway and we'd spend Saturday and Sunday swimming and playing on the beach, golfing and walking up and down the Main Street with all the other weekenders. Then, all of August, I'd spend the month with them, golfing every morning, rain or shine, lounging around in the afternoon, sitting at night on the screened verandah listening to the waves on the beach. God, I loved that verandah. Especially on a rainy summer's night when the air is heavy and sweet with the smell of the cedars and the sand and the lake.

So much for all that.

"Anything else you can think of?"

"It's not as though I haven't done this before, you know."

"I wasn't suggesting ..."

"Stop it, you two." Ben gave me the look and then his mother the look. Then he was up on his feet. "Can't you guys even sit for ten minutes without getting on each other's cases?"

Then he was gone.

Jeannie looked at me. I looked at Katie. I gave her what passed for a smile. She smiled back, then studied her fingernails.

When had she started biting her fingernails?

I was about to ask. But Katie was saved by the clock. The clock said I had approximately six and a half minutes to get to a donut shop half-way across town. I kissed the kids and nodded in Jeannie's direction and wished them all a happy trip. Then I hit the road, trying to figure out the quickest route across town.

The trip from my former home to the Donut Delite took nearly twenty minutes. Angela Merton was lighting up as I crossed the coffee shop to her booth at the back. It was her fourth cigarette. Nervous smoker. It looked like she took about four drags on each cigarette before snuffing it out. The L-shaped butts were cuddling each other in the ashtray. I apologized for being late. "No problem," said Angela. She was lying, and not well. She was checking her watch as I slid into the booth.

Angela Merton was a friend of an acquaintance. She'd been working for The Children's Aid for years. When our mutual friend mentioned to Angela that she knew me, Angela asked her to set up a meeting. She'd read my story, quoting the Tippets, and as my friend told me on the telephone, 'Angela is spitting nails. So are the rest of the people at The Children's Aid.'

Or, as Angela said, once I'd pulled out my note pad: "I'll be damned if I let anyone pin this one on us."

The Children's Aid workers had done everything they could to help Carole Tippet. "And I wasn't one of the ones involved in her case. So I'm not trying to save my own butt." Some of her friends had worked the file and they had done their best. "I'm telling you, it's not right that people are bad-mouthing us on this one. Blaming us."

"Like the parents?"

"Especially the parents."

Since I'd talked to them, the parents had really started shooting off their mouths. They were trying to pin their daughter's death on everyone who'd ever come in contact with her: counsellors, treatment centres, the Children's Aid. Especially the Children's Aid. The TV crews were eating it right up. Night before last, Carole's mother said it was the Children's Aid's fault that her daughter had wound up on the streets, selling her body, getting into drugs. She said if only the society had found the proper foster home, her daughter would still be alive. Stunning. The pretty boy who put it to air didn't trouble himself to get a response from the Children's Aid until the following night. By then, it looked like excuse-making. Cute. It was the oldest trick in the book. Put legs on the story.

"Why do you say 'especially the parents'?"

"You won't have to ask, after you read what I'm about to give you." She patted her purse, which was sitting on the bench at her side. She glanced around the room, then turned her gaze on me. "What I'm about to give you is confidential. Copies of Carole Tippet's files, from the time we became involved. You don't know where you got this envelope. And you never heard my name."

"Agreed."

"You cross me, and you get me fired. You get me fired, there are two little kids whose mother won't be bringing home groceries or paying the rent. Understand?"

I nodded. "I understand."

She opened her purse, withdrew a manila envelope and slid it across the table.

"You've got my word."

"I don't know what your word is worth, Mister Hunter. But I'm about to find out. There are two reasons for my doing this. The first is so that my friends and colleagues don't take the fall for this one. They did everything that anyone could do to help that girl. And the other reason is, I want the Tippets to fry. What those bastards did is unthinkable, it's unconscionable, inexcusable. I've seen and heard a lot of things in my time with the society, Mister Hunter, and this case ranks right up there with the worst of them."

She slid to the end of the bench and stood up. "Shove this right back in their face, Mister Hunter. Then see what they have to say." Angela Merton said goodbye and walked across the room and out the door. I waited a few minutes then I went out into the parking lot and got into my car. I flicked on the dome light and pulled the documents from the envelope and began reading. It takes a lot to turn my stomach, but Carole Tippet's file was doing the trick.

When Carole was first brought to the attention of the Children's Aid, she was six years old. She'd just started school and it hadn't taken the teachers more than five minutes to figure out something was seriously wrong with this little girl. She didn't talk. She flinched any time someone came near her. She sat at the back of the room, biting her nails. She was wild in the schoolyard: if anyone came near her she would lash out at them, a flurry of feet and fists. "Parents indicate she has been a 'problem' child since infancy." I flipped ahead and stopped at a letter from a child psychiatrist: "the patient shows evidence of having survived a significant trauma. The nature of this trauma is not yet apparent. Intensive counselling is advised."

. Carole had been removed from the school and enrolled in what's known in the trade as a "Special Needs Class". Six documents later, she was in a residential treatment program. Report after report written by people baffled by the cause of Carole's severe and debilitating mental state.

Half way through the pile of documents there was a photograph of Carole taken at Grace Hospital the night the emergency staff called the society, and then the cops, when Carole had wandered in through the door. She looked like a refugee from Auschwitz; maybe seventy pounds, bones nudging her skin here and there. She was all bruises and welts, one eye swollen shut, the other looking accusingly at the camera. The doctor at emergency told the cops Carole had been raped repeatedly, probably by more than one person. She told the cops she didn't know who had attacked her. The cops thought she was lying. But no one could get her to talk. The cops called the Children's Aid. Carole was taken back into care although, as the case worker stated, the chances that Carole would stay in a foster home were slim. She had run off repeatedly from every home she'd been placed in. Carole was twelve years old.

I thumbed through the documents.

Deep in the pile, there was a report from a social worker who had visited Carole in the jail. Carole had been sentenced to six months secure custody on a string of charges: theft, break and enter, possession of marijuana, soliciting an undercover cop. When she was placed in her cell, she had gone berserk, 'banging her head against the cell wall until she began to bleed profusely, screaming hysterically, scratching at her wrists until she drew blood'. It had taken three guards to subdue her. She was taken to emergency for treatment, sedated and sent to the psych ward at Hotel Dieu.

"I can't be put in a box again." This is what she'd told the psychiatrist who'd interviewed her the next day. "I asked the client what she meant by this. She would say nothing further."

I flipped back to the photograph taken that night in emergency. I was staring at Carole's accusatory eye when my pager went off.

They'd found Van Allens' Jaguar. It was out at Deke the Geek's, near the airport. Midnight Eddie had heard the call over the scanner. Something about C.I.D. Anytime criminal investigation gets involved in anything, you can pretty well bet there's a story in the vicinity. If you're curious, call. Midnight had, and it was Deke himself who'd barked into the receiver: 'Deke's Towing'.

Midnight and The Geek go back a long ways. They'd first met when Eddie was still a reporter, which was sometime just after the last ice age. Back then, reporters chased a lot of ambulances. So did tow-truck drivers. First reporter on the scene got the best description and the best quotes. First driver on the scene got the wreck. The drivers loved to get their pictures in the paper, and their names mentioned in the story. The Geek knew how to play the game. Midnight had obliged. Which is how friends are made, and contacts established.

When Midnight called, Deke wasn't too talkative, which Eddie gathered was on account of the cops being right there in the office with him because any other time Deke would talk your ear half off, whether or not he had anything to say. "Got a little company Deke?" "Yup." "Dressed in blue uniforms?" "Uh huh." "Something interesting going on?" "Yup." And so on: Eddie firing questions, Deke grunting answers. Eddie put one and two together. A wrecking yard, cars in the wrecking yard, detectives hauling ass out to the wrecking yard tout de suite. Sounded like a body in a trunk to Eddie. "Yup," said Deke. "Thanks," said Eddie. "I owe you one." "Yup, you sure's hell do," said Deke, hanging up on him.

The Jag was parked with its nose against Deke's chain link fence. There were two cruisers and a couple of unmarked cars in the front parking lot just outside the gate. The uniform boys had cordoned off the area with yellow tape. Now they were hanging around smoking cigarettes and drinking coffee out of Styrofoam cups, courtesy of City Catering. City Catering drivers work on commission. They like to put food on the table, just like the rest of us. So any time they spot more than three people standing around, they'll do a U turn and pull up, hoping for the best. When they see the cops they'll pull a U turn just to be nosy. And free coffee doesn't do anything to spoil relations. You never know when you might get stopped for failing to see a stop sign, say. Or running a red light. You can never have enough friends in cruisers.

I bought two coffees, handed one to Garth and headed toward the main gate. Two detectives were cooling their heels over by Deke's shed. The one guy, Lumsden, has the personality of a gerbil. The other guy was Peter Dick. His buddies on the force call him Dickhead. I call him Peter. I'd covered several cases he'd worked on and he'd been helpful and trusting and I hadn't betrayed his confidence and we'd established a certain, shall we say, rapport. He helped me by giving me bits of information which might come in useful. I helped him by making sure he got mentioned in stories where he'd done a good job. He wouldn't volunteer a hell of a lot of information, but he wouldn't lie to me if I'd put two and two together and then asked for confirmation. A few times, he'd told me things off the record and I'd never screwed him by connecting him with things he'd said. Screw one cop, you're finished with the entire department. "What's up?"

What was up was, there was quite likely a body in the trunk of Mister I Sell's Jag.

"Van Allen?"

"That I can't tell you. We haven't opened it yet."

If they hadn't opened the trunk, how did they know there was a body in it? He nodded at Patches the dog. If they had a magazine for junkyard dogs, Patches could be a centrefold. He was a German Shepherd. One of those big ones with hair tufting out in places and matted down in others. One ugly dog. Deke had chained him to the front bumper of a wrecked Chev across the gravel path from the Jag. "Patches started goin' nuts. Sniffin' around the car, lickin' at a puddle underneath it. Finally he got right up on the back of it and tried to scratch his way in. Deke thought it was a little unusual. Gave us a call." Peter nodded in the direction of the two uniformed boys leaning against the front fender of one of the cruisers out front. "They didn't need the dog to tell them. They know death when they get a whiff of it."

"What are you waiting for?"

They were waiting for a warrant.

"A warrant? To open a trunk?"

"This ain't Detroit. If there's a body in the trunk, nine chances out of ten the guy didn't just crawl in there and go to sleep." Murders lead to investigations which lead to bad guys which lead to trials which lead to bad guys spending time in the jug. One little screw-up, like opening a trunk without a search warrant, can mean a bad guy takes a walk. Peter couldn't stand it when bad guys took a walk. Bad enough they got out of jail at all. He sure as hell wasn't going to help them avoid that party, if he could help it.

"How long before you get the warrant?"

"The detective sergeant's on his way."

So was the locksmith. So was Al Sears.

Another client.

"What can you tell me?" Pete bummed a smoke and suggested we take a little walk. Our little walk took us to the back side of Deke's shed. "Close your notebook." I closed my notebook. "Stick it in your pocket." I stuck it in my pocket. He started talking. By the time we

163

returned, fifteen minutes later, he'd bummed and smoked another one of my cigarettes - "I'm tryin' to quit, so I only smoke the ones I can bum" - and I knew the story so far.

The story so far: the car had been towed in the previous afternoon from the airport. It had been angle parked in the short-term lot right out front. An auxiliary cop had ticketed it yesterday afternoon. The parking ticket was marked 2:04 p.m. After he'd put the ticket under the wiper, the auxiliary cop hadn't paid it much attention. When he'd gone off shift, the Jag was still there and when he came back this morning, the Jag was still there. He started paying attention. The night shift guy had stuck another ticket under the other wiper and the overnight guy had written out a third - anything to make quota. The day shift auxiliary called the RCMP and the RCMP called Deke and told him to come and haul it away. This would have been about ten this morning. Deke had dumped it just inside the gate. He figured anyone who owned a Jag would be along before too long to claim it. He didn't want to stick it out back and then have to manoeuvre three junkers out of the way to let the owner drive it off. He hadn't given it much thought for the rest of the day except to think you'd have to be awful forgetful to park a car that nice and that expensive in front of the airport and then forget where you'd parked it. However, as no one had to tell The Geek, the world was full of weirdos and there wasn't much that surprised him anymore. As he liked to say: 'I been around the block a few times'.

So the Jag had just sat there all day long, gleaming in the sun. Then Deke had hauled in a Roadmaster from a no-parking zone down by the casino. Man, did Deke love the casino or what. Sixteen blocks of permit-only parking and 15,000 dumb suckers looking for any quick place to park so they could rush inside and pour their money down the slots. Never give a sucker an even break, is what Deke had been brought up to believe. He practiced this creed, daily. Deke had two trucks doing nothing other than casino hauls. He drove one, his son drove the other. Hundred and fifty bucks per haul. The way he figured it, the only businesses in town that were minting money were the casino and Deke's Towing. Another couple years of this, he'd sell the business to his kid and he'd move to his winter place in Lakeland Florida, spend his days playing golf, fishing, watching the Tigers during spring training and then drink himself into a coma every night.

It was Deke who'd hooked the Roadmaster. When he got back to his lot, he'd backed in beside the Jag. It was when he was unhooking the Buick that he noticed Patches going nuts on the trunk of the Jag. When he went over to kick Patches in the slats, Deke smelled the smell that he'd smelled only twice before. "Put a roast in a garbage can, put the lid on, leave it in the sun, come back the next day, open the lid, and that's the smell we're talking about. Ain't no smell quite like it. And once you smell it, you never forget it." The first time Deke had smelled it, it had been a suicide. The second time it was natural causes. Both those dead men had been sitting in their cars for days before anyone noticed. Which is another weird one, eh? How someone could be dead in a car for two or three days and no one notice. Anyway, as he told me, nodding in the direction of the Jag, you smell that smell you never forget it. He didn't have to lean his nose down near the crack of the Jag's trunk for more than a few seconds. He went inside and called the cops.

The cops had run the licence plate through the computer and the computer had spit out the name they had expected. They told dispatch to call Van Allen's house. The dispatcher had come back with the expected result. No answer.

Meanwhile, Pete and his partner had taken a quick look around. They'd noticed a puddle of something under the trunk. They'd also noticed what appeared to be a smear of dried blood on the rear bumper and a smudge of something at the lower lip of the trunk that might have been blood someone had tried to wipe away. There was a thin layer of dust on the car and there were areas at the edges of the trunk lid where the dust was not uniform, as though someone had wiped those areas. All of which, along with that unmistakable smell, seemed to them reasonable and probable grounds to suspect that something interesting was to be found in the trunk. Reasonable and probable grounds were all a justice of the peace needed in order to scribble his name on the bottom of a search warrant. The detective sergeant was on his way with the paperwork. Another couple of detectives were on their way to Van Allen's house with identical paperwork.

"Let's say it's Van Allen."

"You're doing the saying, not me." Peter spiralled another of my cigarettes over the fence.

"Who do you think might have whacked him?"

"Guy like Van Allen, people would line up and pay for the opportunity. Take your pick."

"Who'd be at the front of the line."

"Drug dealers. Other pimps. Money men."

"The mob?" Peter frowned and tilted his head a bit, thinking it over.

"Let's just say I wouldn't rule anything out, at this point. But wait'll we see what happened to him. If it is him."

Next thing, Alan Sears swung into the lot in his Ident van and a couple of minutes later the detective sergeant pulled in behind him. They and Peter and Lumsden and the uniform boys had a little huddle and a couple of minutes later, Gerry The Locksmith pulled in.

Peter told Garth and me to stand over near Deke's garage until they'd opened the trunk. Garth asked Al Sears if it would be all right to take some long-lens shots. "Just make sure you get my good side."

"Left or right?"

"His arse." This was Lumsden. What a joker.

Peter looked at the Jag. "You never know what to expect."

What you sometimes don't expect is for a trunk to be booby-trapped, but it had been known to happen. And cops definitely don't like people looking over their shoulder when they're doing their job. Makes them nervous. And grumpy.

Alan Sears snapped on his rubber gloves. He told everyone to wait by the gate. He started off by taking a bunch of pictures with his 35. He took pictures of the entrance to the yard and the gravel path leading to the Jag, then he took half a dozen shots of the car itself. Then he leaned in and got some closeups of the trunk. A little too close. He straightened right up. "Whoo-ee." He didn't need to open the trunk to know what he was dealing with. "Something's been cooking." He took his camera back to his van then came back with his notebook. He started scribbling. He kept on for about ten minutes. Then he told Gerry to yank the lock. Then he crooked a finger at one of the uniform boys who came hustling right over. "Constable, do me a favour. Call the weather office. Get me a detailed weather report covering the last 48 hours."

"What do you want that for?"

What he wanted that for was to get the hour by hour temperatures. Then he could figure out the heat inside the trunk. Then he could figure out the rate of decomposition. Then he could figure out approximate time of death.

It took Gerry exactly four minutes and twenty three seconds to yank the lock. It was Van Allen, all right. Or at least most of him. He was lying on his side, his hands behind his back, facing the opening of the trunk. Someone had been busy with the duct-tape: mouth, wrists and ankles. Whoever had killed him had wanted him to die slowly and painfully. They'd removed some essentials and left him in the trunk to bleed to death.

"It'll take more than a miracle to bring this boy back." Alan Sears went to work in the trunk. He ran the barrel of his flashlight over the body, front back and side. He was checking for anything sharp protruding from the body: needles, maybe, or a knife. Given all the blood, he didn't especially want to cut himself. Then he made some more notes about the placement of the body then he brought his camera and fired off a roll of film, taking shots from all angles to show exactly where the body had been found.

"How long do you think it would have taken him to bleed to death?"

"Hard to say. Half an hour, maybe. An hour. Depends if there are any other holes in him."

"Nice way to go."

"Perfect," said Peter. "For a prick like him."

Peter was sitting in his unmarked car. He'd radioed in that they needed the removal service. "Call Fred. Tell him to meet us down at the police garage." The dispatcher gave him the 10-4. "Tell Superintendent Ryan I'll be phoning him." "10-4." What he wanted the Superintendent to do was issue an All Points Bulletin for one Miss Cindy Lou Gilmore.

"You think she might have killed him?"

Peter drew on smoke number four, then dropped the butt on the ground and stepped on it. He exhaled. Sounded like he was sighing. "Let's just say I'd like to have the opportunity to sit down with Miss Gilmore and have a little chat." He was watching the road. "If she's still alive."

"What are the chances she is?"

"Fifty fifty."

She and Van Allen did business with a lot of unsavoury people. They were playing buy and sell in a circle where the wrong move was very likely your last. Peter nodded in the direction of the Jag. "As Mister Van Allen has discovered, to his chagrin." Cindy Lou was a high-grade hooker but she was also Van Allen's partner in the drug trade. She bedded the high rollers, made the sales pitch for Van Allens' pharmacy and banked a share of the profits. Suppliers are not members of The Goodfellows. If Van Allen had allowed a payment to slip his mind and had ignored a polite request for some immediate cash and had thus caused the supplier to get upset, chances are that person might also be a little upset with Cindy Lou Gilmore. "She's either dead, or she's in very deep shit, I'd say. Either way, we'd like to find her."

Alan Sears was pulling the backs from some long thin white forensic centre seals and applying them across the cracks of the doors and the trunk and the hood of the Jag. Then he and one of the uniform boys started wrapping the Jag in clear plastic. The young cop got a little too close for comfort. Next thing you know, he's over behind the next car, sharing his supper with Patches the dog. Alan Sears was doing his best not to smile. The kid came back. But he didn't look to be in any shape to get close to the Jag. Alan waved him off and asked Lumsden for a hand.

Half an hour later, the Jag was wrapped in clear plastic and sitting on one of Deke's flatbeds.

"One last thing." Alan came back from his van with a bottle and a clear plastic bag. He leaned down and scooped a sample from the puddle which had formed beneath the Jag's trunk.

"Blood?"

"Could be. Or could just be juices."

"Juices?"

"Yah. Like when you cook a roast. You get juices in the pan? Same thing."

"I'll think about that, next time we have roast."

Alan put the bottle in the clear plastic bag, made a note on a sticker, peeled the sticker and stuck it to the bag.

"So now what?" We were watching Alan Sears tidy things up in the back of the van. "We'll haul it down to the garage and Al will go over it there."

"And?"

"We'll see what we get from the house."

"And then?"

"And then we hope to find Miss Gilmore, or what's left of her."

I wished him luck, and thanked him for his help.

"I'd do the same for a normal person."

A few minutes later, Willie Van Allen took his last ride downtown. Quite a little procession: a uniform car up front, then an unmarked car, then The Geek, then another unmarked car and the other cruiser and then Al bringing up the rear in his van.

What they got from the house was a murder scene. Dennis Brown had spent half an hour circling the house, taking pictures, making notes. He made a note of the last newspaper to have been delivered at the door (Tuesday's) and the last mail to have been left in the box. Then Gerry the Locksmith yanked the lock - one minute, seventeen seconds - and Dennis went in alone with a video camera, shooting every room and making verbal notes as he went. When he came back out he took the video camera to the Mobile Command Unit out by the curb and told the Detective Sergeant: 'Your scene is in the garage'.

Van Allen had been whacked just inside the big double door. There was a large pool of blood on the floor. There were castoffs on the door and the ceiling and the walls. From the looks of the castoffs - splatters of blood that flew back as the killer yanked the knife out of him - Van Allen had been stabbed several times. Maybe six or seven.

Dennis went to work with his lights and his cameras. Within an hour, he had an identifiable shoe print in the dust on the floor and half a dozen perfect fingerprints. A weapon would have been nice, but the killer hadn't felt like leaving it behind.

From what Dennis could tell, the killer had knifed Van Allen and then dumped him in the trunk of the car and then driven the car out of the garage with Van Allen in the trunk. The right-side tires had gone through Van Allen's blood on the way out. Once the killer had closed the door, he'd hosed down the driveway. The bloody tire-track stopped directly under the garage door.

"Whoever killed him, knew him."

"How'd you figure that?"

"No forced entry. Whoever killed him, came in with him. If not, they had a key, and they were waiting for him."

By the time I got back down to the police garage, the pathologist was just finishing her investigation. The pathologist is a woman named Dora Kinney. She's the best. Anytime Al Sears has a murder, he likes to get Kinney to come to the scene and then do the post. Some pathologists, they bitch and grumble about going to the scene. They show up, pronounce the obvious, then take a hike. Not Doctor Kinney. She'll spend an hour at the scene, looking around, making notes, drawing diagrams. She loves the work and she doesn't mind going to court. And she never makes stupid, lazy mistakes.

First thing she wants to figure out is, what was the mechanism of death. It didn't take her long to find out.

Dennis Brown had been right. Almost. Van Allen had been stabbed five times. All five in the back. From what Kinney could tell, Van Allen had been bending over - maybe putting something into the trunk or taking something out - when he got hit the first time. Whoever killed him just kept on stabbing until Van Allen went limp. Then they just hoisted him in. Then they tied his wrists. He'd really struggled to get his hands loose. The tape had caused some serious bruising as he'd struggled to get free. So he probably figured out what was coming next. What came next was, they undid his belt and his fly and yanked his trousers and shorts down around his knees and performed a little elective surgery.

"He was definitely alive at the time."

For how much longer, Kinney couldn't say.

And, as Al Sears pointed out, "our friend here isn't about to tell us."

Alan Sears was taking a few more shots with his 35. "One thing's for sure. Whoever killed him really hated his guts."

Garth got a couple of terrific shots from the far end of the garage as Kinney and Al Sears were doing their stuff at the back of the Jag. Then he got another couple of shots as Fred and Junior humped the body bag across the room to the door where the body wagon was waiting.

"What'll you do now?"

"Now comes the fun part," said Al. "Now I find the killer."

As we were leaving, Al was half in the trunk, his hand wrapped with Scotch tape, sticky side out, patting the trunk mat for fibres and hairs and anything that could land a killer in jail.

Come back in four hours, he'd still be crawling through that Jag.

If I was a killer, the last guy I'd want on my trail is Alan Sears.

Midnight Eddie could hardly contain himself. It was like he'd been covering the story himself. He wanted all the details, even before Garth headed for the darkroom. We told him what we had, stories and pictures, and he said the entire front, above the fold, was ours. Maybe more. He would've given us three quarters of the page, except there'd been another terrorist attack in the Middle East, more fervent souls blasted to smithereens and into the great beyond, 26 and counting. So he had to put that up front. But the rest of the page was ours and he had three quarters of a page inside where he could turn the story from the front and use more pictures.

Garth and I got right to work. An hour and a half later, Eddie was working on the layout. He'd outdone himself:

MUTILATED CORPSE STUFFED IN TRUNK

Immediately below the banner, there was a subhead:

SUSPECT IN PROSTITUTE'S SLAYING FOUND IN ABAN-
DONED JAGUAR He played two of Garths' shots right below the headline. The first was a nice grainy long-lens shot of a bunch of cops standing around the Jag, just after they'd opened the trunk. The second showed Freddie and his helper and the bagged body. My story wrapped around both the pictures and turned to the inside. Inset into the body of the story was a head and shoulders of Van Allen, cropped from the shot Garth had taken down by the river, when Cindy Lou's car had been found on the riverbank.

Brilliant.

"Hey, Huntzie."

When I turned, Freddie was shuffling through the junk on his desk. "There was a message for you." He stirred the papers around, lifted things up, moved things to the left, moved things to the right. "Why can't I ever find anything?" He kept looking, but it was pretty clear he wasn't going to be able to find what it was he was looking for.

"Who was it?"

"Betsy."

"Never mind. I've got her number."

Eddie made like he hadn't heard. He kept rooting around his desk.

"Eddie."

He looked up.

"Forget it. I've got her number."

"There was something else. Another envelope."

"From Betsy?"

"No. That broad I told you about. The one who came by earlier. She came by again. Left an envelope for you."

"What'd it look like?"

"Just an envelope. Letter size. White. Had your name printed on the front."

Now we were both rooting through the junk on his desk.

"Why'n hell don't you clean up this mess?"

"One of these days I will."

We gave his desk the once over. We lifted every piece of paper on the desk and then went through them all again. Eddie finally gave up. He lifted his visor with one hand and ran the other hand through what was left of his hair. "I'll be."

"You'll be if you don't find that fucking envelope."

"Payola?"

This was the rim rat. I gave him a look which suggested that if he knew what was good for his health, he'd refrain from further smart ass comments. He went back to editing the story in front of him.

172

"You go make your phone call." Eddie lifted his garbage can onto his desk. "I'll keep looking. I know it's gotta be here somewhere."

You could feel the chill, right through the phone line. Betsy was in one of her moods. One of Betsy's moods I wasn't in the mood for. I hated to be abrupt. But abrupt was what was called for. "No, Betsy. I'm not coming back. No. Not tonight. Not tomorrow night. Not any night in the foreseeable future."

"Why not?"

"Because I've moved out."

"It's all a misunderstanding. I never meant for you ...."

"Betsy, we've been through this. It wasn't a misunderstanding. You told me to pack my things and shut the door behind myself and slide the key under the door. There was nothing ambiguous in those instructions. Even a moron could have understood those instructions. I followed them to the letter. I'm out. And I'm staying out."

"Why are you angry with me?"

"I'm not angry with you."

"Well then, pack up your things and come back ...."

"Betsy, listen to me. Listen very carefully. I've moved out. And I'm not moving back. You and I are the past tense. Do you understand?"

"You don't love me?"

Boy. She knew how to put it to a guy. Why do women do that? Huh? Beats me, but they'll do it every time. They back you into a corner and then hit you with the L word. It's like they want to make you squirm.

"Well?"

"It's not that I don't love you, it's just ..."

"What's that supposed to mean? Do you, or don't you?"

"Right at this moment, Betsy, at this point in time, I guess I'd have to say I'm not sure."

That was it.

She was crying, now. She wasn't making any noise, but I could hear her crying regardless. That silent kind of crying women can do when their eyes well up and their noses turn red, that if you were sit-

173

ting there in the same room, you'd be sunk just watching.

"I'm just being honest. You don't want me to lie to you, do you?"

"Yes, as a matter of fact. I wouldn't mind it the least little bit if you lied to me. If you don't know, just lie and say yes."

"I can't lie."

I was sitting with my feet up on the corner of the desk. I'd already put two cigarette butts up on their filters on the desk and watched them die out. Now I put down a third. When I looked up, Midnight was waving an envelope at me. He was holding it in his left hand and pointing at it with his right and mouthing the words 'found it'. I swung my feet down.

"Betsy, I gotta go."

"You can't leave me."

"Betsy, I already have left you. We're all done."

"You're not coming back?"

"No."

"Ever?"

"No."

"Never."

"Never."

"You asshole."

From the sounds of it, she broke the receiver in half.

Midnight was right. The letter had been there, somewhere. Somewhere under a bunch of scrunched up copies of news stories and an empty waxed-paper coffee cup in the bottom of his garbage can. It was a plain white envelope. Used to be, before the coffee stains. My name was printed out in block letters on the front. I turned it over, held it up to the light, then ripped the end off, careful not to rip the contents. The contents amounted to a single sheet of plain white paper upon which there were three lines, printed in block letters. Very neat.

Want the REAL hookers story?

Meet me. Airport Motel. Room 122.

Come alone.

174

"Love letter?" Midnight was trying to read the note. I folded it and put it back in the envelope.

"Yah."

"Some guys have all the luck."

"That's me, Midnight. The original Mister Lucky."

"If she's got a girlfriend, count me in."

"I'll be sure to do that." I picked up the phone and dialled.

Kenny picked it up on the second ring. "Who is it? And whaddya want?"

I told him.

"I'm on my way."

-Eleven-

The Airport Motel is out on the strip, half a mile down from the airport itself. It's an L-shaped place, two storeys with a fenced pool on a patch of lawn near the office. The owner is a guy named Roger Clemens. On the wall behind the counter there's a picture of the other Roger Clemens, the pitcher, from the days when he was with the Red Sox. It's signed: 'To Dad, Love Roger." It's Motel Roger's idea of a joke. If people want to believe he's the father of the famous Roger Clemens, that's fine by him. Now and then, someone will bring in a Boston Red Sox cap or a Red Sox pennant and ask him to sign it. He always obliges: "Roger Clemens."

Once, when the Sox were at Tiger Stadium, Motel Roger managed to flag down the real Roger. He gave the pitcher a picture of himself, standing in front of The Airport Motel. 'To Roger Clemens from Roger Clemens.' He told Clemens that if he ever needed a nice clean room for the night, he could have a room on the house. Plus free coffee in the morning. Clemens said he'd take him up on it. Then he told Roger to stay right where he was. A few minutes later, Clemens came back out of the dugout with a photo. 'To Roger Clemens from Roger Clemens.' Motel Roger put that photo in a big frame and hung it up in his living room. Then he called The Spec and wondered whether we'd be interested in doing a little write-up on the two Roger Clemens. Norm Weatherall had left Midnight Eddie a note telling him to send The Wonder Boys out to do a little bright. Roger was pretty excited when we showed up. And a little surprised that we'd bothered. 'Must be a slow night, eh?' Then he'd told Garth and me to come behind the counter and into his living room, which is right

176

behind the office. He stood by the mantle while Garth took a picture of him and his picture from Roger Clemens. Pretty cheesy. To either side of the photo, there's all manner of Red Sox paraphernalia: pennants and T-shirts and caps. On the mantle there are baseballs and mugs and a batting helmet. Most of the stuff was a gift to Roger from his regulars. The regulars get a big kick out of staying at Roger Clemens' motel. Roger had cornered a couple of them, so we could talk to them.

Thanks to his regulars, Roger can light up the No Vacancy sign by noon, three, four sometimes five days a week. Most of the regulars are salesmen and most of them reserve the same room, time after time. Some of them phone from down the road first thing in the morning, just to make sure they don't have to go looking for a place to stay once they pull into town. Some guys, as soon as they know their route schedule, they'll write Roger and book their room for so many days a month, right through to the end of the year. Roger treats his people right. He puts snacks in the room for the guys pulling in late. He drops morning papers outside the door for all his regulars. And he's got free coffee and free muffins and donuts in the office first thing in the morning.

Roger runs a tight ship. No quickies. No Prom Parties. No teenagers, unless accompanied by their parents. No drunks. No bikers. His Noisy Party Policy is taped to the counter top: One complaint, you get a warning. Two complaints, you get the boot. Roger gives single females the third degree. The last thing a motel needs is that kind of reputation. If Roger has his doubts, he'll recommend a nice clean cheap place just down the road.

The Mystery Lady had passed Roger's inspection, which was saying something. She was driving a burgundy Crown Victoria with a Hertz sticker on the bumper. I parked beside it, in front of room 120. I knocked on the door of 122. No answer, no lights. I knocked again. The curtains of Room 124 fluttered shut. Then you could hear the safety chain sliding back. The door of Room 124 opened. A woman stuck her head out, looked at me, looked at my car, looked around the parking lot. She nodded for me to enter.

She slid the safety chain back in place and checked to see the door was locked. She brushed past me and walked to the middle of the room and turned to face me. She was about five three, five four and wouldn't have weighed more than a hundred and ten. Her hair was short and stylish, brown with streaks of blonde. She was wearing a pale yellow satin blouse and chocolate coloured leather pants and matching high-heeled shoes. She had very small hands, whose nails were long and elegantly painted. She had a weakness for rings. There was one on each finger. The biggest, a diamond solitaire, she wore on the pinkie finger of her left hand. You couldn't help but notice. The pinkie was a stump, cut off at the first knuckle. The diamond had to be close to a carat. Altogether, a very classy lady. Even if she was wearing a tad too much makeup. Especially on her forehead.

"I'm Cindy Lou Gilmore."

"I thought you might be. Nice to see you're still alive."

Cindy Lou sat on the end of one of the twin beds.

"Nice to be alive. For the time being." She looked me over, from the shoes on up. Then she nodded in the direction of the chair by the window."Mind if I smoke?"

I told her I wouldn't mind at all, in fact I wouldn't mind having a smoke myself.

Cindy pulled a pack of cigarettes from her purse, and a cigarette from the pack. Then she dropped the pack in the purse and pulled out her lighter. It was a Zippo. She flipped the lid back and spun the wheel in two quick motions - very practiced, very smooth - then snapped the lid shut. She did it all with one hand. Her left.

She dropped the lighter back in her purse.

We sat there for a moment, looking at each other.

I pulled her letter from my shirt pocket. "The real story?"

"I thought you might be interested."

"I'm all ears." I pulled my tape recorder from my trouser pocket. "You don't mind?"

"Not at all."

"Where shall we start?"

"Why don't we start by having a drink. After the last few days, I could certainly use one. Whiskey?"

I told her whiskey would be fine.

"Neat. Or ice?"

"Neat."

She came back from the washroom with two plastic glasses, each half filled. She handed me one and then extended hers toward me. "Here's to a real story."

"I'll drink to that."

Cindy sat back down on the end of the bed.

I pulled a chair between us and set the recorder on the seat and pushed play and record.

"Where should we begin?"

Cindy Lou thought we should start with the fact she was as good as dead. "Unless the cops can find a guy named Luther Cross. And find him in a hurry."

"Who's Luther Cross?"

"He's a pimp. He's an asshole. And he's got a very twitchy finger. This one." She made her hand into a revolver and pulled the trigger. "He's killed two people. One was my partner, the other was supposed to be me. Now that he knows he missed me, he won't be happy. He knows that I know enough to send him up the river for a long, long time. So I suspect he's a little anxious to ice me. And since he's already killed a couple of people the past couple of days, I don't think he'll be shy when it comes to killing again."

"Details?" I took another sip of whiskey - Canadian Club from the taste of it - and waited.

Cindy Lou lit another cigarette from the tip of the one she was smoking, snuffed the short one, drew on the new one and exhaled. Sounded like a sigh. She took a sip of her drink and set it down on the bed beside her.

"Melissa McBride was a nice girl. Not bright, which isn't necessarily a drawback. But not loyal, which is major drawback." She'd worked for Willie Van Allen for a few years and then got unhappy with the arrangement and shopped herself around until she found a higher bidder.

"The higher bidder?"

"Luther Cross. Dumb mistake. Very dumb. But I'll get to that in a minute." When she'd taken the walk, Melissa McBride had underestimated the proprietary feelings of Willie Van Allen, which she shouldn't have, considering she'd worked with him for more than

179

four years. "Willie's not the kind of guy ..." she paused, and looked down and then took another sip of her drink and set it down. "He wasn't the kind of guy who liked to lose things. What's Willie's is Willie's, eh? Like, forever. Or until he loses interest. He hadn't lost interest in Melissa McBride when she took a walk." To be fair, Willie Van Allen had warned Melissa she shouldn't even think about going to work for someone else. "I know. I was in the room when he told her." Melissa had asked for a meeting with Willie. She wanted a bigger cut of her earnings. "Willie told her at her age, the shape she was in, she should be happy getting what she was getting. She sure as hell wouldn't be getting anything more." Melissa wasn't very happy and said so. "She told Willie, 'I either get a bigger cut or I take a walk'." Willie had been very calm, very collected. And very firm. "He didn't threaten her or anything. All he said was, 'that would be a very stupid thing to do Melissa'. He said 'I'd think about that very carefully'. Like I said, she was nice, but she was dumb. She split and went to work for Luther Cross."

Melissa McBride had made two crucial mistakes. First, she left Van Allen. No pimp likes to lose a broad. Second, she crossed the street to work for Willie Van Allen's main competition, a guy who'd put the word out that he was going to drive Willie off the streets.

"Willie never liked to lose any of his broads, eh? He tended to take it personal. He especially didn't like to lose a broad to an insect like Luther Cross. It put him in, let's say, an awkward spot. If you know what I mean?"

I told her I could see the point.

Normally, a situation like this, Willie would've laid a beating on the broad. "I've seen him do it dozens of times. Girl steps out of line, he thumps her, tells her to smarten up, get back into line. End of issue. But this, eh? this was different. This was serious. Other broads were watching." Some of those other broads had been having second thoughts about working for Willie. A few were agitating for a better cut of their earnings. A few wanted better spots on The Alley. A couple wanted to climb up the ladder, get off the street, move to the casino or work the hotels. The usual bitch and gripe. "Nothing you normally can't handle. But a broad crosses the street, maybe the others start getting ideas. One thing Willie hated was when the girls started getting ideas. "Plus, he was pissed Luther was poaching. And he had to put a stop to that right quick."

In short, he had to send a message.

The message was a body in a ditch in the west end.

"You're saying Willie Van Allen killed Melissa McBride?"

"Stone dead."

"How?"

"Beat her head in with a rock."

"How do you know that?"

"I was in the car, watching."

"Where did he kill her?"

"In a field off Albert Road. Between Albert and Walker. The old Canadian Bridge property."

"With a rock?"

"He knocked her around first. Then he finished her off with the rock."

"And you were watching."

"The whole show."

"Did you try to stop him?"

"Do I look crazy?"

"And then?"

"And then we wrapped her up and trunked her and carted her down to the west end. Dumped her in the ditch where they found her."

"We?"

"Yah. We."

"Did you help him kill her?"

"Willie never needed any help when it came to killing people."

"Is that a yes or a no?"

"No."

"Whose car?"

"What do you mean, whose car?"

"Whose car did you use to take the body to Balmy Beach."

"Mine."

"Why yours?"

"There's a lot of Mustang convertibles around town. There aren't that many Jags. If you know what I mean."

"What'd you wrap her with?"

"Blanket."

"Where's the blanket."

"Tossed."

"Where?"

"Into the river."

"And that was it for Melissa?"

"That's all she wrote." Cindy lit another cigarette. She was watching me, watching her. I lit up as well, then sipped at my drink and set the glass down. "And Van Allen killed her because she'd crossed the street, started working for Luther?"

"That's the long and the short of it. Mostly."

"What's that mean?"

"I think she was beginning to piss him off, generally."

"In what way?"

"Just general ways. She was a whiner. She was also sneaky. I think he started to get the picture that she'd stab him in the back the first time he turned around."

"You?"

"Me what?"

"Is that the way you felt, too."

"She wasn't any concern of mine."

"But you were her supervisor, sort of."

"Willie dealt with her. He dealt with all the street girls. I dealt with the girls working the casino and the hotels."

"What kind of relationship did you two have?"

"Willie and me?"

"No. You and Melissa."

"No relationship. She was just one of the girls in the stable."

"And that was it. She just got a little too pushy, and a little too greedy?"

"That just about sums it up perfectly."

Which brought us around to Luther Cross. When it came to people whacking his girls, Luther was not what you'd call a card-carrying Christian. He did not believe in turning the other cheek. And once Melissa had signed on with him, she was definitely his property. "He was pissed with Willie, to put it mildly." And one good turn deserved another.

"You were the target?"

Cindy Lou nodded her head.

I pointed to the tape recorder.

"Yes," she said. "I was the target."

"But Carole Tippet got whacked instead."

"Let's just say she was in the wrong car at the wrong time in the wrong place."

"Which means?"

"Which means, it should've been me who took the hit, not her."

"You set her up?"

"I didn't exactly set her up. We had a little business deal."

"Which was?"

"I got a call from this guy I never heard of. He wanted to make a buy. Normally, I don't mind taking new customers. And he had references. But there was something about him I didn't like. You know how you get an inkling sometimes?"

I told her I knew what she was talking about.

"Well, I got an inkling with this guy. He didn't sound quite right. Plus, he called the day after one of my people tells me she hears Luther's going around sayin' he's going to square things up with Willie Van Allen. So I put one and one together and it didn't add up. Or it added up too easy. So I went looking for Carole."

"You got her to make the sale, in case it was a setup?"

"You could say that."

"Carry your purse, drive your car?"

"Yah."

"Why would Carole do that?"

183

"She owed me."

"Owed you for what?"

"Let's just say she was in arrears."

"To the tune of?"

"Several dollars."

"She was willing to risk her life for a few bucks."

"It wasn't a few. And she didn't know she was risking her life. I told her it was just a regular deal. Get the cash, hand over the goods, take off."

"Wouldn't she wonder why you'd have her dress up and pretend to be you?"

"Carole Tippet was not what you'd call a clear thinker. Plus, I told her if she makes the sale, I'd wipe her debt and give her a couple of days' worth of H. For two day's worth of H, Carole Tippet would've ridden to Bolivia and back on a mule."

"So off she went?"

"Off she went."

"In your clothes and your car?"

"Yup."

"And?"

"Luther iced her." The icing had taken place in the parking lot near the tracks back of Jackson Park. Carole had driven in, parked under the overpass, left her parking lights on and waited. She hadn't had to wait long.

"How do you know?"

"I was watching."

"You were watching?"

"Me and Willie. We came in by foot from the far side of the park. We were about maybe twenty feet away, behind one of the pillars, when Luther pulled in." Luther pulled his Lincoln alongside Cindy Lou's Mustang. He got out. Carole got out. He opened his trunk, she opened her trunk. She asked to see the cash. He asked to see the drugs. "You first." "If you insist." Luther had leaned in to his trunk. When he turned around, he had a briefcase in one hand. It was the briefcase Carole was looking at. She should have looked at Luther's other hand.

184

When he hit her with the tire iron it "sounded like when you whack a melon with a stick. Kind of a sick soft thud." Once she went down, Luther hit her a few more times. "Then him and his thug popped her into the trunk of my car. The thug got in and drove my car. Luther followed in his car. Like a little funeral procession."

"So Willie whacked Melissa because she went to work for Luther Cross?"

"Correct."

"And Luther whacked Carole Tippet, thinking he was whacking you and getting even with Willie?

"Correct."

My turn to light up. Cindy was watching the flame. I was watching her. "So." I exhaled, then took another sip of my whiskey. "Who killed Willie Van Allen?"

"I don't think it was The Pope."

I pointed at the tape recorder. "I need you to be a little more specific. Who killed Willie Van Allen."

"Luther."

"Luther Cross?"

"The only Luther I know."

"Why would Luther want to kill Willie Van Allen?"

"With Willie out of the way, he doubles his stable. Plus, he can get involved in some lucrative sidelines."

"Such as?"

"You're not really as dumb as you sound, are you?"

I pointed at the tape recorder.

She looked at the tape recorder, then at me. "What I'm telling you is, Willie had a big stable. None of this nickel and dime stuff. Plus, he had a very serious drug business on the go. Plus he had protection services. All of which add up to a very good reason for Luther to knock him off and move in, in a big way."

"How do you know he killed Willie?"

"I was about fifteen feet away at the time."

"You were watching?"

"Nope. I was hiding."

I told Cindy Lou I was getting a little confused. I told her I thought maybe we ought to back up just a little. She shrugged, raised her glass, discovered her glass was empty, then spent a couple of minutes pouring us each another.

"You were hiding. Where?"

After they'd left Jackson Park, Cindy and Willie had headed home. They figured the Mustang was going to turn up sooner than later. And they figured the cops would want to know a little bit about Cindy Lou. Good guess.

"When the cops called, Willie made out like he was my boyfriend. Answered a couple of questions, then asked a couple of questions, then he headed down the river to make out like he was real worried. And so on. Mostly, he didn't want anyone coming out to the house, start snooping around." Willie wasn't back home more than an hour when Luther called. "He thought he and Willie ought to have a little meeting. See if they couldn't come to some kind of agreement. So Luther came around and they had a little chat.

"And you were hiding. Where exactly?"

"Just off the garage there's a hall leading to the kitchen. Just inside the door to the garage there's a big walk-in closet. I was standing just inside the closet."

"And you could hear everything?"

"I could hear everything I needed to hear."

"Which was?"

Cindy Lou pulled a tape recorder out of her purse. She held it out toward me and pressed the play button.

"No, Luther. Please." There was a grunting sound, and then a whimper. "Please." There was more grunting, then a muffled scream. "Please Luther, don't ... I'll do anything. I'll ..." Then there was the sound of scuffling and grunting. "Oh God. Oh God. Please. Help me." "God ain't in the neighbourhood, Willie." "Oh please. Please. Dear God." Then there was another scream and then a faint cry. "Fuck you, Willie." Then the tape went dead.

"You taped Willie getting murdered?"

"I wasn't planning on it. We figured Luther'd say something stu-

186

pid. Something we could go to the cops with, if we had to."

"Where was the recorder?"

"On a shelf, right beside Willie's car."

I looked at Cindy Lou. She looked at me. We just sat there for another minute, staring at each other.

"You don't believe me?"

"You've got to admit, we're straining the limits of credibility here, Cindy."

"Tapes don't lie." Cindy Lou lit another smoke. She was looking past the match, and right at me, as she did so. She was not wearing what you'd call a friendly look. And I got my first glimpse of a woman I wouldn't want to cross. She had a deadly set of eyes.

"I just want to get this all straight, one more time." I went through the scenario, just as she'd painted it, detail by detail. When I was done I looked right at her. "That's the story?"

"That's not the story, Mister Hunter. That's the way it all happened. That's the truth. And you seem to have a problem with it."

"I've got a couple of problems, actually. Starting with Melissa McBride. The way I hear it, Melissa didn't want to leave Willie Van Allen at all, much less cross the street to work for Luther Cross."

"Who told you that?"

"Melissa's sister."

"What the fuck's she know?"

"She talked to Melissa a few days before the murder. Melissa told her a lot of interesting things."

"Such as?"

"Such as, Melissa told her sister she was working her way up in Willie's organization. In fact, she was pretty soon going to stop working the streets, period. She was going to be Willie Van Allen's right hand lady. And she mentioned to her sister that she'd put someone else's nose out of joint, more than a little."

"Whose nose?"

"Yours."

Cindy Lou laughed. She tapped her cigarette against the edge of the ashtray, then tapped it again. When she looked up, she was looking over my shoulder, like she saw someone behind me. "That's a joke." She drew on her smoke, then exhaled, then drew on it again and stubbed it in the ashtray. When she looked up, she looked right at me. "She was dreaming. Technicolour. There's no way Van Allen would've taken her off the street. And there's especially no way he would have moved her up the ladder. She was a cheap trick. Period."

"Why do you think she would've told her sister all that then?"

"Hookers are notorious liars. Always want to do a little make-believe. The sister was probably on her ass about the work she was doing. Maybe she just wanted the sister to believe she was going on the up and up. Who knows. But I can tell you this, she walked. I know it. Ask some of the girls down on the street. They'll tell you."

"I did."

"And?"

"I got another problem."

"What'd the girls tell you?"

"I'll get to that in a minute. This other problem I've got, maybe you can help me with."

"What problem?"

"Let's say Willie Van Allen did kill Melissa. I've got a problem understanding how he could have done that."

"I already told you how he did that. He beat her head in with a rock is how he did it. I was standing right there watching him."

"I thought you said you were in the car."

"What I meant was, I was right there. I watched him kill her. So what's your problem?"

"Everyone I talked to who knew anything about Willie Van Allen said he was gutless. All hot air, no action. Everyone. Even people he threatened. Everyone says he always had someone else doing his jobs for him."

"I knew Willie Van Allen better'n anyone. And I can tell you this: Willie Van Allen was a ruthless little sonofabitch. You piss him off, he'd go through a brick wall to get you. And anyone who says he was gutless is full of shit."

"I've got another problem."

"What with?"

"The part about someone setting you up for the hit."

"What's your problem with that?"

"It just doesn't add up."

"What do you mean, it doesn't add up?" Cindy Lou Gilmore would be a prosecutor's delight. All of a sudden, she was very twitchy. Couldn't sit still. Couldn't maintain eye contact. Kept looking past me at the door of her room. She fiddled with her cigarette pack and then she fiddled with her lighter. Altogether, not a very happy lady.

"What I hear, it wasn't Luther who put out the hit on you. It was Willie Van Allen."

"Willie?"

"That's what I heard."

"Who'd you hear that from?"

"A couple of people, actually."

"What kind of people?"

"People who spend a lot of time with their ear to the ground."

"Well, their hearing ain't so good. Why would Willie put out a hit on his own partner?"

"I don't know. Why would he?"

"If he had've, I could tell you. But he didn't, so I can't." Cindy Lou was half way through another cigarette. Apparently she didn't much like the taste. She butted it, then used the butt to push some of the other butts around in the ashtray. Then she dropped the butt and looked at her watch. "Listen." She finished her drink and stood up. She set the glass on the bedside table. "I gotta hustle outta here in a few minutes."

"What I hear is, the hit was worth ten thousand dollars. Which seems like kind of a lot of money when there are guys in town who'd do the job for a couple hundred. He must've wanted you dead in a big way, and a big hurry."

"Why would he want me dead?"

"That's the part I can't figure."

"You can't figure it, because it wasn't true. Willie and I were just

189

like this." She crossed the first two fingers of her left hand. "He couldn't operate without me. I did all the paperwork. I hired all the girls. I lined up the customers for the buys. I did all the banking. He'd have been lost without me."

"Word on the street was, he already had a replacement."

"Melissa McBride couldn't run a shoe-shine stand, never mind an operation like Willie's and mine. She didn't know shit from putty. You can ask anyone. She was nothing but a slut, and a dumb one. Period. If she lived to be eighty, she'd never have moved off the street. No way."

"I didn't mention Melissa McBride."

Cindy Lou stood up and grabbed her purse. I shut off my tape recorder, put it in my pocket and stood up as well. We were facing each other in the centre of the room. "I gotta get out of here." She grabbed her purse and shouldered it. "You gonna use this or not?"

"Oh yah," I said. "You've given me some terrific stuff here. Once I get these loose ends tidied up. But loose ends, eh? I'm worse than a seamstress when it comes to loose ends. Even one will drive me crazy."

"You'll be able to print all that, about Luther?"

"The managing editor's going to have to go over it all. And then our lawyer will have to give it the once over. But let's put it this way. I think they'll be very interested to hear what you've got to say." I made my way to the door, put my hand on the doorknob. "And speaking of you."

"What about me?"

"You willing to talk to the cops?"

"I'm not a big fan of cops."

"They're definitely going to be interested in talking to you."

"They can be interested all they want. The one I'll talk to is the prosecutor. And only with my lawyer."

"But you'd be willing to testify against Luther, in court?"

"You bet your ass I'd be willing." She snuffed her cigarette.

I opened the door an inch or two. "How can I find you, if I need to?"

"You can't. But I'll keep in touch."

We shook hands. "Thanks." She nodded. "Take care of yourself." She grinned. "You don't have to worry about me. I've been taking care of myself all my life. I'm a pro at taking care of myself."

I stepped out the door, then turned to face her.

She took a step toward me.

"Freeze." Cindy Lou turned to her left, toward the voice. She found herself looking down the barrel of a .45.

"Not a move." She turned to her right. Another .45. "You're under arrest, Miss Gilmore." Peter Dick started rhyming off her rights. Kenny came grinning out of the darkness.

Cindy turned to look at me. "You prick."

I smiled and shrugged my shoulders.

"You fucking prick."

Off to my right, I could hear Garth's motor-drive whirring and whirring and whirring.

Page One.

191

-Twelve-

MaryMary was holding the front page at a distance. We were in what she called The Salon. Living room, in any other house. But this, of course, was not any other house. The drapery was velvet, or it looked like velvet: sort of a maroon with lots of purple tassels along the edges. The drapes were hooked back on either side of the windows but the windows were covered with blinds pulled right down. There were paintings on the walls. They were either very old and very expensive, or very good fakes. But with the tiny little lights hooked to the tops of their frames, you couldn't tell. There were bookshelves and cabinets against the walls and lots of big overstuffed chairs and sofas. It felt like we'd gone back in some time machine to the nineteenth century. Or the eighteenth. MaryMary was sitting at the edge of the big sofa in front of the window. She looked at the picture on the front page and then looked at me and then looked at Garth and then back at me. "For a friend, he sure don't take your good side."

"Lemme have another look."

Mary turned the page so I could see.

"I dunno, Mary, looks pretty good to me."

The picture was six columns by eight inches right under a 72-point eight-column screamer:

SPEC REPORTER LEADS COPS TO ALLEGED KILLER

There I was, smirking at Cindy Lou who was glaring at me, with Peter Dick on one side and The Gerbil on the other, their revolvers pointed at her head.

"The thing you gotta realize, Mary, he's got no good side."

I gave Garth the finger.

192

"I dunno." Angel was sitting in the armchair to my right. It had doilies on both arms, Angel was sticking her nails through the holes. She reminded me of a cat. Fluffy and blonde. "I seen a side I kinda liked."

"Who wants a refill?" Mary set the paper on the coffee table and stood up and looked around the room. All the hands went up. Beer for Kenny Koster. Beer for Midnight. Beer for Garth. Scotch for Roger Clemens. Whiskey for Peter Dick. Soda water for The Gerbil. Double Canadian Club for yours truly.

"Cash, boys."

I put a couple of bills on Mary's outstretched palm. "Buy one for yourself, Mary."

"What about me?"

"And one for Angel."

"Angel's working. No drinkin' durin' workin' hours."

"What about I pay now, she can drink later."

Mary nodded. Angel smiled. "You're a sweetheart, Huntzie. Honest to God." Oohs and ahhs all around the room.

"Lemme have a look at that, will you?"

Kenny grabbed the paper from the table and tossed it to me. "You're gonna wear the print off the page, Huntzie."

Yah, well.

Love that headline. Love that picture. I turned to Garth. "You make me a print of this baby?"

"Eleven by fourteen. Suitable for framing."

"I always did like you, Garth."

"Spare me."

"Isn't that the nicest word in the English language. I stabbed my finger at the little box above my byline. EXCLUSIVE.

"How long we gotta suffer through this crap?" Kenny Koster was shaking his head.

"Only another few days." Garth stood up and reached over and grabbed the paper out of my hands. He straightened it out and admired his handiwork. "You gotta admit, only a genius could take that shot in the dead of night without a flash."

MaryMary arrived, finally.

We raised our glasses.

Angel raised an empty hand. "Here's lookin' at ya, baby."

"What I want to know," said Roger, "is how you knew it was her."

"Midnight told me."

"I told you what?"

"That my mystery lady was Cindy Lou Gilmore."

"I did like shit. I didn't know who she was."

"But you described her."

"How'd you know what she looked like. You never laid eyes on her before you walked into that hotel room."

"Motel," said Roger. "Please."

"I didn't need to know. I only needed to look at her hands. Her left hand."

"Her little finger?"

"Exactly."

"How'd you know it was Cindy Lou."

"I asked."

"Asked what?"

"Asked one of my pals down at the cop shop."

"You got a pal, at the cop shop?" This was The Gerbil.

"I got pals in the strangest places."

"Well, it wasn't this pal." This was Peter Dick. He tapped himself on the chest. Once. Twice.

"This pal shall remain nameless."

"And what'd he tell you?"

"He told me how come Cindy Lou's father could give a positive ID without laying an eye on the body of his daughter. That did kind of spark my curiosity. How could you do that? Easy, as it turned out. He asked the coroner to describe the left hand on the body. The coroner had to go back and have another look. He told Mister Gilmore there wasn't anything unusual about the left hand. Gilmore told him, and this is a quote: 'if there ain't anything unusual about her left

194

hand, then it ain't my daughter'. Gilmore had cut off Cindy Lou's little finger, at the first knuckle, when he slammed the car door on it. She'd been eight at the time. As far as he knew, little fingers don't grow back.

"If you knew it was her," said Roger, "weren't you scared?"

"Nothing for me to be frightened of. She may have iced a few people, but she sure as hell wasn't about to ice me. She needed me. If she could pitch her story to me, I was going to buy her a ticket to ride."

"I still don't get it."

"Pretty simple," said Kenny.

And it was, really.

Cindy Lou had been telling the truth about one thing: hookers are notorious liars. And she'd lied her way through her first and final exclusive pretrial interview with the press. After five hours in a 10-by-12 interview room at headquarters, she'd sung a different tune.

To wit:

Melissa McBride had taken a walk on Willie Van Allen. But it hadn't been voluntary. Once Cindy Lou had twigged to the fact Van Allen wanted to cut her out of the picture, she took Melissa aside and laid out the options: Melissa could stay with Van Allen and get whacked the first time she turned her back. Or she could cross the street and go to work for Luther Cross. Melissa had walked.

Van Allen hadn't been pleased. He went looking for Melissa. He was even less pleased after he found her and had a little chat and Melissa told him what Cindy Lou had told her. When Willie came home he told Cindy to pack her things and get out. She was finished. And as soon as she was gone, Melissa would be moving in and taking over.

Cindy could hardly believe her ears. After all she'd done for Willie Van Allen. Where in hell would he have been if she hadn't been around to show him the ropes, eh?

Et cetera.

Half an hour later, Melissa was dead and half an hour after that, Cindy had dumped the body in the ditch in Balmy Beach.

Melissa's body was still in the morgue when Willie put the word out he'd pay big bucks to anyone who'd take care of a little problem of his. A problem named Cindy Lou Gilmore. And it wasn't just the fact that Cindy Lou had whacked his new number one property which pissed him off.

What really got to him was, Cindy Lou whacked Melissa after she'd cleaned out her closets in the big house in Southland Gardens. Her closets he didn't much care about, except that at the back of one of those closets was a bureau and in the bottom drawer of that bureau there'd been a couple of hundred thousand dollars worth of cocaine.

So, Willie had put out a hit on Cindy Lou.

Put out a hit on anyone, and a guy like Luther Cross will probably be the first to hear about it. Luther has a pretty good set of ears and he's your consummate businessman. He doesn't care whether he works for a friend or an enemy, so long as the employer pays in cash. And ten thousand bucks for one dead hooker was too tempting to turn down.

Luther went right to work. That part of Cindy's story was true: he'd put out a call for Cindy, asked about buying some drugs, set up the meeting, and she'd smelled the rat. She dispatched Carole, then Luther dispatched Carole.

Cindy Lou watched the whole thing, just like she said. And just as she'd said, it was Luther who'd done the killing.

And as soon as Luther had finished off Carole Tippet, Cindy had stepped out of the shadows with a deal on her mind and a gun in her hand.

The deal was: if Luther took care of another piece of business, Cindy would forget she ever saw Luther raise a hand against Carole Tippet.

What kind of deal, Luther had wanted to know.

Get rid of Willie, Cindy had said.

With Willie out of the way, Cindy could liquidate their assets. Luther could liquidate his and they could take the money and run.

Where to? Luther had wanted to know.

Somewhere sunny, she said. And somewhere where they don't believe in extradition.

Luther said it sounded like a plan to him.

Only there was one thing.

What was that, she'd wondered.

How did he know he could trust her?

She told him to look in the trunk of the Mustang.

What he found in the trunk of the Mustang was a briefcase. What he found in the briefcase was two hundred thousand dollars, in small bills, payment in full for the drugs Cindy had stolen from Willie.

She told Luther he could keep the money. Kind of a down payment to seal their 'business deal'. She told him to put the briefcase in his Lincoln, then she wondered if he thought he could trust her now.

Luther slammed the trunk lid, wiped his right hand on his pant leg and they shook hands.

Next item of business was getting rid of the body. Cindy told him to put it in the trunk of her Mustang, then get in his Lincoln and to follow her out to Balmy Beach. Cindy had driven her car just a little too far, not noticing the riverbank. She and Luther wrestled Carole's body out of the trunk, dumped it on the riverbank, then hopped in Luther's car and headed for town.

They were back at Luther's place, having their second celebratory drink, when they heard the call on Luther's police scanner. They headed back to The Beach, parked the Lincoln a couple of blocks up from Water Street, walked down and mingled with the crowd and watched the action. They watched Al and Dennis wrap things up at the scene; they watched Willie have his little chat with Tubby Taylor; they watched Deke the Geek drive off with Cindy's car, then they wandered off into the night.

Next stop: out to Willie's house for a little chat. Luther went to the door. Cindy stayed in the Lincoln, slumped down out of sight. As soon as Willie and Luther went in, she got out of Luther's car and followed them inside.

Luther said he'd come to collect his earnings. Ten grand in small bills.

Willie's first mistake was telling Luther, no body, no money.

His second mistake was turning to show Luther the door. He was a little surprised to see Cindy standing just inside the door. He wondered what was up and, while he was wondering, Luther nudged him in the back with the business end of his switchblade, then marched him into the garage.

Cindy Lou's tape was the genuine item. She'd recorded the whole encounter, just as she said she had. Well, not quite the whole encounter.

Once Luther had shivved Willie two or three times, Cindy snapped off the tape recorder.

Luther handed her the blade. Cindy did a little surgery, for old times' sake. Luther stuffed Willie in the trunk of the Jag, drove the Jag to the airport, parked it, walked in one door, came back out another and took a cab downtown to The Hilton.

Cindy Lou took Luther's Lincoln.

She told Luther she was going to shuffle some money into some offshore bank accounts where no one would find it. Then she'd meet him at The Hilton, they'd have a pleasant evening and catch an early-morning flight connecting to L.A. connecting by a red-eye special to a place where they could spend a little time soaking up the rays.

Luther said it sounded good to him.

Say this about Luther Cross. He was big. He was mean. He could stick a knife in your gut, pull it out, wipe it off and walk off, whistling. He was also stupid as a stump. Or, as Peter Dick put it: "If Luther was a light bulb, he'd be about a 15 watter." Peter Dick shook his head and laughed.

Even a nitwit could have seen it coming. Well, most nitwits.

"With Luther out of the way and with Van Allen dead, the town was hers for the asking. That's why she was so keen on getting you to buy into this story about Luther Cross."

And which was why, before dropping my envelope off at The Spec, she'd put another envelope - with a note and a hotel room key - under the windshield wiper of a cruiser parked outside the downtown police headquarters.

Luther was sprawled on the double bed in the honeymoon suite, wearing only a smile, when the cops used Cindy Lou's key and walked in without knocking. "That bitch. I can't believe it. That bitch." If he said it once while he was dressing, and while he was going down the elevator, and while he took the ride down to the lock-up, must've said it a couple of dozen times. "That bitch. I can't believe it."

He finally believed it, as the door of the cell clanked shut. "She set me up."

"They'll make a lovely couple in the prisoner's dock," said Peter Dick.

'Yes they will," said Kenny Koster.

"Charming little lady."

"Charming as a snake."

"But she very nearly pulled it off."

Well, no, as a matter of fact.

Unhappily for Cindy, Melissa had been a scrapper and a scratcher. There was enough of Cindy's hair and skin under Melissa's nails to constitute a positive ID.

And there was enough of Cindy's blood on the seat and the floor of her car to put her at the scene where Carole's body had been found. Al Sears wouldn't have much trouble proving that the cut on Cindy's forehead could only have been caused by her forehead hitting the steering wheel when the car went over the riverbank and onto the beach. And Leslie Ambrose told Pete Dick she could positively identify Cindy and Luther Cross as the people she'd seen on Water Street when her dogs had wakened her with their barking in the middle of the night.

When it came to Willie, Cindy'd been just plain stupid. Or blinded by jealousy.

Whatever.

"Revenge is mine, saith the Lord." And as The Gerbil said with a cockeyed smile, "we oughta leave it to Him."

"That's real poetic," said Angel.

The Gerbil smiled and nodded and raised her glass. He was right.

Cindy Lou's surgical procedure had been her big mistake: the surgery, and the fact that she wanted Van Allen to be alive to experience it.

Cindy Lou had to undo Van Allen's belt and his fly before she could haul down his trousers. She couldn't have made things any easier for Alan Sears. All he had to do was look for the upside down finger and thumb prints on Van Allen's belt. He suspected, rightly enough, that those prints might be on file.

And he had himself a killer.

The fingerprints were a bonus.

The moment Van Allen realized what Cindy was about to do, he'd lost control.

Cindy could wash her hands half a dozen times, but all the washing in the world wouldn't remove all the traces of urine and blood hidden under her nails and in all the crannies of all those lovely rings she wore.

Case closed.

Which called for another round of drinks.

Midnight said it was his turn to buy. "I insist."

He was the only one insisting.

It was just about five a.m. when Garth and I pulled into his driveway. The living room light was on.

"Not a good sign," said Garth.

"No," I said, "I'd have to agree."

The front door opened just as Garth was fumbling with his keys.

Mrs. Garth did not look happy.

But it was me she was looking at. "Your son called." She handed me a piece of paper with a number written on it.

I hit her with about six quick questions.

"Relax, Huntzie. It's not life and death. Their car broke down. He wanted you to call him."

"Dad?"

"Were you sleeping?"

"No." Say this about Ben. He can't lie worth shit. He was yawning halfway through 'no'.

"Where are you guys?"

"In a motel."

"Tell me a story."

Pretty short story, actually.

Jeannie and the kids had got off in good time and a couple of hours later, they were in the parking lot down by the beach in Grand Bend. They spent half an hour going up one side of the main drag and down the other. The kids went into a video arcade. They all grabbed a bite to eat. Then they went back to the car. The car wouldn't start. Wouldn't even turn over. Wouldn't even groan.

An hour or so later, the greaseball from the local garage told Jeannie it was probably the alternator. Then he'd tried to explain what an alternator does - or did, when it was working - and why he couldn't possibly get a replacement until Tuesday at the latest. Jeannie paid him ten bucks for his trouble and called another garage. Same diagnosis, same bad news about a replacement. "The nearest dealership's in London. And there ain't no way they can ship anything out until next week at the earliest. You folks got a place to stay?"

On the May 24th weekend?

In Grand Bend?

Luckily for Jeannie and the kids, the garage man had a sister-in-law who runs one of the motels along the highway. He made a call, then he hooked the Olds and towed it to his garage, dropped it in the lot and drove them to his sister-in-law's motel.

"We were trying to get you last night. Where were you?"

"Working on a big story, pal. I just walked in."

"What kind of story?"

"The dead hookers story."

"Cool ...."

Next thing I knew I was speaking to Jeannie. Very sleepy. But not that sleepy. "Not more dead hookers, I hope."

You could hear the kids giggling in the background.

"Sounds like you've got yourself a situation, there."

"Yes," said Jeannie. "That's about exactly what we've got."

"What're you going to do?"

"I don't know. Bill, the guy from the garage, he said he'd make a call to London this morning, see if he could get an alternator shipped up on the bus. But if not, looks like we're stuck."

We sat there, the two of us, staring at our respective ceilings.

I don't know what was on Jeannie's ceiling. But I couldn't take much more than a few seconds of Suzie's mournful face. I turned in my chair and faced the far wall.

"Well," I said.

"Yes?"

"I was just thinking that, maybe ...."

"Maybe?"

"It's Saturday morning, right?"

"Yup. It's Saturday."

"I don't have to be back at work until Tuesday night."

"You've got the weekend off?"

I could hear Ben in the background. "YES."

Then I could hear Katie in the background. "YES what?"

"Dad's coming to get us. He's gonna take us ...."

Jeannie clamped a palm over the receiver. Then a second or two later: "Sorry, I couldn't hear you for all the hollering in the background."

"I was just saying, I don't have to be back at work until Tuesday night. I was just thinking, you know, maybe I could ... well ..."

"We're at a place called The Dunes Motel."

She gave me directions.

I told her I had one little item of business to tidy up. "Should take me a couple of hours. What time is it, anyway?"

"Five thirty, by my watch."

"Should take me until seven thirty. Thereabouts. Then I'll hit the road. I'll call you when I'm heading out the door."

"You sure you want to do this?"

More YESSing in the background. "I told you he was coming."

"Sure I'm sure. See you about nine thirty. Nine thirty or ten."

"Huntzie?"

"Yes?"

"You want our room number?"

"Oh yah. Shoot."

"One twenty two."

"One what?"

"One twenty two."

"You are not going to believe this."

"Believe what?"

"Never mind. I'll tell you when I get there. Go back to sleep."

"Fat chance. With these two in the room." She palmed the receiver again. But I could hear her telling them to hush up before the neighbours started banging on the walls.

"Huntzie?"

"Yah?"

"Thanks."

"Thanks for what? I haven't done anything yet."

"Thanks anyway."

"Okay, bye."

"Huntzie?"

"Yah?"

"Drive carefully."

"Actually, I was thinking about zipping along like a bat out of hell. I was pretty careful yesterday. Hate to be predictable."

"I don't think that's anything you have to worry about."

"Bye Jeannie."

"Bye Huntzie."

-THIRTEEN-

"Thought you were long gone." Norm Weatherall was sitting at his desk, eyeshade down over his forehead.

"Just wanted to go over tomorrow's story, one more time."

"Be my guest."

"You got a proof?"

"Sent it back. Tell them to pull you a fresh one."

I went back to the composing room. Rusty Gibbons was in the midst of doing the corrections. I told him I'd wait until he was done, then I'd give it the once-over myself. I read over his shoulder as he was making the changes. You had to like the headline:

THE SHORT, SAD LIFE OF CAROLE TIPPET

"This story begins in mid-December, seventeen years ago. It begins with a birth announcement published in this newspaper. Tippet: Suzanne and Harold are delighted to announce the birth of their daughter, Carole Elizabeth, seven pounds, six ounces, at Hotel Dieu Hospital. A baby sister for Harry Jr. and James.

"The story ends in a field in Balmy Beach earlier this week. It ends with a front-page story, in this same newspaper, recounting the discovery of the body of a teen-aged hooker.

"It's what happened between the beginning and the end that will break your heart."

From there on, it was just a matter of reworking the information in all those files that Angela Merton had delivered to me. I mentioned Carole's early troubles at school and her numerous involvements with treatment programs. I ran through her troubled history while in the care of the Children's Aid Society. I quoted from the reports filed by social workers and foster parents and psychologists and psychiatrists. I listed, conviction by conviction, her entire criminal record.

I quoted from three reports written by experts who were baffled as to the cause of Carole Tippet's serious psychological problems, including one social worker who had dealt with Carole for more than three years: "Everyone who has ever worked with Carole Tippet will report that she is an extremely likable girl, very bright, very personable when she wants to be. And everyone who has ever worked with her will also report that she is one of the most disturbed youngsters they have ever encountered. As Carole tends to be very closed when it comes to her background, we can only guess as to the cause of her severe disturbance."

It was James Tippet who had eliminated the need for guesswork.

He accomplished that while the two of us stood on the front step of the funeral home, having a smoke.

I saved his remarks for the end of the story, right after this quote from a psychologist:

"Carole Tippet is a severely disturbed young girl, one of the most troubled I've encountered in my practice to date. Although we have had numerous sessions, and although I seem to be establishing a rapport with her, I have so far been unsuccessful in determining the cause of her apparent childhood trauma. Her past remains a mystery."

Standing on the front step of the funeral home, in the time it took him to smoke two cigarettes, James Tippet cleared up the mystery:

"My father was pimping her from the time she was nine. She was pregnant when she was eleven. Could've been one of the customers. Could've been my father, for all I know. She didn't really know. She didn't really know what 'pregnant' was, until then. Her mother took care of things. On the kitchen table. After that, Carole didn't have to worry about getting pregnant any more. Six months later, they were pimping her again."

James paused and spiralled his smoke onto the lawn and lit another. "That's not the worst of it," he said.

The time she wound up in hospital, raped and beaten to ratshit. "That was my father who did that. My father and his drinking buddies. They took turns with her. And when she finally had enough - three or four of them - and started screaming, my father beat her. Fists and feet. And he told her if she ever told anyone who'd done it, he'd kill her." James had looked over at me, then had looked at the street. "And that's still not the worst of it."

The worst of it was this: "From the time she was a little baby, a week or two after she came home from the hospital, until the time she was about four, they kept her in a closet in the basement. In a card-board box, in the closet. They couldn't stand the crying, I guess. I remember her crying a lot that first week. Then they put her in the closet and every time she cried, they hit her. She stopped crying after that. But they kept her in the closet, anyway. It was my job to take her food. I can still remember the look she'd give me when I opened the door. That little smile she gave me as soon as she realized it wasn't my mother or father who'd opened the door. She'd reach her little arms up for me. She wanted me to pick her up. But I couldn't. At least I didn't. They told me they'd beat me and put me in the closet with her if I picked her up or touched her. I can hear her little whimper as I shut the door. I've been hearing it for years. I should've grabbed her and run out of that place. But I was scared. I didn't know what would happen to me.

"It never occurred to me to wonder what would happen to her."

What I couldn't figure was, why her? Why Carole?

Why weren't the boys ever locked up, or beaten up?

Pretty simple. "My mother had an affair, a year or so before Carole was born. My father found out about it. There was a big storm in the house for weeks. She swore it was all over, that she'd seen the last of the guy. Next thing you knew, she was pregnant. My father never believed he was the father. He always figured my mother and this guy had had one final fling. As far as he was concerned, Carole was no kid of his."

"So he made her pay?"

"No," said James. "He wanted my mother to pay for it." He drew on his cigarette and then pulled it from his lips and looked down at it and flicked it onto the lawn. Then he turned and went back inside.

"You want this, or not?"

Rusty was holding a proof of the page.

There were seven mistakes. Typos, missed punctuation. What I used to call 'little' mistakes until Norm Weatherall overheard me and, in a megaphone voice, said 'there's no such thing as a little mistake'.

After I'd finished correcting the mistakes I read the proof over one more time, for good measure. Two more typos.

Then I looked at the pictures.

James Tippet had given me a grade-school snapshot of his sister. They'd blown it up to two columns. Directly below it, there was a two-column black and white of the scene where they'd found her body. Beside these pictures, there was a four-column blowup of the picture which Angela Merton had given me: the shot taken in the hospital when Carole Tippet had turned up, more dead than alive.

That one accusing eye.

"Hell of a story, kid." Norm was standing to my right, looking at the proof. "The shit's going to be in the fan over this one."

"To paraphrase a friend of mine: 'I hope the bastards fry'."

"Get ready to answer your phone."

I stood up. "I'm not going to be anywhere near a phone this week-end."

"You going into hiding?"

"Next best thing. Going to the cottage."

"You and the lady friend?"

I shook my head. "Nope. Jeannie and the kids."

"Jeannie?"

I nodded. "Yup."

"Well," said Norm.

That was all. Just 'well'.

I handed him the proof. "Have one of the nitwits go over this one more time, will you? If you can find one who can read."

He said he'd do that.

"And close your ears. I'm about to make a personal call on the company tab."

"I'm having a little trouble with my hearing these days, Huntzie.

207

I'll have to get that checked out." He gave me a fake punch to the shoulder then took the proof over to the rim. He slid it across to my favourite rat. "Here. See if you can find a mistake the Prima Donna missed."

"My pleasure," said the rat, with a little ratty grin.

"Hello?"

"I'm on my way."

"Already?"

"The kids there?"

"Ben's gone over to the restaurant. He was starving."

"Katie?"

"I'll get her."

Jeannie called Katie's name.

"Is that Daddy?" I could hear her thumping across the room.

"Hi Daddy."

"This is Willoughby's Taxi Service. Did you order a cab?"

"Yes we did."

"A long-distance cab?"

"Yes we did."

"Well, we're just about to dispatch that cab right now. You sit by the window for a couple of hours, and you should see it pull up right in front."

"Daddy?"

"Yes."

"You're goofy."

"That's only one of my many endearing traits."

"Daddy?"

"Yes."

"Hang up so you can get driving. I'm bored."

"You and Mom and Ben go for a walk. By the time you get back, I'll be there."

"Honest?"

"If you walk far enough. Let me speak to your mother."

"Bye, Daddy."

"Bye honey."

"Drive careful."

"Carefully. Careful is an adjective. Carefully is an adverb." "Don't crash is what I mean."

Katie handed off the phone.

"I'll second that."

"Second what?"

"Katie's advice. Don't crash."

"I'll do my best."

About The Author

Paul Vasey, the award-winning journalist and novelist, lives and works in Windsor, Ontario. His previous books include *The Sufferer Kind, Lord, Lord, Into Thin Air,* and the popular and controversial non-fiction work exposing the real lives behind young offenders called *Kids In The Jail.*

Vasey is the morning host of a CBC program based in Windsor called *Morning Watch.*

AGMV
MARQUIS
Québec, Canada
2000